"Hey, Kid," I said. "It's been awhile since I saw you last. Someone told me you were back east."

I pushed through the men and shook hands with the kid, who was trying to control his fear. "Come on over to my table and let's catch up on what your family is doing," I said.

The apparent leader glanced my way and nodded. "I have some business with the kid," he said, a challenge in his eyes. "Doesn't it look to you like he's a sissy son-of-a-bitch?"

I looked the boy over and smiled. Then I turned back to the big fellow. "Hell, Stud, you've got me there. I really couldn't tell you how a sissy son-of-a-bitch looks," I answered, "but then I'm not the one running around with a sissy son-of-a-bitching gang."

The big fellow was turning back toward the boy, whose mouth was bloody. As my words sank in, he quickly turned. "What the hell are you trying to say?" he growled.

I had taken the kid by the shoulder and steered him over to my table. I turned my head toward the bar. The bartender was watching the action. I held up my bottle of beer, pointed to the kid, and turned around to take my seat with my back to the wall. Before I could sit down, the big fellow had taken a couple of steps toward us. His face was tight with anger and he forced the words through his clenched teeth. "Draw, you son-of-a-bitch," he snarled. His hand gripped the butt of his forty four.

"If you don't like sons-of-a-bitch, keep your mama out of the kennel," I answered.

Sputtering with rage, he pulled his gun. So did I, and it was the last thing he ever didn't see.

Seeker's Valley

This is a novel of the Wild West and the battle to carve a ranch out of a country dominated by a man who wanted it all.

Gun-smoke, romance and intrigue dominate this unusual but realistic story of how one lonely man returned to a country that had been empty when he rode through it a few years earlier. The man was named Easy Seeker.

Easy had returned to the Bend of the Rimrock to claim a hidden valley he had discovered while searching for his missing sister. The valley was now occupied by a man and his beautiful daughter, Earlene. It soon became apparent that the man and the girl had met before, for one fleeting but memorable moment.

Easy's sense of justice and fair-play soon caused him to lock horns with the villain, a big rancher who took what he wanted and wanted it all. With the steadfast loyalty and help of Earlene and her father Brad, assisted by Rodney, an English boy he had saved, Easy took on the big rancher and his army of gunfighters.

Love and passion, eroticism and lust, gun-smoke and a blood drenched valley serve as the setting for this battle-ground that took the entire country in the Bend of the Rimrock out from under the thumb of Burly Dobbins and moved the citizens from poverty to prosperity.

Author of:
Reflections of Love
The Beckoning Hand
Third Book from the Sun

Library of Congress Control Number: 2012939149

ISBN 978-0-9723911-2-2

First Printing

Notice:
This book is a work of fiction. Every place, person, incident, event, time line and/or episode is a product of the author's imagination. Any resemblance to any actual person, place, thing or event is purely coincidental and bears no historical significance or resemblance to actuality.

This book is dedicated

To May

To the characters that I have created
and come to know intimately;

To the places that I have created
and come to love dearly;

To the circumstances that I have created
and the suspense they have given me;

To the nature that surrounds me
and has given me such pleasure;

To the fantasies in which I live and have lived,
and experienced so much fullness;

To the dreams that I have dreamed
and the people and things that have populated them;

And to those I love and those who love me in return,
and those who wished and/or tried to love me.

*A very special thanks to Cathe Ferguson
for the endless hours she spent in
editing this book and offering encouragement.*

Thanks again, Cathe!

CAST OF CHARACTERS

1) **Easy Seeker**
   A man young in years, but mature and solid in judgment and action. He came west seeking his lost sister. A strange attraction brings him back to the Rimrock country after giving up his long search.

2) **Earlene Rogers**
   The daughter of Brad Rogers and the partner in the &RR (&Ours) ranch

3) **Brad Rogers**
   Owner of the &RR ranch, along with his daughter, Earlene Rogers

4) **Pat Donahue**
   Owner and proprietor of the Vacaville Bar

5) **Arnold Smith**
   Jack of all trades, owner of the blacksmith shop and livery stables

6) **Burly Dobbins**
   Owner of the X-Pan-D, the biggest ranch in or around the Bend of the Rimrock

7) **Rodney Hampton**
   A boy scarcely out of his teens, scouting the west for a good investment for his father, a rich English gentleman

8) **Torch**
   A man just a little too fast with his mouth and a little too slow with his sixgun

9) **Hatch**
   A gunfighter who was disgruntled because he thought he had taken a back seat to Torch for too long

10) **Paddy O'Reilly**
    Proprietor of the general store and mercantile

11) **Todd Russell**
    Sheriff of Rimrock county

Chapters

Chapter One
Prologue
A little about the lay of the land

The Rimrock ran in a straight east – west line from north of west, and toward a little south of east. There was one big exception. As the Rimrock neared the wandering River, it seemed to make a desperate leap toward the cooling waters. Then, like a fickle lover, it changed its mind and looped nearly back upon itself, forming a large, teardrop-shaped mesa as it returned to its previous alignment.

The high ground that was left behind resembled a peninsula that reached into a sea of short grass country. It was here that the desert gave up its attempt to conquer the grassland. The sand stopped and the grass started and ran for hundreds of miles to the east until it met the wooded black land, which ran on to the piney woods.

The Rimrock served as a curious replacement for the foot hills that generally begin before a mountain range. It enclosed the Wandering River Basin on the north, while the nearly limitless grassy plains enclosed it on the south.

There were many unusual formations in the area where the Rimrock and the desert to the west and grassy plains to the east fought an endless battle to dominate the area that was known as the Bend of the Rimrock.

The mountain's east slope consisted of layers of parallel rock strata, tilting upward at a gentle angle from the surface of the prairie to the south and east. Slabs of granite, alternating with colorful sandstone, erupted through the earth's crust which left vertical walls and striated bands of different rock formations that resembled stacks of tombstones of varying thicknesses and colors.

The mountain ridge curved in a great circle from the north toward the west, and then back to the southeast. Hidden in its rugged terrain on the west side of the bend was a green valley about seven miles long and three miles wide. Each end abruptly pinched together, like a Havana cigar. It was invisible to any passer-by, as the entrance turned sharply and appeared to end.

There were two similar valleys on the east side of the bend. The one on the west was an undiscovered Eden. One of the valleys on the east side was a cattleman's paradise, where the &RR ranch was located.

Just east of the &RR was the other hidden valley. It would have been another cattleman's paradise, except for the lack of running water. An old dry river bed cut a shallow swath through the deep grasses until exiting the valley through the narrow throat of the entrance and wandering off toward the Meandering river. It crossed a land rich in grass, but without water for livestock.

High up on the nearly sheer slope that lay just east of the crumbled stone wall where the dry river bed emerged, were scattered clumps of stunted brush that clung to each small out-cropping of rock which had gathered enough soil over the ages to furnish a toe-hold to the hardy shrubs. They clung stubbornly to the cliff-sides, roots projecting into whatever crack or cranny that was available.

Chapter Two
Return to the Rimrock
(In the beginning)

Pulling my horse up beneath the scanty shade of a rocky out-thrust along the Rimrock wall, I reached for my last remaining canteen of water. I had exhausted, my regular canteen, along with a two gallon canteen that I carried for my horse. This last two gallon canteen was being carried to be prepared for any eventuality. I was the man who always had an ace in the hole. In this case, it was a second two gallon canteen.

The main line of the rocky bulwark traveled in a general east and west direction. At this one point, way out in the middle of no-where, that bulge added a two day ride to what would have probably been a three or four hour ride if one had been able to ride directly across, instead of having to take the huge detour.

As it were, I still had six hours to get to that odd deviation. I raised the large canteen to my lips, having to hold it with both hands.

Suddenly my horse made a great lunge and I dropped the canteen, grabbed the reins and brought him under control. I leaped from the saddle to grab my canteen and nearly landed on an angry, buzzing rattlesnake. It had bitten my horse on his left front fetlock.

I shot the snake and looked quickly around for my canteen. I was sick with fear, for the canteen had landed in a nest of rocks that held it upside down. I grabbed it and shook it. To my dismay, it was completely empty. In the blink of an eye I had lost my entire water supply to the thirsty desert sand. On top of that, I had a horse with a quickly swelling fetlock and a three day walk ahead of me if I cut straight across the desert for the Wandering River. I couldn't believe my bad luck!

I thought of hiding my saddle and leaving my horse to die in the desert as I made my way south toward the river, but I'd had the horse for three years, raising it from a raw bronco colt. Calliope was the best horse I had ever straddled, and I just couldn't bring myself to leave him.

I put the stopper into the empty canteen and hung it on my saddle. Picking up the reins, I started walking. Calliope, head hung low, was scarcely able to stagger along.

I knew that if we stopped and I tried to give him time to recover, thirst would become a greater enemy than the snake bite was. In order to survive, we had to keep moving.

It is curious how one's psychological quirks manifest themselves. I had had a good drink of water at the time the sleeping snake must have awakened and struck my horse. Here I was, less than half an hour later, and my knowledge that there was no water was feeding my thirst as though I had been two days without the precious liquid. If my canteen had been full, I probably wouldn't have had the least urge to drink.

However, there is a lot of difference between straddling a good horse, on the one hand, or on the other hand, shuffling along through the sand, winding around the spiny bushes and cacti, waiting for a sick horse to follow you. My horse had to be suffering from thirst, for I hadn't had a chance to dismount and pour him a hat full of water before the snake struck. I could just imagine how good it would have felt to clap that wet Stetson back on my head after he had drunk. I could nearly feel the water trickling down my face and running down my chest and back.

For hour after weary hour, I struggled along, half dragging Calliope. Just thinking about the miles ahead of us seemed like a gulf too big to be crossed. Yet, cross it we must, and the only way to get a job done is to do it. No matter how far it was, each step brought us one step closer. My feet were blistered and aching, yet, looking at the sun, I estimated we had only come about six or seven miles.

I decided it would be best to seek shelter from the sun in the shade of an enclave in the Rimrock during the heat of the day. As soon as the sun set, I could walk through the night. The Rimrock would offer shade until about noon before the sun passed the line of the Rimrock and shone directly on me again.

It would be better to conserve my strength while I had strength to conserve. I estimated that it would take a couple of days to get across the open prairie. I wasn't sure as to whether it would be smarter to continue straight on now to get to water quicker, or to rest. One thing for sure was that I couldn't do both.

The way things were appearing right now, in another hour or two, my horse would probably drop dead from the combination of rattlesnake venom and thirst. I figured that I was damned if I stopped and damned if I continued. I sat for a minute, watching my horse raise and lower his injured foot, while his head drooped in agony. He was breathing air in quick shallow puffs that he must have felt were coming from the ovens of hell. I raised my arm to shield my face as a whirl-wind danced along the edge of the Rimrock, carrying stinging bits of sand, grit and chaff.

The errant wind must have carried some scent with it, for my horse jerked his head up and tugged against his reins. I tugged back to bring his head around, but he refused the pull and jerked me half to my feet as he turned toward what appeared to be just another shadow in the irregularities of the rocky wall. I climbed staggeringly to my feet from where I had collapsed with my back against the rocky bluff. I allowed him to lead me behind a huge fallen rock, more by my weakness than by my will.

As we rounded the rock, I suddenly realized that what had appeared to be a crack was actually a bend in the wall which was outlined against another rock wall about fifteen feet beyond the first. As Calliope pulled toward the gap between the walls, I saw it was a large crack in the Rimrock.

By this time I was so tired and so near death from thirst and fatigue that I tried to turn my horse loose, but the reins were looped around my wrist and I had no choice but to follow. I found it easier to allow the horse to drag me onward than it would have been to pull him to a stop.

The crack soon became a widening cleft as I followed the newly energized horse for a few more yards. Somehow I managed to muster enough strength to pull him to a stop before climbing up and throwing myself across the saddle.

*

Coughing and spluttering, I raised my gasping mouth above the surface. Coolness surrounded me and I was choking. I finally got a breath of air and was able to look around. Instead of barren desert, I caught a glimpse of green.

It took moments to realize Calliope was standing spraddle-legged in a pool, drinking great gulps of water. I splashed a double handful of water across my lips and into my mouth, stood up and half dragged Calliope out of the pool before he foundered himself.

Staggering back to the water, I drank a couple more mouthfuls. I had never tasted anything so good before in my life.

Once I felt a little more refreshed, I went back and unbuckled the cinch, permitting the saddle to drop to the ground. Leaving it where it fell, I led Calliope back and allowed him a couple of more swallows of water, clipped the end of my picket rope to the hackamore, tied the other end to a branch, and promptly collapsed in sleep.

I awoke the next morning to find myself in a valley about two miles wide, surrounded by some aberration of the Rimrock. I had entered through a narrow opening that amounted to a crack running up into the high ground from the lower elevation at the foot of the cliff. It appeared like a part of the Rimrock had split off and slid about three miles away from the high ground, with each end of the valley it formed still connected to the higher ground at the two ends.

The end where I had entered was a narrow crack through which an opening barely existed.

The valley narrowed before ending about five miles away. Looking back toward the entrance, I saw that I was inside the valley a couple of miles. Lush, sub-irrigated grass filled the fifteen or twenty sections of land. It was in strong contrast to the desert that stretched away toward the west in the direction from which I had come.

The pond of water where I had spent the night was fed by a small spring, gurgling from the base of the valley's north wall, where the valley ended and the high ground began. It seemed as though a large oval bubble had somehow been created in the rock which formed the high ground as it reached the point where some primal upheaval had separated the high ground from the low ground.

I had plenty of food in my saddle bags and I'd been traveling for several days; the thought of hunkering down for a couple of days rest was too great to pass up. I started a small, smokeless fire of dried willow branches. My horse was busy cropping the green grass, and meat was sizzling. Grease dropped into the sputtering fire, where little blue blazes darted upward in the puffs of smoke. I was overcome by the sudden strong urge to finally have a home. This valley would make a wonderful spread, but it was just too hard to get cattle to market from here.

When I was finished eating, I saddled up, more to test my horse's foot than anything else. Surprisingly he scarcely favored it. I headed up valley toward the far end. It was an hour of riding filled with a strange sense of being the first man to ever cross this fertile grass. Lost in dreams and reverie, time abruptly ceased to exist.

I was roused from the trance-like state by the growing sound of a roar. I raised my head and saw a sight, such as I had never dreamed of.

The valley was closed off at the end by a rock wall of jumbled gravel and broken stone where a cascade of water burst from the side of the cliff. It emerged from a hole about eight or ten feet in diameter, and formed a pool perhaps one hundred yards in length and the entire width of the valley, which was only about twenty yards wide at this point. The huge jumbled boulders that formed the eastern end of the valley were the only part of the valley's circumference that exhibited this tangle of rocks. All the rest of the wall was solid stone. The wall of jumbled rocks was much lower than the solid walls of the Rim Rock.

I was wondering where all of the water was going, for the torrent that was raging from the hole in the north wall was great enough to soon overflow the banks that confined it. I began walking around the small perimeter of the lake and soon heard the sound of another waterfall, only this time it was muffled by the south wall where the water was filtering out of the lake through jumbled rocks that formed the canyon's end. As I walked around the lake the precise place where the water was disappearing was out of sight behind a promontory of stone that jutted out from the south wall.

I had whiled away the entire day, lost in reverie and filled with a peace that was foreign to my character, or at least buried deeply in my soul.   Calliope was standing in the shade of the setting sun, content with the grass he had eaten. Taking my cue from him, I decided to spend the night at this idyllic spot, promptly abandoning my earlier plans to ride back to the spring where I had spent the night before.   That would have given me a little head-start on my trip on southward in the morning, around the southern bulge of the Rimrock, and back northward to where it resumed its eastward march across the country. However, time was the one thing that I had plenty of. I felt that I might as well take advantage of it while I could.

I disrobed and washed all of my dirty clothes in the clear water. A leaf floated by and was pulled by an invisible force toward the spot where I surmised the underground river continued.

When I finished washing my clothes, I spread them over the willow branches to dry under the warm summer sky. The air trapped by the valley walls mixed with the coolness of the air around the pool. The cooling mist from the waterfall made it heavier than the arid desert air, so the temperature felt just right to my naked skin.

I threw my saddle down on a carpet of grass in the shade of the willows. In spite of the hard pillow, it wasn't long before I drifted off to sleep.

My dreams were pleasant, and I awoke with a feeling of well being in marked contrast to the previous long journey across the sand and heat that brought me here.   The willow leaves softly brushed against my body, and I was so comfortable that I longed for sleep, despite my ravenous hunger.

Smiling, I luxuriated in the warm air that felt more sumptuous than a quilted blanket to my bare skin, and in the relaxing touch of the delicate leaves which rustled about in the breeze. As I dozed off, I was suddenly overcome with fantasies, brought on by the isolation of the perfect Eden in which I was so sensuously engulfed. It was easy to imagine I was the only living human being on the face of the earth.

The fatigue that I had experienced, along with the warmth of the day and the fantasies alive in my mind made me lay, half awake but half dreaming.

In the morning, when I opened my eyes, I was shocked to see the startled face of a beautiful nude girl peering down at me! I rolled away from the willow branches and leaped to my feet as fast as I could, but I spun around to see only vacant space where I had expected to see a girl.

I knew that I must have been dreaming, but the dream had seemed so real that I felt compelled to check the other side of the willows just in case she was hiding there. There was no way on earth that anyone, let alone a nude girl, could be out here fifty miles at least from the nearest habitation. Satisfied that I was alone, I lay down again.

I couldn't help thinking how real the girl had appeared. Of course it had to be my imagination, I reasoned. The mind must have a way of sometimes conjuring up images that are so beautiful and ideal they are seldom found in reality.

It could have been the loneliness of the long journey, I thought, coupled with the natural desires that can rise, unbidden, in one's imagination. I couldn't rule out the hormonal influence that I admit had taken root in my increasing sense of loneliness, either, which had heightened in intensity as the previous evening had worn on. Those thoughts flitted through my mind, but in a minute I was fast asleep.

The combination of the willow leaves brushing against my body, together with a dream that was possibly the continuation of the one I must have been having when I dreamed of seeing a naked girl a few minutes earlier combined to cause me to have a wet dream. It brought me fully awake in the middle of my ejaculation. I rolled over and got to my feet and waded out into the pool and washed the residue from my body. Then I walked over a few yards from my campsite and looked out across the green grasses as I took a leak. My piss had never fallen on such green grass or in such a lovely setting.

I turned back to the dead ashes of my earlier fire and squatted down, laying the small wooden debris and branches that would start the larger pieces burning. Then I reached over to my blue denim pants and got a match and lit the fire.   As the fire grew, I stood in its warmth for a minute. The cool water had chilled my skin.

I put my coffee pot on and started bacon frying in my skillet.   As soon as I had my breakfast started, I stretched the kinks out of my body, turned and sprinted toward the pool, dove in and felt the cool water close over my nakedness once again. I swam briskly to the far end and back. Now I felt totally rejuvenated and ready to face the day. All my problems had magically dissolved like a nightmare that disappears with the advent of light. Or, I chuckled, like the way the remnants of my dream with the beautiful girl had disappeared.

Picking up my pants, I stepped into them, pulled on my shirt and boots, took the bacon out of the pan and put some biscuit dough in and set it to frying in the embers that had formed.

The peace that surrounded the valley was profound, and as my bread fried, I couldn't help wondering about its potential. Ample herds of cattle could grow fat quickly on such rich grass, bringing large sums of money at the market. Still, cattle have no value if you can't sell them.

Suddenly I thought I saw a movement near the rim of the strange jumble of rocks that formed the canyon's end, but upon a second look, I saw nothing. Maybe it had been a deer, or even a cougar. More than likely, it was my imagination. When it was ready, I sat down to a meal of bacon, pan fried bread, and hot beans. The taste was as good as the aroma and I could only hope it would last me longer than it took to enjoy the flavor.

I spent the rest of the day, lazily meandering along the Rimrock, studying the different grasses and clovers while I enjoyed my unexpected little vacation. I had always had an interest in rocks and formations. Shortly after noon, I fixed up another meal and took a siesta. When I awoke, the sun was low in the sky.

I ate some left-over beans and bread, with a slice of cold bacon. Then darkness plummeted upon the valley as the sun dropped behind the western wall of the Rimrock.

The next morning, I had eaten breakfast before sunup and was saddled up and riding back toward the entrance.

Chapter Three
&RR (And Ours) Ranch
Earlene sees more than her cattle

Earlene Rogers rode along a path about two hundred yards out from the creek that ran through the center of their ranch. She would make an occasional foray to one side or the other, checking small bunches of cattle which grazed the lush grass.

She and her father ran the ranch alone, except during the spring and fall calf crops. Then they would hire riders to help them bring the cattle to the corral to do their branding and castrating. The steep sides of the valley, one mile to the west, formed the boundary of the ranch. Their valley was located in the midst of a peculiar indentation in the Rimrock which supported a rare stream that cut through the middle of it and ran south to the Wandering River.

This stream was the only good source of water between the Rimrock and the Wandering River. The lower end of the ranch pinched in to a width of about two hundred yards. They had built a rail fence out of mountain cedar to keep the cattle from straying southward and even more important, to keep the X-Pan-D cattle from grazing their lush grasses. A hundred yards beyond their fence, the Rimrock bent to the east. Ten miles to the south, the Wandering River paralleled the Rimrock.

She frowned as she thought of how appropriate the brand was for the Dobbins ranch. The brand consisted of an X, joined by a short bar to the handle of a pan, which in turn was joined by a short bar to the center of a D.

Although the brand was generally read as X-Pan-D, it was universally pronounced as the EXPAND ranch. That was the perfect description of what Burly Dobbins was doing. He had eX-Pan-Ded his ranch from where the desert sands ended about five miles or so west of the huge mesa known as Promontory Point, on the south side of the Wandering River, to where the east fork of the Wandering River, known as the East Fork, flowed out of the South Cedar Breaks. That was about ten miles to the east.

The South Cedar Breaks were formed of rough hills and gullies and a thick cover of Mountain Cedar. Scanty grass grew in the little glades. Several small ranchers ran cattle in the South Cedar breaks, for water rose from the hills and flowed in several creeks down into the Wandering River.

Until recently, Dobbins' X-Pan-D ranch had only grazed cattle on what everyone had considered to be his own graze.

His ranch consisted of about one hundred and fifty square miles of good grazing. That was about 96,000 acres of prime grass. What made this such a splendid ranch were the creeks flowing out of the breaks. It should have been all that anyone could ask for. Burly was not just anyone.

Recently, he had moved a herd of cattle north of the river and they were now grazing on the land along both sides of the creek that flowed through the &RR valley. They were mixing with the stock of the few ranchers who were grazing their cattle along the north side of the Wandering River. He had accused some of them of stealing his cattle.

Earlene knew that was just a prelude to sending his hired guns to clear the ranchers off the north side. She also knew that despite the fence across the entrance to their ranch, the &RR, it was just a matter of time until he would also move into their valley.

He had approached her once at a party that one of the merchants in town had thrown for his daughter's birthday and asked her for a dance. She had refused him. He asked her why she appeared hostile to him.

She had answered that she didn't dance with land hogs.

He had stood for a moment, looking her over from her dark hair to the soles of her feet. He then told her, "Every small rancher's daughter in the Wandering River country seems to have a different opinion of land hogs than you do. You can ask any or all of them, if you want to verify that fact. None of them were able to convince me that they should have the land they are squatting on. Still, even a land hog wouldn't bother his own father-in-law. Some land hogs place a very high value on a woman as good looking as you are." Earlene had turned and walked away, feeling his eyes caressing her body.

The approximately five thousand acres comprising their own ranch was an average width of a mile and three quarters. It ran back into the mountains for about four and one half miles. It was highly coveted by Dobbins, because it furnished the only truly good shelter for cattle during the winter that was known to exist in that entire area. It also was sub-irrigated and had the capability of growing both hay and corn. She and her father were also talking of trying out some wheat. This could give them some good winter grazing and would cut down on the amount of hay that it would be necessary to put up each spring and summer.

Their own spread was the only one on the north side of the Wandering River that didn't border on it. There had been several who claimed land along both sides of the stream that flowed from their valley. They had disappeared when the X-Pan-D ranch moved cattle onto the land they had grazed. The cattle that grazed the north side of the river seldom grazed over two miles from the river, because of the long walk for water.

The strip of good grass that lay between the river and the Rimrock was useless without water, other than the couple of miles adjacent to the river. That land adjacent to the river was occupied by half a dozen more small ranchers, each having a couple of sections of land. This was sufficient land to make up a solid economic unit, if not overgrazed. It was obvious that it was not sufficient for them and the big herd that Dobbins had moved in.

When Dobbins had moved his herd across the river, it had robbed every small rancher in the area of his feeling of security. Everyone was aware that he was beginning to make offers for the small ranches on the north side of the Wandering River. Each offer had been made with an ominous overtone that sounded somewhat like an "or else." No one wanted to test Burly's "or else" out to see just what it did mean.

The ranchers grazing the land along the creek that headed in their own valley had mysteriously disappeared, along with all but three or four that grazed the north bank of the river. Burly made no secret that all he wanted in life, as he often and loudly repeated was, "a small ranch with all of the land that adjoined it". His smile, as he made his joke, only contributed to the uneasiness of the few ranchers left on the south side of the Wandering River in the South Cedar Breaks, and a couple of small ranches wedged in between the Wandering River and the south flank of the mountain that formed the west boundary of their own brand, the &RR, plus those along the north bank of the river.

Earlene and her Dad were both proud of the brand and the ranch name, read as "And Ours", a corruption of "And Rs" referring to the double R, with one R being for Brad Rogers and the other for Earlene Rogers.

Earlene's musing hadn't prevented her from keeping a close eye on the cattle, and as always, taking a loose count. Their ranch house was at the lower end of their ranch. It was approximately ten miles to the Wandering River. It would have been difficult for anyone to enter their secluded ranch, without being seen, because of the narrow entrance which was commanded by their ranch house and the cedar pole fence they had erected.

Earlene and her father had left the ranch house at the same time, with her father riding about four hundred yards west of the creek that bisected their ranch into two similar sized plats of land. He then returned about four hundred yards east of the west boundary. Earlene rode up the east side of the creek, about four hundred yards out, and returned about four hundred yards west of the outcropping that formed their east boundary.

In this way, the two were able to cover every square inch of their property. The creek started near the upper end of the ranch. It began from springs that gushed from several cracks in the wall of the valley along their west boundary. There was no place on their ranch where cattle would have to walk more than three quarters of a mile to find water.

The land was sub-irrigated from the mountains, and the grasses grew high enough to have nice hay fields along the creek. They were planning on fencing in some hay fields along the lower end of the ranch, near the house. This was going to make the winter feeding of the cattle easy to accomplish when the snow was too deep for the cattle to graze. They had a field fenced off for growing corn near the creek below their house, and they intended on expanding it before winter set in.

The mountains surrounding their valley had the Rimrock all along the southern side, as though the forces that had squeezed the mountains out of the bowels of the earth had also forced up a plateau. This plateau created a weird formation all along the south side, as instead of having foot hills climbing up to the mountain range, the Rimrock gave a very abrupt beginning to the mountains. It also sheltered them from the frigid blizzards that often took a heavy toll on the cattle of the area that was generally referred to as the Bend of the Rimrock.

All in all, the Rogers' ranch, though not large, was large enough to afford a very good living. Even more important than the size, was the fact that its location made it easy to run. It allowed the more intense cattle raising of a stock farm, rather than a pure ranch. Instead of relying on sheer numbers of cattle, they put their efforts into up-grading their stock. They picked out the best twelve percent of the heifers each year to replace the cows that were beginning to age or become less productive. The second twenty percent were sold to small ranchers to upgrade their stock. The balance was sold with the steers. They kept eight range bulls, and brought in new bulls every four years, selling their older bulls to small ranchers who were anxious to upgrade their own herd.

They had a small bull pasture, and turned the bulls out only during the proper time to have a crop of spring calves and a crop of fall calves. By turning out four of the bulls to take care of the cows coming in heat for fall calves, and a different four bulls to take care of the cows coming in heat for spring calves, each group of calves was sired by different sets of bulls. Each two years, the groups of bulls were rotated, so that the bulls that bred the cows for spring calves the first two years would breed the cows for fall calves the second two year period. This prevented most interbreeding. Their bull calves were sorted before any castration took place, with only the top twenty percent sold for breeding bulls, and the rest castrated for market.

The butchers in the nearby town of Vacaville had contracts to get all of their beef from the &RR ranch, as did the town's restaurants. The &RR ranch raised enough corn in the creek bottom to feed out enough beef to supply the town of Vacaville with the finest of corn-fed beef. They were considering feeding out enough hogs to have monthly income from furnishing pork to the area. They had to weigh that consideration against selling corn to the valley ranchers for their horses.

Earlene reached the end of the canyon. The day was hot and she decided that she would take a swim in her own private hide-a-way. She rode her horse up the hidden path that she had discovered behind a thick growth of Birch and Willows.

This path could not be detected by anyone looking straight at it as it led up the face of the cliff-side, sloping upward from left to right at a moderate slope. It was well above eye level for a person on a horse when it emerged from the grove of trees that hid its beginning.

Reaching the top, she continued along a high stone ridge that angled very slightly to her right. She picketed her horse by the ridge, removed her bedroll, and spread it out on the soft, thick grass and proceeded to undress.

Her body was firm and slim. Smooth, supple muscles moved beneath her even tan, evidence that sunbathing was a frequent routine for her. Taking a bar of soap and a towel from a kit in her roll, she walked lithely beside the ridge for a short distance until she reached the canyon.

The musical sound of a not-too-distant waterfall came to her ears and the slight feel of mist lifted above the rim of the precipice and cooled her body. She turned left along the precipice, walked along the edge until she reached a pathway, then descended to the cool floor of the canyon.

She bathed in silence at the water's edge, basking in the sunlight. Lathering her hands, she slowly and sensuously smoothed the foam over her small, perfectly shaped breasts. She washed thoroughly;

then, using a brush that she had rolled up in her towel, she lightly scrubbed her back, arching in pleasure as the soft bristles caressed her skin.

She cupped her breasts in her hands and her forefingers traced tiny circles around her erect nipples. Shaking her fantasies away with a toss of her dark hair, she stepped off into the water.

She floated lazily on her back for a few minutes and then stroked as silently as an otter across the pool to a small grove of willows. When she reached the trees, she stepped out of the water. She hadn't taken more than two steps before she was taken aback by something she had never expected to see. About fifteen feet away a man was sleeping in the grass beneath the willow trees. With his face in repose, he appeared to be very young. He was lying on his back with one arm thrown over his eyes.

Earlene had never seen a nude man's body before. She had seen boy babies and even small boys naked, but this was far different to small boys. She had knowledge of how one must appear, but one's imagination never captured the true picture. None of the books she had ever read had dealt with *that* part of a man's anatomy. All her friends in school had liked to talk about such things, but none of them had first hand experience.

She had been raised around livestock and knew very well all about animal procreation. She sometimes got a strange and excited feeling when she watched the cattle and horses breed.

For a moment she stood, paralyzed by surprise and a mixture of unidentifiable emotions. She took two steps back to the edge of the water, as silently as possible. Suddenly the man's eyes opened and looked straight into her own. He appeared to be very startled. In an instant he rolled from beneath the willow boughs and sprang to his feet. Before he could turn to face her, she had dived into the pool and was swimming beneath the surface toward the hidden path. A moment later, she was around the promontory and out of sight.

Swiftly she gathered her things and quickly ran up the path to her horse. Her skin had dried in the summer air as she started to dress. Instead, she fumbled around in one saddle bag and pulled out her binoculars, and ran back to the precipice, feeling as guilty as a peeping Tom.

She found a vantage point between two stones near the rocky ridge and crawled to the edge for a closer look. She raised her head carefully, just enough to allow her to look through the opening between the two stones. The man was moving around, peering under branches and searching through the brush. He had a baffled look on his face as he looked first one way, then the other. Eventually he must have decided he had been dreaming, for he gave up and lay down once again and closed his eyes.

It appeared that he was immediately asleep. It was also obvious that he was involved in some fantasy or dread, for his male organ was very erect, and straining against the flesh that held it secured to his body. Earlene could see the willow leaves drag back and forth over his pubic area, and the man's body began to make slight movements that raised his hips and subtly thrust them upward.

A minute later his hand seemed to become part of the action of the breeze, for it wandered down and began making light stroking motions, alternating with what seemed to be hard squeezes.

Earlene suddenly realized she was also lightly stroking herself. She couldn't stop! Her hand was in time with that of the man she watched.

The man's hips thrust up forcefully and the man's hand was grasping his organ tightly and moving it vigorously.

Her hand was also vigorously moving on her own organ and her finger had joined in as though of its own volition. She place the entire weight of her body on her hand, which was imprisoned between her body and the soft grass.

She saw the man's ejaculation begin, with the product of his body spurting onto his stomach and pubic area. She felt her body convulse and stiffen with pulse after pulse of pure pleasure racking her body and taking control of both her body and emotions.

She still had to keep the binoculars directly on the man; his swollen member was rapidly beginning to wilt and lose its rigidity. Her own body was falling into a state of relaxation more profound than any she had ever experienced.

She had noted and marveled at the way a bull's great instrument of reproduction was thrust inside a cow with the power of an ax hitting a log. A few hard thrusts, a time of fighting against withdrawal, and then as the bull dismounted, that great tool retreated from the cow and immediately withdrew back into its sheath.

She had also watched as a stud horse entered a mare as though his member was a battering ram being rammed into a door, making an aperture through which it entered, followed by several thrusts and then a period when his head was laid tightly against the side of the mare's shoulder, caressing her side as she often turned her head back as though entreating him to continue. Still, a minute later, would see that same battering ram slide slowly out, its strength depleted, still partially engorged, with its head swollen to the size of a saucer as it sort of sucked against the vacuum being created in the mare. Then it would swing down below the stud's belly, still huge but quickly losing mass, and then disappearing back inside his sheath.

How could so much pass through her mind in such a short period of time, while her own body retreated from its initial tension to the loss of stress it felt now?

How could the man's organ have surrendered to that same lassitude she felt, when a moment before it had looked as though it were a permanent and indestructable as one of the great mountains thrusting up into the clouds?

She was beginning to feel the pressure of time, but yet she lingered.

The man lay there for a moment and then arose and waded out into the water and washed his belly and pubic area off. It was hard for her to believe that the same tool of production that swung loosely between his legs in front of his scrotum was the same piece of flesh that had challenged the world but minutes before.

Then he came out of the water and used his hands to dash the water from his body. Walking a few steps from the remnants of his campfire, he began to urinate.

Earlene was fascinated to see him stand and urinate. He moved his penis as though drawing designs in the grass. She wondered how it felt to be able to hold one's self like that and urinate in any direction one desired by merely moving that piece of pliable flesh around to aim it at any place one wished. She felt somewhat guilty over having spied on a man in such a private moment. However, she would never again see the stranger who had invaded her private refuge!

As he turned back toward the burned out ashes of his campfire, she rushed through dressing and quickly eased her horse down the path to the bottom of the &RR and continued her inspection of their cattle.

She did feel some kind of a difference in the usual sensuous feeling generated by the saddle pressing against her, or bumping when the horse stepped into a low spot. She had felt this all many times before, but they seemed to have a different meaning now.

Chapter Four
The arrival

It was a long and dusty forty mile trip around the southern end of the Rimrock. As soon as I passed the place where it bent back in a northeasterly direction, the desert disappeared and a good stand of Curly Mesquite and Gramma grass began.

This was great land for grazing cattle. The grass grew up in the spring, cured in the summer and fall and kept a large amount of protein and food value for grazing in the winter. When it was not overgrazed, it was some of the best cattle country in the world. It was also short on water in many areas. This was one of them.

I followed the Rimrock northward. I planned to explore every little enclave, hoping to find one that would extend into the high ground and broaden into a canyon or valley that would furnish cattle a good wintering place and also make it easy to handle them, alone or with one puncher.

The ideal would be a small to medium sized spread that was enclosed within the high ground with a fairly narrow entrance that I could someday fence. I could build near the open end and ride out each day to keep the cattle pushed back toward the interior until I could put a fence across the opening.

When I had passed through this countryside seven years earlier, I had discovered such a valley. It was green and well watered from a large spring which flowed from the Rimrock at the upper end of the valley. It was ideal for what I had in mind.

I had also discovered another such valley, but I hadn't had time to explore it. No water was flowing in the part that I saw, but the grass was sub-irrigated from the higher ground which surrounded it.

I had some sort of a built-in affinity for that place. If it had water, I preferred it to the one that I had seen that did have water. The trouble was, I couldn't remember exactly where; only that it was a day's ride from where I now rode. The valley that held my hidden oasis where both Calliope and I had rested up had only one drawback. The desert walled it in as securely as did the Rimrock itself.

I took my time and explored every little cul-de-sac. All of them were shallow and showed little promise of what I was seeking. It was late in the afternoon when I came across a line of trees and bushes following the course of a stream that flowed from the narrow mouth of a canyon. As I rode closer to the canyon's entrance, I saw a pole fence stretching from side to side. It was about a hundred yards inside the canyon.

A large sign was over the gate proudly displaying the names, Brad Rogers across the top and Earlene Rogers across the bottom. Between the two was written, "& OURS RANCH". At each end of the sign, the brand, &RR was burned into the wood. It was easy to see that the name, & Ours, was a corruption of the brand.

This was the second of the valleys I had discovered when I had ridden through this area several years before. It was also a blow to my hopes that this area would still be unsettled, and my heart fell with disappointment. The watered place that I had coveted was now taken. Was the same true of the larger valley with the old river bed? Had I arrived too late to realize the dream I had carried with me ever since my previous trip?

If it turned out the valley I had my heart set on was taken, or if the land proved to be too dry, perhaps I could find something along the river that lay a few miles to the south. I decided it would be worth my while to introduce myself to the owner of the property to see if he could shed any light on the subject. If nothing else, perhaps he knew of some land in the area that might still be available.

I opened the gate and led my horse through, replacing the bars behind me. It seemed the perfect place. I hated to have missed such an ideal opportunity, but opportunities seldom wait until we can take advantage of them.

As I rode along, I passed several head of cattle which turned out to be only a small portion of a good-sized herd. I rode a little further until I came across a ranch house surrounded by some out-buildings.

I was ready to approach the house when I saw a man riding toward me. He had a rifle in his right hand, with the barrel resting on the horse's neck, just in front of the saddle horn. He appeared tense, even at this distance.

I pulled up my horse with its body quartering across his line of travel. Both of my hands were resting on my saddle horn. The man's rifle was pointed at a forty five degree angle, but there was no question he was ready to use it.

I hooked my right leg over the saddle horn so that I was more directly facing him. I leaned over with my crossed hands on my knee and watched him as he rode up. It also made it easier for him to see that I meant him no harm. He rode up, looked me up and down and said, "You're a little off your range, aren't you?"

"It's hard to say", I answered, "Since I don't have any range yet". I cuffed my hat back and grinned at him. "It looks like you have some good grass here. From the way you're holding your rifle, I'd say that it is not improbable that someone else has their eye on it too. Either that or someone has been helping himself to some of your beef. I just rode around the Bend of the Rimrock and didn't see any sign of cattle being moved.

It would be a long way to market that way, seems to me."

The man was beginning to relax a little. "Well, no one has been rustling my stock. I suppose the man with his eye on mine has his other eye on my range and thinks he might as well get it all intact. He doesn't see any need in rustling the stock."

"Yeah, it seems like this country is full of those hombres who want it all," I said. "I was through here one time, about seven years ago. There wasn't a ranch in this whole country. Now people are fighting over land that no one wanted at the time." I took off my hat and let the cool breeze that had just sprung up cool my sweaty forehead.

"Well," he said slowly, "there weren't any people around here when I arrived five years ago. This valley's off the beaten trail. I just accidentally stumbled onto my place. It may not be big, but I think it's the best place that was ever created".

He had been occasionally scanning the prairie with glances over his left shoulder, toward where his valley reached into the Rimrock. "Here comes the other half of this spread," he said, as a girl suddenly rode into view. She crossed the creek that divided the little valley in half, and as she drew nearer, the man's face brightened. A moment later she pulled her pony to a stop, her alert eyes quickly appraising me, my horse, the man to whom I was talking and the general atmosphere.

I noted caution in her posture, which was relaxing as she saw the man I was talking to smiling fondly at her. The man reached over and held out his hand. "Sorry I'm so late in introducing myself," he said. "I'm Brad Rogers. This is my daughter and partner, Earlene.

You may have noticed the brand on the cattle. It is called the 'And Ours' in these parts." He pointed to the brand on the left hip of Earlene's horse. "There's the '&', and those two Rs make it the And Rs brand, but we've always called it the And Ours, for the first R is Earlene's part of the Roger name and the second is mine.

You see, this ranch isn't just hers, it isn't just mine, it's ours or you might say, Rs." You could see the love shining from his eyes as he let his eyes swing from the horse's brand to his daughter.

"My name is Seeker, Easy Seeker." I returned her smile with one of my own."

"Aw Dad," she grinned, "You know the first R is yours!" She held out her tanned hand to me. I took it and felt a handshake as firm as a man's. She left her hand in mine just long enough to show friendliness before withdrawing it. "What brings you to our little out of the way valley?" The question was casual, but one could see intentness as she listened for the answer.

"It's a long and convoluted story", I answered. "It's neither a quick nor easy one to tell."

"Well, your name *is* Easy," she said, a twinkle in her eye. "Telling a long story shouldn't exhaust you over-much". She shot a quick glance at her father and said, "Dad, why don't we ask Mr. Seeker to supper. It's getting about time to think of eating, and we are only ten minutes from home. It's *hard* to think of poor *Easy* having a *hard* time *easing* up on some unsuspecting rabbit to *ease* his hunger." She put a little accent on each variation of the words easy and hard. Then she laughed and told me and her father, "Come on, let's go chow down!"

A few minutes later, we arrived at a small, but well built log house. The corrals were neatly and efficiently arranged, just down the slight rise from where the house set. The house appeared to have four rooms.

When I entered, it was into a fair-sized and comfortably furnished living room which in turn was separated from a kitchen by a well worn table which butted against the wall on one end and served to make the one big room appear as though it were two.

The kitchen was clean and neatly arranged and it was plain to see that the Rogers were building to stay. Two doors opened off of the east end of the living room. I imagined that they were a bed room for each of the Rogers. In back there was a well-built porch that ran the width of the house on the north side. It made a cool place to sit and look out over the verdant valley to where the wandering stream disappeared toward the distant end of the canyon, some three miles or so away.

The front porch ran the width of the house on the south side, where we'd entered. It commanded a view of the narrow entrance to the valley. The house was located less than a quarter of a mile inside the pole fence that separated the valley from the land outside the valley, where I had been riding.

I had one big surprise when I walked out the kitchen door onto the porch to wash up for supper. A well had been dug before the porch was built. The porch was built to enclose the well within the wooden flooring. A pitcher pump was conveniently located just outside the kitchen door.

I started to make a comment on the convenience of the well and pump, something that was a real novelty in that part of the country. It was also very unusual to find water at a shallow enough depth to allow a well to be dug by hand. "Wow!" I exclaimed. Talk about convenience. I have always been lucky to find a mud hole to bathe in," I said.

"It didn't look like you were having any trouble finding a good place to bathe the day before yesterday", she said, turning to hide her blushing face.

Her words hit me like a bolt of lightning. How could this girl possibly know where I had been bathing the other day? I decided she was purposely being enigmatic, for there was no possible way she could have been in two places at the same time unless she had wings.

The thought hadn't even crossed my mind that she had actually seen me in the valley at all. How could she have possibly seen me at my oasis and returned to this spread when it was a two day journey from here? I chuckled to myself, for if she had wings, they were surely well hidden. Her clothing accented nothing but the beautiful body of an athetic young woman in great shape from her ranch work.

It suddenly occurred to me that if she had been watching me in the valley that day, she would have seen everything I was doing! She would have seen me washing my clothes, taking my nap, and cooking my meal. Not only that, but she would have seen me doing those things as naked as the day I was born!

I finished drying my face and with a swipe of my hand, brushed my hair back as Earlene joined me on the porch.

"I'm almost afraid to ask you what you meant by your remark about me having plenty of water the day before yesterday," I said, rushing my words and speaking in a nearly muffled voice.

In an attitude of mirth, she seemed to ponder my remark. Then, with a curious expression on her face, she said. "Easy, please wait here a moment. I'll be right back." She left the porch but returned with a crystal bowl.

"Please pump this full of water," she said.

I obliged, wondering what in the world she was leading up to. "Here you go," I said, handing her the bowl full of clear and shimmering water. The stars were reflected in the still water and the moon drew a miniature but nearly occult trail over its surface. The cut crystal reflected those lights into a myriad of sparkling dots.

Earlene took the bowl and told me, "I'm a witch and this is my crystal ball." Then she gave a chuckle that seemed a little strained to me. She closed her eyes, stretched her arms out like a cross and slowly brought them around to point toward the rising moon.

"Oh, Luna, carry me back to the past. Carry me to the place where this man spent the night, two nights ago. Oh, Luna, bring me into that time and let me see what happened." She was speaking in a sing-song voice that was nearly hypnotic, and her face looked exotic in the starlight.

As she dropped her head down, she furrowed her brow. "Now," she intoned, "the past is being revealed. Please do not move or speak to break my trance."

I stood enraptured, knowing that what she was doing was impossible, but still captured up in the moment of time.

Earlene moved her hands over the bowl of water and then caressed the sides of the bowl as though it were an omnipotent gateway to the supernatural. "I see a hot and arid land. I see a man and horse toiling through the heat. By chance, they found an unknown entrance to an enchanted valley. This valley can only be seen by a chosen few. The only man who has ever been privileged to enter its forbidden portals now stands by my side, awed by your power, Oh Luna. Reveal to me his actions that evening."

She stopped speaking for a moment and began humming in a gripping drone of sound. "Continue, oh Mistress of the Moon, Maker of Tides and She Who Exposes the Truth. Reveal to me the innermost thoughts and actions of this man."

I found myself captured by something that I was afraid would disrupt all of my beliefs and convictions, but I maintained my silence.

"Luna, Wise and Wonderful, please unveil to us what this man did. What were his innermost thoughts? What emotions pulsated through his heart on that special night?"

She gazed into the bowl as though the water held some magical power. Suddenly she turned to me and looked deeply into my eyes. Her face was flushed and her eyes were burning with some strange combination of emotions.

When she looked back into the bowl, she intoned, "I see a tired and lonely man; a man with a wounded soul who was granted entrance into an enchanted Eden. Then he undressed and washed his clothing in the bewitching waters of the sacred pool. He lay down at the edge and immediately fell into a trance-like sleep."

I was shocked by what I had heard and afraid of what she had seen, but I didn't want to interrupt, either, for along with my fear of her disclosure was a far greater sense of disappointment that she might not have seen the rest of what happened.

"As he lay sleeping under your spell," she continued, "his dreams became erotic and infused with sensuously explicit feelings. Luna, Oh Luna," she cried, "please don't take the vision away. Please disclose to me the rest of this man's innermost feelings. Expose his every hope, desire, and goal that he has never expressed, even to himself."

She shook her head as though awakening from a trance. A moment later, she turned to me and said, "Easy that is all that has been revealed to me."

Suddenly she turned toward the door. There was no sign that she even remembered the remark she had made moments earlier. I heard the click of the bowl as she set it on the cabinet. A moment later she returned. I was not sure, but it seemed there was a smile hidden so deeply inside her that it could not quite break free and shine from that lovely face.

She went straight to the well and pulled up a bucket. Its lid was fashioned out of meshed wire that was fastened to the bail on either side. The bucket, itself, was perforated on the bottom and sides. This allowed it not only to sink easily when lowered into the water, but it also allowed the water to quickly drain out when it was raised above the surface. The bucket was used to store food and the cold water in the well kept it refrigerated.

The bucket rose to the top of the well and she displayed to me jars of milk, cheese and other things that tasted better and remained fresher when cool.

Another light rope reached down into the water on the other side of the pump. "I assume that one is for your extra milk and cheese," I said.

Earlene smiled and told me, "Well then, your assumption is wrong. If we want to cool something that is too light to sink into the water, or that will get wet and soggy if it were to get wet, we've another way of treating it. Wait a minute, while I pull it up and show you."

She began to pull the other line up. It was threaded over a light pulley. There was a loop in the line that could be placed over a big spike that was driven into one of the porch posts that supported the roof. It was tied at a point in the line that would allow whatever was in the container to be lowered only deep enough to be covered with water, without sinking deeper into the well.

I reached over to take the line from Earlene and pull up whatever was on the other end. She shouldered me aside with a smile and continued pulling it up herself.

When her shoulder struck mine, I felt a jolt go through my body. My face reddened as I thought of the impossibility of her gazing at my nude body in the little oasis a couple of days earlier. One thing was for sure. Crystal water or no crystal water, everybody knew there was no such thing as a witch. Didn't they? There's a big difference between being bewitching and being a witch.

I suddenly recalled the nude girl I had seen in a dream I had that night. Maybe it hadn't been a dream at all. Maybe I had caught a glimpse of Earlene as she had unexpectedly stumbled upon me just before I awoke. Anyway, I was positive even a witch couldn't just disappear.

By the way Earlene was struggling with the rope; it was obvious that the weight on the line was considerably greater than it had been on the previous line.

A moment later, the mystery was solved as a five gallon cream can rose to the surface. The girl effortlessly swung it over to rest on the stone rim of the well. I could immediately see that the reason for the extra weight was some kind of heavy iron pieces from a farm implement that had been fastened to the cream can.

The girl explained to me, "See, Easy! The cream can with its lid keeps water from getting in on things that don't easily go into jars to make them water proof. My bread, for example, sure couldn't stand getting wet. These weights make the cream can heavy enough to sink beneath the water's surface, despite being mostly full of air. This lets me keep more things fresh."

As Earlene explained all this to me, her father suddenly joined us. "That's all Earlene's invention," he said proudly. "I've never seen nor heard of anyone else using such a method."

He laid his hand proudly on his daughter's shoulder. Earlene smiled and said, "OK, enough of that! Let's eat a bite." She took the items out of the bucket; then her father and I followed her into the kitchen.

Earlene served sliced beef sandwiches on homemade lightbread for lunch, and poured each of us a tall glass of cool buttermilk. She then placed a jar of plum jam on the table. "For your information, this jam came out of a thicket that grows further back right here inside our own little valley. We can be pretty self sufficient when we want to be," she remarked with a touch of pride.

A few minutes later we all pushed back from the table and Earlene turned to me and said, "Okay, let's hear that long and convoluted story!"

Staring at my coffee cup, I sat in silence for a moment while I gathered my thoughts together. Finally I said, "It's hard to know where to start. I was born in Connecticut. My dad had a small fishing boat. Mother worked right alongside him when he was busy fishing. I was lending a hand from the time I was old enough to form a memory.

Our joint dream was to save enough money to come west and take up a piece of land. We were all used to hard work and we were naturally happy. We enjoyed working in the fishing industry together and watching our savings slowly add up. That is, all of us enjoyed it excluding my sister, Alice.

She was two years older than I was. When she was seventeen, she was able to get a job in a clothing factory. She worked long hours for little pay, but she didn't mind contributing her share to the family coffers.

One night, she didn't come home from work. A girl who worked in the factory brought a note that Alice had written. She had asked her to give it to Mother and Dad when she got off work. The note explained that a man had stood in front of the factory trying to hire two girls to work as maids for an English family that was traveling from New York to St. Louis, by way of New Orleans and the Mississippi River.

They offered much better wages than the factory paid. Alice was one of the two chosen. She asked if she could run home and leave a note for her family. She was told that the steamboat for New Orleans was leaving immediately. They told her she could mail a letter from New Orleans. She scribbled the note and sent it by the girl who delivered it.

We never got any further word. Dad went to the dock and was told that a steamboat had left for New Orleans at a time that coincided with the time the English family was supposed to leave. However, no one knew anything about an English family. They did verify that a man with two girls from the factory had boarded the boat, along with another hardcase. Dad was unable to find out anything more.

"I promised Dad that I would go to New Orleans to see if I could pick up her trail. That was nine years ago. When I arrived, I found a dockworker who remembered them booking passage from New Orleans to St. Louis. When I got to St. Louis, a merchant said that he vaguely remembered outfitting a party of two young women, a gunman and another tough looking fella who were joining a wagon train. He was able to give me a rough description of the men.

"After asking around, I finally found someone who served as a guide for the train. He said that to the best of his recollection, the men and girls had left the train where the Oregon Trail forked off toward the California gold fields. I searched for several years without one single additional clue."

I stopped talking for a moment, trying to retrace the steps of the fifteen year old boy I had been when I started, all the way up to the twenty four year old man I had become.

Brad sat quietly listening, his face reflecting his understanding.

Earlene must have seen the pain in my face, for she quickly asked me, "Easy, how was it you came to pass through this area seven years ago? That would have made you a year younger than I am now."

"I ran into a man who had had a store in St. Louis. He had sold out and come to California in a wagon train. He remembered the second man who had been with the big gunfighter when they took the two girls and headed for New Orleans.

He had seen that second man kill another fellow who had made advances to one of the girls they were escorting. It seemed that he had a thing going with the girl." I paused for a minute, thinking back. Then, anticipating the question, I added, "No, it wasn't my sister.

The man who was telling me the story said that the girl I had described as my sister was quite stand-offish, and had as little to do with the rest of the group as she could. The first man seemed interested in my sister, but apparently, they had no romantic relationship. Anyway, to make the story a little shorter, it gave me a trail to follow, for the law put a price on the man's head and he evidently started back to St. Louis. He took some out of the way trails, and one of them brought him across the desert and he began to follow the Rimrock. I caught up with him about a day's ride east of here."

"And what happened then?" the girl asked.

"He had just cooked up a mess of beans with some fried bacon and bread. He invited me to eat with him, and I did. Then I asked him what he knew about my sister, and what his intentions had been for the girls after they were fed the fictitious story about the job with the British family."

I tried to speak calmly, for I wanted to find out where the other man was headed with the girls.

"He just grinned and said my sister had been the victim of a run-away wagon that had slammed into a tree and turned over. There were no survivors, including Alice. I asked him where her body was and he said she was buried in a grove of trees along the trail and that the spot was marked with a wagon wheel, half buried in the ground. A board with her name was tied to the spokes.

"I told him that he would have to ride along with me so he could show me where she was buried. He laughed and told me she was buried in hell and that if I didn't leave, he would lose his patience and send me straight to hell with her.

I told him that I would let him go if he would show me her grave. He laughed again and asked me what the hell I meant when I said that he could go free if he came with me. I told him that I would kill him if he didn't.

He said that it wouldn't be that way. He stood up and I stood up. He laughed and told me to go for my gun. He fell into the fire when I shot him. I rode back this way, thinking that the buzzards would have a meal of cooked meat.

"Back on the trail, a half day later, I changed my mind and went back and gathered the man's belongings, rolled him up in a tarp and took him back to the sheriff. I gladly accepted the reward money and sent it back to my parents.

"Two months later I received a letter from a lawyer. My parents had sold their boat and were coming west to find me and to buy that ranch we'd always wanted. It turns out the river boat they were on blew up between New Orleans and St. Louis. I had a check for the boat money and the reward money which is what I'm using now to put towards a ranch when I find the one I'm hunting for."

The profound silence that fell between us at that moment was filled with sadness and empathy. Finally I said, "When I get my ranch, I intend to bury my parents and my sister on it."

I expected both of the Rogers to invite me to move on down the trail, but surprisingly they didn't. Earlene shook her head without saying a word. Brad made the comment, "I suppose that pistol you're packing is for more than show, judging by what you have just said."

"I suppose one could say that," I answered.

A moment later Earlene began again, "So that's what brought you back to this country?" she inquired. "It seems to me that you came a long way to get to this particular spot to find a ranch."

I glanced up and met her eyes. "Yes, that's what I came back for. You see, I had found a valley similar to this one, just a little east of here, as I recall. It was nice, but had no water. Then I discovered this valley, and it was this valley that brought me back.

 There are other reasons in addition to the valley. One of them is that it was near here that I found out that my sister was dead. It was near here that I killed one of the men who were involved in coaxing her to leave Connecticut. This is also the place where my parents got as near to justice as they'll ever get for their daughter."

"I can understand a young man coming back for this valley", Brad said, "but what are you going to do now that you know it's already been taken?"

I shot a glance at Earlene. She still had a look of unsatisfied curiosity. "Yeah," she said, "So what do you do now?" She poured the three of us another cup of coffee.

I stirred some cream into my cup, rather morosely. "I really can't get that other valley out of my mind. It looked like an old river bed came right down through the middle of it. Maybe I could put a dam across it and catch enough water for a few head of stock. I just don't know. There is some additional kind of a pull that I really don't understand. It is as though the valley is reaching out to me, as though there's another reason for my being here that I've yet to discover and haven't even put into words in my own mind. I doubt that I know what it is."

I put the cup to my lips and took a tentative sip. Then I went on, "I had a dream the other day. I won't bore you with the details, and it was quite private, anyway, but one thing's for sure. There's no other place that I know of where I could find neighbors as nice as the ones I've met here on the &RR. Maybe I came back to find such neighbors."

No one said anything for a minute. I sat there blowing on my hot coffee, taking small sips every so often. Earlene was looking at me with an expression like I had never seen before.

"You know," Brad said to Earlene, "Easy must be referring to that narrow opening in the Rimrock, just around that jagged bend where that old wash runs down to the river."

"Yes," Earlene answered back. "I was just sitting here thinking. There isn't another place that answers that description. However, I had no idea that it opens up into a valley. I thought it ended just a hundred yards into the cliff-side."

"I've heard there is a small town near here," I said, half asking and half stating.

"That would be Vacaville," Brad said. "I have one piece of information that you need to know before you make any plans to settle here. There's a range hog named Burly Dobbins that has a big ranch on the other side of the river. He has made it plain that he plans to take up all of the land from the Rimrock to that ridge of hills about ten or twelve miles south of the river. He brags he is going to graze all of the land, beginning from where the desert starts and running all the way back east on both sides of the river from here on east to the east fork of the river. He just might do it, too."

He was silent for a moment, and then added, "He already has the south side. That's the side that has water. The only reason he hasn't taken this place already is because, along with the water and the sheltered graze, he's made it clear that he wants Earlene, too. I've seen the way he looks at her when we're in town for supplies. I'll tell you right now, Easy, in no uncertain terms, he'd have to kill me first, 'cause I sure as hell won't let him have either, as long as I'm living."

"I can't tell you how much I appreciate your hospitality," I said. Tomorrow I intend to get a close look at that piece of ground with the old river bed. I intend to look it over tomorrow. I'll see if it looks as good as I remember it." I stood up and grabbed my hat.

"We won't even hear of you leaving at this time of evening," Earlene said. "We need a good neighbor. If those of us on this side of the river were to band together, we might be able to hang onto our places." She stood up briskly. "Take your bedroll and spread it on the back porch. You can eat breakfast with us in the morning, if you think you can stand any more of my coffee."

"If there were ever anything that I could stand, it would be another cup of that coffee," I said.

Brad grabbed his hat off of a peg in the wall. "I'll walk out with you and we'll put your horse into the corral. A forkful of hay and some corn shouldn't hurt him, either." He led me outside. I took my bedroll from behind my saddle, threw it on the porch and we walked to the barn.

"How worried are you about that Dobbins fella?" I asked, now that we were alone.

"How worried can a fella be?" he answered.

When we reached the pole corral, I draped my saddle over the top rail. We said little as we walked back to the house. He went inside and I carried my bedroll around to the back and spread it out on the porch.

As I drifted off to sleep, I felt a strong affinity with the stars that hung over this troubled country. In my dream, I saw the naked form of a girl as she stood watching me wake up.

You know how dreams can be. They can take the desires that one doesn't even know exist and build them into a fairy tale of happenings that are very seldom found to be a part of real life; real life just can't eliminate all of the doubts and the buts, ands and ifs that dreams sometime provide. I started trying to figure out how Earlene had been able to make such an accurate summation of my evening in the secret valley the other night.

I awoke the next morning without a clue as to how she had been able to tell me what I had done. She had had some fun at my expense playing the part of a witch, though. What a sense of humor! For that matter, what a sense of innocence to "read" my past without shame.

I also knew, deep in the recesses of my mind, that she knew every move I had made as I camped beside those clear waters. I didn't know how she knew, but I knew that she knew. In the darkest and most profound parts of my mind, where my most precious secrets resided, I could find no answer. I knew that she had to have seen me. I could not resolve the question of how she had gotten there and back again so quickly. I hated to broach such a delicate subject, but I had to know the answer to that question.

The naked girl that I saw *had* to have been a dream. In my dream, it had been a startled face that I had seen. It was looking through dark hair with water streaming down. It was human nature that now made me attribute Earlene's face to that wet body. One thing was a fact. It would have been impossible for her to could have been that far away from the &RR, and still have been here at her ranch when I arrived.

There was a second fact, now that I thought of it. She surely had the body that would do justice to any dream.

Chapter Five
My lost valley

We must have all been running on the same clock, for as I got up and stowed my bedroll, I could hear people stirring around inside the kitchen. I had just finished washing up when the back door opened and Earlene came out to draw up the breakfast ingredients from her ingenious improvised cooler.

Ham, eggs, lightbread and hot coffee were on the menu for this morning. I went in and got the water bucket and pumped a fresh bucket of cool water; then Brad and I chatted of ranch related topics as Earlene prepared breakfast.

A few minutes later we sat down to ham and eggs with hot coffee. Before retiring the night before, Earlene had asked me how I like my eggs cooked. She brought them hot off the skillet when I joined the two at the table, and they were made to perfection.

We sat in silence as we enjoyed our meal, which surprised me. However, I supposed it was because the hard-working people from these parts were used to rising early and working hard, not wanting to waste time on idle chit-chat.

I pushed back from the table and was about to say my goodbyes when Earlene spoke. "Easy, I've been thinking. It takes me and Dad about three hours to make our rounds of the ranch, barring finding something that has to be taken care of. We have our crops in and it is between calving, branding, and our other seasonal chores. We are enjoying our easiest time of the year, so it wouldn't be putting us to any trouble. Why don't you make the rounds with us, and then we can ride with you to your lost valley? We can save you time by taking you straight to the right place."

I looked questioningly at Brad, and he nodded. "It sounds like a good plan to me", he affirmed. "If you feel you have the time to spare, you can see what we are in the process of doing with this little spread. We have some real plans, and think we have just the place to make them all feasible."

I was curious as to how a such a well watered place would look. I was sure the high ground surrounding the valley would contribute to the sub-irrigation. "I would like that," I agreed. "It will give me a goal to work toward on my own place."

Brad smiled as he noticed that I was already using the possessive 'my' when I spoke of the valley that I had only seen one time, and very superficially at that. I smiled back at him, so he would know that I knew he had noted my presupposed claim to the place.

At the barn, when I reached for my bedroll, Brad stopped me. "Why don't you wait until we get back before loading your horse down with all your gear?" The thought of my twenty pound bedroll loading my horse down made all three of us laugh. I understood his offer, however, and opted to leave it behind when we rode out.

We rode out of the ranch yard and Brad spoke. "Here is where we split up. I always ride out the far side of the creek and Earlene takes this side. We go up canyon near the creek on each side, and return on the on the side toward the Rimrock. That gives us pretty good coverage of the place.

We each carry binoculars. That saves us some riding and helps us make a rough count of the cattle each day. Earlene, why don't you take Easy with you and explain to him what we're doing? We'll get back while it is still early and you and Easy can go look for his valley while I cut a few more posts." I felt a flush of happiness that Brad had divided us up so that Earlene and I would be riding together. My happiness was doubled as I noted the faint blush of color cover her tanned cheeks.

Earlene was eager to chat as we rode along toward the Rimrock. She explained about the plans they had to farm the land along the creek, and how they were going to fence off the cropland from the pastureland. The new cropland would run adjacent to what they had already fenced off for corn.

They also had plans for cross-fencing which would enable them to separate the steers that would be going to market from the springing heifers and the yearling calves. It would also allow for rotational grazing. I could see the enthusiasm in her face as she spoke and I couldn't help thinking what a great partner she would make.

Our horses had stopped of their own volition as we reached the end of the canyon. Earlene made no effort to turn back toward the house and I had hardly noted that we had stopped.

I had kept putting off asking her how she had gotten from her home to the little oasis that I had discovered and how she had returned to her ranch to arrive ahead of me. I was reluctant to mention it because of the way she had apparently seen me so up close and exposed and I didn't want to embarrass her; yet I loved the sense of excitement it stirred in me whenever I contemplated the question.

Earlene must have read my mind, for she said, "Easy, I know that we met under what were rather strange circumstances, and I'm sure you're wondering about how it was possible that I appeared to be both there and here at nearly the same time." She looked at my face to gauge my reaction, but continued before I could answer. "Let's tie our horses here in this little grove of trees. I want to show you something."

She swung off her horse without waiting for an answer, slipped the bit out of its mouth and clipped a picket rope to the bridle to allow it to graze. She took something out of her saddle bag that was wrapped in a soft cloth. She didn't volunteer what it was and I didn't ask. I had already picketed my horse by that time and I followed her slim body as she walked behind the screen of birch, willow trees and a plum thicket to the wall of the canyon.

Even though I had been looking for a way up the cliff, when it suddenly appeared, I nearly missed it. Over unknown ages, the rain that had fallen on the highlands above had worn down what had started out as a crack, into a chute that seemed made for a trail. Without wasting time on words, Earlene climbed agilely up the passage way. I could see signs that a horse had been ridden up that same trail.

We were both breathing hard from the climb when we reached the top. My breath had also been accelerated by watching her firm body move ahead of me. Not that I didn't try to keep from looking!

At the top, going left, the land ran level for maybe fifty yards before it tilted up toward the first mountain. I could see the shoulder of another mountain, with a third in the distance that seemed to be trying to peep over the two nearer peaks.

On the right, an outcropping of stone formed a ridge that slanted off at an angle from the valley. It barricaded a clear view of the land beyond. Further along the ridge, the rugged mountains began, angling off directly on our right to a distance of several miles. In front of us, only about twenty five or thirty yards or so, there was nothing to see but a yawning emptiness of space.

The ridge bisected the end of the emptiness that had to be a canyon. Earlene grabbed my hand and said, "Come on, Slow Poke!" She tugged on my hand and led me at nearly a trot to the edge of the rim where we stood. I had to do a double take before I realized that we were looking down on the oasis where I had spent the night a couple of days earlier. The sound of the waterfall was clear in the morning air.

"Come on," she shouted. "You ain't seen nothing' yet!" She jogged off to the left and started down a trail to the bottom. No wonder I hadn't seen her from the willows where I had taken my nap while my clothes were drying the other day! It was completely hidden from view!

"Let me guess," I said. "This is your own private little swimming spot, isn't it?"

"As right as rain," she answered. "As you can see, the trail is an easy way down. I had never, in all the years we've lived here, seen another human being either here, near here, or anywhere in this vicinity. I had never been so surprised to see anyone in my life as I was to see you that day! This is the spot where I had initially undressed, and then returned to after my swim to lie down in the sun for a few minutes to dry off."

"I went down the trail, slipped into the water and swam across. You were," she said, turning her head enough to mask her face, "lying there sleeping as naked as the day you were born. I watched in amazement to see any human in this area that I considered my secret hide-away. I know that you had considered it as pristine and private as I do and did.

"You must have been awakened by the strength of the dream you were having." She was speaking with no sign of embarrassment or of shame. "I couldn't help looking you over as you lay there so soundly sleeping for a moment, before you began to awaken. It was so obvious that you must have been having some kind of dream, from the way you stirred and stretched yourself awake. I had just started backing away to leave as silently as possible, when you began to stir. Suddenly you opened you eyes and saw me before I could retreat. You rolled over, but I was leaving as fast as you were trying to get up.

"I slipped back into the pool and swam underwater to the other side of that strange rock in front of us." She pointed to a bulge in the wall. "As you can see, it blocks our view of the willows, so when you were at the willows, your vision was blocked from this trail.

"Once on land, I ran up the trail as fast as I could go. I was planning to saddle up and head back to the ranch, but something stopped me." She smiled then and said, "Come with me for a moment."

She turned and walked toward an area where the stony ridge bisected the end of the canyon. When she came to a particular spot, she raised the cloth wrapped package, removed her binoculars and when she handed them to me, I knew the rest of the story.

I put the binoculars to my eyes and focused on the willow trees which appeared close enough to touch. Directly in front of them was the place where I had stood and urinated.

"I'm not sure I understand. Are you telling me you stood here and watched as I did all those things that I did?" I was amazed that a young woman would make such a confession.

"No Easy, I didn't stand here and watch you. I lay in the grass in my bare hide and watched you. To put it bluntly, I was an active participant in your entire ritual. Girls are as much a part of nature as are men. We are not impervious to the same feelings that men have.

"I would have never been able to tell such a thing to anyone else but you. Why to you? Because I have an advantage over you. You had lain yourself stripped bare before me, unknowing and unsuspecting. I had to give you an even start with me, if you're going to be our neighbor and friend."

I stood for a moment, dumbfounded by what she had just said. "Well, you still have an advantage of me, then. You have seen me completely. I have only seen a fleeting glimpse of you, while I was still actually sleeping."

"Sorry, Easy. My sense of fair play doesn't extend quite that far. When I saw you, I had no inkling that anyone was within fifty miles of here. I had once walked quite a ways down the valley to see where it went. It looked like it dead ended up ahead. I couldn't go all the way to the end, for I was afraid I would sunburn." She blushed as she knew that I was picturing her walking nude and barefooted through the grasses.

I looked at her for a moment, meeting her eyes. Licking my dry lips, I started to continue on that subject, but I decided that would be taking advantage of the circumstances.

Instead I remarked, "I wouldn't be a bit surprised if we were the only two people on earth who have ever stepped foot inside this canyon. "It's completely hidden from view on one end, and even from the entrance, you think you're just in a little cul-de-sac. If I can't do something about the lack of water in my lost valley, I plan to come back here to start my home.

""We'd better get a move on before Dad thinks a bear has eaten us." She licked her lips as she turned toward the path. Maybe I wasn't the only one whose heart was beating a mile a minute.

"What lies on the other side of that ridge?" I asked, jerking my thumb toward the stony outcrop.

"I've never been over the ridge," she answered.

"It will just take a second for us to look over to the other side," I said, sweeping my left arm in a wide gesture that included everything that might lie beyond. "Do you think we have time to do that without your dad worrying?"

"We have time," she answered. "You know, Easy, there were many times when I would have done some exploring on my own, but by the time I complete my swim and sunbathing, it's late. Besides, since I'm usually undressed when I'm here, I wouldn't want to navigate around those rocks without my clothes on.

"Do you know I have never even mentioned this valley to anyone, not even to my dad? I never wanted to linger over-long for fear he might show up, thinking I needed help with something."

We clambered over the rocks and through the stunted shrubs that grew around them until we reached the top. There, backed up to the narrow valley that housed what I was always referring to in my mind as "My Oasis", was the valley we were looking for! "The lost valley! My valley!" I shouted excitedly. It was separated from my oasis by twenty or thirty feet of jumbled rock. The wall so formed was much lower than the walls of the Rim Rock.

It was easy to imagine that, at one time, the run-off from the waterfall had flowed serenely through my valley and into the Wandering River. I could scarcely wait to ride into it from the narrow front. My sense of discovery was honing my excitement to a fever pitch. I turned to Earlene and we grabbed each other in jubilation.

We went down the trail to the &RR ranch floor in a scrambling run. Seconds later we'd coiled up our picket ropes and were loping back along the Rimrock that encircled this ranch and the other two valleys as well. We both kept our eyes open for any stock that needed tended. Since we were in a hurry to get back to meet Brad, we felt lucky that we hadn't seen a single thing that looked amiss.

Half an hour later, we were back near where we'd split off from Brad earlier. We were surprised to see that we were a little ahead of him. It seemed impossible that we'd learned so much in such a few short minutes. We had so much to tell her father, we could hardly wait for him to join us.

When he finally arrived, the three of us rode back to the house together. After a cool drink of water, and a refill of our canteens, Earlene and I took leave of Brad and started loping our horses along the edge of the Rimrock. We were able to see the brush along the old dry river bed while we were still half a mile from the entrance to the canyon.

The mouth of the canyon was a little wider than I had remembered. It was probably about fifty yards across and just looked like a sandy, brushy enclave that bent to the right and stopped a couple of hundred yards ahead. In fact, the old river bed angled off to the right, doubled back to the left and headed straight up canyon toward its near intersection with the &RR and my oasis.

The land was sub-irrigated and lush with Curly Mesquite and Gramma grass. Wild Wheat and Fescue were mixed in among them, especially on the shadiest areas of the valley. Bees buzzed among the clovers and flowers. The only thing missing was water, and that was a lot to be missing. The thought crossed my mind, however, that it was strange to see so many bees when there was no sign of water.

We rode slowly, taking our time, talking about the plans Earlene and her father had for their spread, and the plans I had for my valley. We reached the end of the canyon, and by riding toward the eastern side, we could see the promontory where we'd stood only a few hours earlier. As we searched the area, we discovered a pool of clear water that was steadily seeping through the jumble of stones from the other side of the rocky wall.

When we were done exploring, we turned back toward the &RR. The sun was beginning to creep lower in the sky as we approached the house. Night fell early on this ranch, for the west canyon wall hid the sun earlier than on the flat lands outside the valley that extended southward. The mountains that the Rimrock followed were already darkening and the timbered slopes were merging into a cloaked area of unexplored mystery.

It had been hours since breakfast, so we were both starved by the time we arrived at the ranch. We fixed a quick dinner, and then sat down to a meal of sliced beef and hot bread smothered in plum jam and sweet butter.

I remained mostly silent while Earlene gave an animated account of what we'd discovered to Brad. He listened attentively to the details that were flavored by the fondness you could see on his face as he watched her tell of what the three of us could do, as though we'd all been planning together for ages.

It took little coaxing for me to spend the night. Once again I spread my bed roll on the back porch. I climbed into it, lightly covered in the cool valley air. Cooler air flowed down from the higher elevations that began just back of the Rimrock. It was as though this valley were blessed by design, rather than a freak upheaval of nature.

I was dead tired, but I had trouble sleeping. My mind was churning with plans for the future. The jumbled rocks that formed the wall between the combined valleys were also posing questions for which I planned to find answers.

As I started to drift off to sleep, a feeling of belonging surged over me in a manner I had never known since leaving home so long ago. Then I was lost in a dream. Once again I felt myself making the long trip that I had made while trying to retrace my path of seven years earlier.

I awakened in the still of the night and listened to the sound of coyotes howling in the distance. Always before, they had sounded so lonely that they touched my soul. This night, however, they sounded happy, as though they were singing. I soon fell asleep again. Oh! How different were my dreams this time!

Chapter Six
Entering Vacaville

The next morning I saddled up quickly and just as I finished securing my bedroll, Earlene surprised me with an invitation to join her and her father for breakfast. Since a hot plate of ham and eggs was too good an offer to pass up, I was more than happy to accept.

I had a hard time containing myself, for I was anxious to get to town, so after a hurried meal, I said a brief goodbye to Earlene and her father. I expressed my gratitude once again for their hospitality, and apologized for my quick retreat. Before running off, Earlene handed me a sliced beef sandwich she had previously packed for my lunch. I thanked her and set out for Vacaville.

A couple of hours later, I splashed across the river and started up the short main street of the town.

A quick glance up the street showed a rather large dry goods store, several cafes, a leather shop, and a saloon, a blacksmith shop that seemed to go with a corral and livery stable and a scattering of other businesses. The houses were mostly on three short streets running east and west, making three corners with the main north-south street. I was surprised to find such a large community.

I stopped at the blacksmith shop and asked the smith if he owned the livery stable. He answered in the affirmative. I asked him if he had a good pack horse for sale. Again, he glanced at me and nodded. He hit a couple of more licks on a horseshoe he was shaping, wiped off his sweaty face, and took off his leather apron. "You said a pack horse." he repeated me. "I assume you wouldn't want a mule."

"No, I guess not," I replied. "I want a horse that will double as a cow horse when needed." He nodded his understanding and pointed to a dun horse standing near the hay rick.

"Let's have a look at him," I said. We walked over to the horse and the smith put a loop over his head. I opened his mouth and checked his teeth. He was a six year old. I ran my hands over each leg, noting how docilely he took the inspection. I then ran my hands over the rest of his body, noting no problems and asked the smith if he had ever ridden the horse himself. He again answered with a nod, bridled the horse, flung a blanket over its back and followed it with a saddle. He cinched the saddle down expertly and tossed me the reins. "Try him out. Are you gonna be around here for awhile?" he asked.

"I plan to stay here, and take up some land," I told him.

"Well, that calls for two statements from me," he mused. "I try to mind my own business. I make a good living as a blacksmith. I don't have to deal in animals that I wouldn't be happy to keep. I don't give them away, but I don't try to rob you, either. If you're staying here, I'll guarantee the dun to be sound in every way and with no bad habits. That's my first statement."

My second statement may seem like I'm butting into your business. I'm just making friendly conversation that is between you and me and the gate post. If you're planning on taking up land, you're biting off a big mouthful. We have a rancher near here that has a motto. He says that all he wants is a small piece of land and all of the land that adjoins it. He means what he says, and repeats it frequently."

"He has a big piece of land and is working on getting all of the land that adjoins it. That includes *all* of the land, both claimed and unclaimed. I mention that just in case you're interested in land but not interested in probably having to die for it."

I mulled over what he said for a minute. He didn't strike me as a man who just talked to hear his own voice. I judged he was a good man and not a timid one. If things were as he said they were I was sure Burly Dobbins wouldn't take very kindly to what the blacksmith had just told me. On the other hand, Burly might be happy if I moved on, saving him the effort of chasing me off. One can never tell about these things.

I looked up and said, "I truly appreciate what you've told me. The gate post will pass it along before I will. I want to shake hands with a good man. I know one when I see one."

We shook hands and I told him, "My name is Seeker. Easy Seeker. I passed through here several years ago before this town was here. I have some strange attachment to a place back under the Rimrock. I hope that no one even thinks of taking it from me, 'cause sometimes I lose my temper. I don't start trouble, but if it comes, sometimes I don't give it a chance to leave."

"My name is Arnold Smith. You don't have to tell me any blacksmith jokes, 'cause I've heard 'em all. At least a good portion of them," he grinned. "Well, the way I look at it, fore-warned is fore-armed."

I paid for the dun without a quibble. "I'll leave him here for now, but I'll be back to pick him up in a little while. The first thing I'm gonna do is buy a beer and wash the dust out of my throat. I also need to pick up a pack saddle and some supplies. Then I think I'll pay a visit to the land agent."

"If you only need the pack saddle until you get a camp going on the land you settle on, I have one here you can borrow. You can bring it back when it is handy to do so. That is, unless Burly finds out you're taking up land here. Then you may not have the chance." He grinned at me, but it was evident that he was serious in his repeated warning.

I raised a hand toward him and grinned back. "Just so you don't worry too much about your saddle, I wasn't just talking to hear my teeth rattle when I said that I can lose my temper pretty easily when someone crowds me. When I say 'my temper', I don't mean my cool," I tossed out.

Smith looked at me for a moment. "You know, I believe you," he said.

"I just thought of something. I'm going to need a big, strong sign for the gate that will one day lead to my ranch. Who would I have to see about making one for me?" I asked.

He smiled and said, "I'm the jack-of-all trades in this town. I can make an angle iron frame and put a good sign inside it. If you want your brand stamped on it, I can do that, too. I can also make your branding irons. If you want painted letters, however, I'll get the butcher's son. He's a real artist when it comes to painting signs."

"That sounds great," I told him. "However, as strange as it seems, I don't know what I want on the sign yet. I'm toying with a couple of different ideas. I'm in a big hurry for it, if you can do it, for I want everyone to have no doubt that I'm staking my claim, even though there will be no name on it for now."

"I'll put it at the very head of my list," he told me.

*

I walked into the bar and stepped to the side of the bat-wing doors until my eyes were accustomed to the dim interior. There were about a dozen men scattered around at various tables. About half a dozen other men were grouped together near the right hand end of the bar. They seemed to be raw-hiding a young man in new Levis and a flannel shirt.

I strolled over to the bar and ordered a beer. The bartender kept shooting worried glances toward the commotion. He sort of shook his head as he handed me the bottle.

I took it to a table against the right hand side wall, not far from the group of men. I noticed that no one seemed inclined to help the kid, as the men began roughly shoving him from one to the other. It was easy to see the kid was scared, but he did his best to keep cool. I was disgusted to see that no one appeared ready step in to help.

I took a couple of swallows of my beer and got up as though I had just noticed them. I walked over to the group with a smile on my face.

"Hey, Kid," I said. "It has been awhile since I saw you last. Someone told me you were back east." I pushed through the men and shook hands with the kid. "Come on over to my table and let's catch up on what your family is doing."

The apparent leader glanced over and nodded at me. "I have some business with the kid," he directed at me, a challenge in his eyes. "Doesn't it look to you like he's an eastern sissy son-of-a-bitch?"

I looked the boy over and smiled at him. "Hell, Stud, I really couldn't tell you," I answered. "I'm not the one running around with a sissy son-of-a-bitching gang."

The big fellow was turning back toward the boy, whose mouth was bloody. As the meaning of my remark dawned on him, he turned back toward me. "What the hell are you trying to say?" he growled.

I had taken the kid by the shoulder and steered him over to my table. I turned my head toward the bar. The bartender was watching the action. Holding up my bottle of beer, I pointed to the kid, and turned around to take my seat with my back to the wall. Before I could sit down, the big fellow had taken a couple of steps toward us. His face was tight with anger and he forced the words through his clenched teeth. "Draw, you son-of-a-bitch," he snarled. His hand gripped his gun butt.

"If you don't like sons-of-a-bitch, keep your mama out of the kennel," I answered.

Sputtering with rage, he jerked his gun. So did I, and it was the last thing he ever didn't see.

I holstered my Colt and continued to watch the group who had been harassing the kid. "Is the fracas over?" I inquired quietly.

"It is as far as I'm concerned," one of the punchers answered, "but I'm not so sure that's how the boss will see it when he hears about this."

"Your boss must be a little on the chicken-shit side himself to hire that sorry excuse for a human. Whoever that dead guy is, he looked big enough to stomp his own snakes and old enough to know when to fold his hand," I answered. "The kid and I are gentle peace-loving folk and don't take kindly to being raw-hided. I want you all to remember that, the next time you see either one of us. When you see the kid, whether I'm with him or not, you'd better remember what just happened. You start trouble with either one of us and you've started trouble with both of us."

I started to sit down and drink my beer, but looked back at each person there, square in the eyes. "I'll remember each one of you," I told them. "I'm taking up some grass here, and I won't tolerate any hassling. I want you all to pay particular attention to the word *any*. I mean any, in the same vein as *none, zero, zilch* and I don't just mean serious hassling. I mean play hassling, hassling by staring, muttering, or accidentally walking into one of us. I mean jokingly, drunkenly, mistakenly or just by plain bad luck. I mean whether you do it singly, in pairs, in a group or with all of your friends and acquaintances."

The men shifted their bodies and shuffled their feet.

"Am I understood?" I asked. No one answered. "Hey Stud," I said, looking the toughest appearing man squarely in the face, "I want to know if I'm understood?"

"We understand you," he squeezed out through lips so tightly squeezed they were blue. "Come on, fellows," he told the group, "Let's go."

*

Burly Dobbins and his bunch were working cattle about a mile upriver to the west of Vacaville. They were moving more cattle across onto the north side range, when he looked down stream and saw Hatch and the rest of the men who had accompanied him to town ride into his camp. He immediately noticed that Torch wasn't leading the bunch. He also saw that Hatch had apparently assumed command, for he directed the other men to catch fresh horses out of the remuda. Hatch then came straight to his boss to report what had happened.

Burly hid his anger, for he had a reputation as one whom was never rattled by circumstances. He listened impassively while Hatch told the story. It was not lost on Burly that he related the whole story in a way that highlighted what he perceived as the failure of Torch. The inference was that he would have done a lot better job had he been the one in charge.

After listening to the happenings in town, he called his segundo over and told him to continue with the work, but to pick him out four more men for a job that might require a little gun-play. He told him to have them saddle up and be ready to ride in ten minutes.

A few minutes later, Burly and his men were on their way back to town.

*

The bartender stood over the dead man and shoved his body with the toe of his boot. "Burly Dobbins is not gonna like this a bit," he said to me, "but Torch had it coming. He always was a mean son-of-a-bitch. He had every intention of killing the kid. I guess old Robert Burns had it right when he said something about the biggest plans of a fella going astray, or some such thing."

He appraised me quietly for a minute. "You have shown you can handle yourself," he said slowly, "but Burly will be after you with enough men to put you six feet under the sod, if you hang around here. I'd sort of hate for that to happen. If I were to hazard a guess, I'd say they'll be here within in a few minutes. They're working only about a mile up the river."

He held out his hand and I reached up to shake it. "My name is Pat Donahue," he told me. "I own this bar. Those men are from the Dobbins spread. Spread is a good name for it. It is spreading all over this neck of the woods. He sure doesn't take kindly to anyone even hinting that they might settle here."

"My name's Seeker," I told him as I extricated my hand. "Easy Seeker." I took a sip of my beer and added, "They call me Easy because I'm so easy to get along with. Thanks for the advice."

Donahue turned and walked back behind the bar.

"Mister," the kid said, reaching out a hand for his bottle, "You sure saved me from an early grave." He took a swallow of beer and grimaced as he wiped his sleeve across his cut lip. "I came out here from England, by way of New York and then St. Louis. I've been looking for some sort of investment opportunity for my father.

"When I was over at the land office asking about how the range here lays, Mr. Dobbins was there and told me that there wasn't any land available within a hundred miles of here. That was this morning. My name is actually Rodney Hampton." We shook hands briefly and he continued.

"He left town and the land agent told me that I would be wise to leave too. I was planning to go back to England to report to my father, anyway.

"Later, while I was in here talking to Mr. Donahue," he nodded at the bartender, "that gang of men rode in and immediately started making fun of my 'funny way of talking'. It seemed that they had come in purposely to start trouble with me."

"Well", I told him, "I think they found all of the trouble they could handle." I finished off the beer and then said, "I have business with the land office before I leave. I'm going to get on over there before they close." I stood up to leave, and the kid got up too.

"Do you mind if I tag along?" he asked me. "I hate to admit it, but I prefer not to be here by myself when they come back," he said, referring to the bunch that had left a few minutes earlier.

"Not at all", I invited him. "I personally don't think they're too liable to come back."

Donahue had been listening from his post behind the bar. "I wouldn't bank on that", he told me. "As I just told you, when Burly Dobbins hears the news, he's gonna ride in and bring enough of his crew to make sure you don't ever give him any more trouble. He's always claimed to nip trouble in the bud. Your best chance is to high tail it from here as fast and as far as you can. If he doesn't come himself, he'll send Hatch with a dozen men. He doesn't use half measures."

Most of the other men in the bar had gone back to drinking, and the poker game toward the end of the room had begun again. I could see by the glances I was getting that I was the subject of a lot of the conversation. The men seemed to have a friendly feeling toward me.

The bat wing doors flapped and a tough, capable looking man with a star on his chest entered the bar. He was flanked by two other men who moved with adept motions to a place on either side of the bat-wings. One of them was a man in his early twenties, but something about him projected an image of maturity beyond his years, a capability that came from more experience than would normally be associated with his age.

The other man was an obviously experienced lawman. His keen eyes had swept the bar room the instant he entered, and I knew they had missed nothing. For all of the confidence the pair of deputies exuded, my eyes turned back to the man who had entered the door first. I quickly surmised that this was a man who fit the job of a lawman like a worn glove fits the hand that has worn it thin. After a quick glance around the bar room, he looked at me with neither friendliness nor animosity.

Before he spoke, the older of the two deputies placed his hand on the English kid's shoulder and told him, "Let's step out here for a moment" and led him out the door.

The sheriff walked over and looked me straight in the eye. "Tell me what happened", he ordered. He hooked his heel on the rung of a chair and jerked it out from under my table and sat down across from me. He listened without speaking while I told him my story. He turned to address the bartender. "What happened here, Donahue?" he asked.

Donahue sketched out the story pretty much as I had told, except that he added what I had told the group who had been with Torch as he tormented the kid.

"I suppose that you're aware of what will happen now," the sheriff stated. "I wonder if you really know what you have gotten yourself into."

I said, "Yeah, Sheriff, I have a pretty good idea. I wonder if this Dobbins fellow has any idea what the repercussions will be."

The Sheriff looked at me contemplatively. "I really doubt it," he said after a minute. "I think I might have an idea," he finally told me. "However, I think I will wait a day or two and see what has developed before I go so far as to actually believe what I now suspect."

The deputy returned with Rodney. He gave a nearly imperceptible nod to the Sheriff, who put both hands flat on the table and started to get up. The action was interrupted by the deputy's next remark. "Sheriff, Dobbins and a bunch of his riders are coming up the street. We may want to listen in to what he says and to see what his actions are gonna be."

"Yeah, I guess we might, at that," he remarked. The two deputies positioned themselves at opposite ends of the bar so in case of gunfire, they wouldn't be firing toward one another. When the deputy had returned with Rodney, he had brought two shotguns in with him. He had given them to the young deputy, who now handed one back to the older man before crossing to his end of the bar. This all happened so unobtrusively and efficiently that no one seemed to notice.

Hoof beats stopped outside the bar. There was the flurry of sound as saddles creaked, horses stomped around as the riders dismounted and tied them to the to the hitch rail, and of muted conversation. Boots stomped heavily across the board walk. The bat-wing doors slapped against the wall as a bull of a man slammed them back. This was the picture of Burly Dobbins as he entered the bar, a crowd of punchers behind him.

He glanced quickly around the room and his eyes settled on me. He crossed quickly to me. He overlooked the sheriff, who was leaning against the wall about ten feet over from my table. "Are you the son-of-bitch who shot Torch?" He bit the words off like the end of a good cigar.

"Is that the name of your litter-mate?" I asked. "It seems your mothers were playing in the same kennel."

Burly apparently was so shocked by the audacity of someone speaking to him in this tone that he was momentarily stunned. He straightened up and I could see that he was on the verge of drawing. "Easy, Boy", I told him. "Let's not get off on the wrong foot. We might have a lot in common."

"I doubt the hell out of that," he spit out.

"Whoa! Whoa!" I smiled at him. "Have you ever been on a cattle drive?"

"Hell yes! What in the hell are you trying to say?" His voice was thick with rage, but there was a note of curiosity as to what I was getting at.

"I was just wondering if you have ever ridden around a herd of cattle, singing 'em to sleep."

"Of course I have", he snarled. What in the hell are you driving at?"

I had been smiling at him in an ingratiating manner. "It isn't the thing I'm driving at", I told him. "It's the thing I'm aiming at. The thing I'm aiming at is your little prick and those two peanut sized balls that you're so obviously proud of. It is the fact that if you even tense a muscle or call me a son-of-bitch again, you'll be minus your little girlish appendage and from here on, you'll be singing to those cattle you herd in a nice soprano voice while your crew of ewes calls you Betty instead of Burly. You must be a dumb son-of-bitch to walk up to a table without getting down on all four paws to see what is pointed at you."

Burly was rash, and Burly was rabid with rage, but Burly wasn't completely without brains. He made no such move. The tough guy who had been so enraged when I faced him down after I shot Torch, called out from the group of punchers, "Can I kill him, Mister Dobbins?" Burly just stood there, making no answer.

"We're gonna kill you before we leave town tonight", he finally said.

Suddenly the sheriff stepped forward, startling Burly and his men for they hadn't been aware of his presence until then. "There will be no killing in this town," the sheriff said. "If you're gonna fight, fight out on the range."

Burly's crew began to mutter, looking toward the man who had offered to kill me.

"What should we do, Hatch?" one of them asked. It was the first time I had heard anyone call him by name.

"Hatch can go back to his kennel and hatch another chicken killing-dog-of-a-brother to come back and help him when he grows up," I told the man who had asked the question. "I'm not shutting your boss down because I think he would rustle my stock, since I'm not raising chickens. Still, he might come after my baby calves if there were no moon and he thought I'd gone visiting back east or some place where he would have plenty of time to hide before I got back. However, he might send some of you boys out to do it for him. That is, if any of you are left to try it, if your boss misbehaves."

Burly broke in before any answer could be offered. "I want to make you a solemn promise," he grated. "There is not room on this range for the two of us."

"Well Son," I told him, "I can understand you being so solemn about your promises. I felt the same way when I was a kid, wandering around in a man's world. You did surprise me when you told me you're leaving this range, though. I had the feeling that you were trying to make this country your home."

"I don't know how in the hell you got the idea that I'm leaving. I own this country!" He was nearly foaming at the mouth.

"Well, dog-gone it, you said the words yourself. Wasn't it you who admitted there won't be enough room for you now that I've arrived? I know everybody heard you." I scratched my head, as though completely baffled.

"You're a dead man! I give you my solemn promise..."

I cut in before he could finish his statement. "There you go again, getting all solemn. You need to lighten up. Children like you should be happy and care free. You're a cute little tyke, but you seem a mite spoiled. I'm gonna be dropping by O'Reilly's store a little later in the day. I'll get you some licorice sticks if you'll promise to try to control that terrible temper before it gets you in trouble."

"You're dead..." he began.

"You sure have a limited vocabulary. Is that one phrase all you can say? Excuse me! What I meant to ask, is that one phrase all you can solemnly promise?"

I turned to the sheriff. "Sheriff, you have heard him threaten me. I have a solution that will make it unnecessary for you to become involved in something that is about to become personal. If sonny boy Burly and his cute and cuddly little puppy dog, Hatch, want to hatch up a problem for me, let us make a contract with you. That contract would be that we absolutely swear to not fire even a single shot in this town."

The puzzled sheriff answered, "I have no idea what you're asking, Seeker. Are you saying that I should stay out of it, if you're not in town making trouble?"

"That's exactly what I'm saying, Sheriff. I came here to raise cattle. The last thing I want is for these coyote pups to be killing my day-old calves or stealing my cook's chickens. That may be about all they'd have the guts to tackle, but I intend to protect what's mine". I noticed Burly Dobbins' blanched face as I surveyed him and his hard-bitten crew. Finally settling on Hatch, I could see the hate radiating from his mottled face.

"There's an old saying, Sheriff: *All is fair in love and war*. Before this thing turns ugly, I'm offering an olive branch to Baby Boy Burly and his faithful Puppy Dog Hatch. If they stay on the south side of the river, I'll let 'em be."

Looking deeply into Burly's livid face, I addressed my next sentence directly to him. "Dobbins", I said. "Let's put an end to this here and now. I'm asking you, man to man, to shake hands with me. There's no use in our fighting over such a minor thing as the killing of your bully boy, Torch. You stay on the south side of the river, and I'll stay on the north side. But let me warn you, if you let just one cow cross to the north side of that river, you'd better get it the hell back to the south side quicker than I can pull a trigger.

"You can rest assured I won't bother anyone living on the north side, and the only time I'll need to cross the river is when I ride into town for supplies.

"I trust you're a man of sterling character and proud enough to live up to any promise you make here in front of all these witnesses. That is to say, especially if it's one of your *solemn* promises. After all, you don't want to be known as a liar and a coward, do you?

"Sheriff, while everyone is in such a good humor, before any trouble starts, I want first to offer the peace pipe to Baby Boy Burly and his Hound puppy Hatch. If they stay on the south side of the river, I will let 'em be."

I looked deep into Burly's livid face and directed my words straight to him.

"Dobbins", I said. "I would like to ask you, man to man, to shake hands and make up between us. You stay on the south side of the river. I will stay on the north side. If you have one cow on the north side of the river, you had better get them to hell and gone across to the south side."

"I won't bother anyone who has a spread here on the north side. The only time I will cross the river is to come into town for supplies. I can tell that you're a man of sterling character and proud enough to live up to any promise you make here in front of all these witnesses, especially if it's one of your *solemn* promises. You don't want them to know you for a liar and coward. Will you shake my hand?"

I stood up and slipped my gun back into its holster and stuck out my hand.

Burly was sputtering. "I will see you in hell first," he gritted.

"Oh, I'm so sorry to hear you say that, Dobbins. Especially since I have to assume it's another of your *solemn promises.* I had hoped that you would be smarter than you look." I shook my head in mock sorrow.

"Oh, you'll be sorry, alright. Sorry you ever rode into this country," Burly said, and suddenly all of the wild rage was gone. He smiled at the sheriff. "Sheriff, I'm gonna accept Seeker's offer. Not his offer to shake hands, but his offer to declare war on one another when we are outside the town limits. All is fair in love and war. Those were his words. I'll hold him to them. I'll expect you to respect his words also." He waited until the sheriff gave a reluctant nod of his head, and turned toward me, a look of triumph for future actions already on his face.

Before he could speak, I said, "Well, Burly, I want every one to remember that I gave you a chance to make peace. When I ruin you and either run you out of the country or kill you, I don't want everyone," I stopped talking and looked at the group of men in the bar and swept my arm out in an all inclusive gesture, and picked up where I had left off, "I don't want everyone to pity you for your poor judgment.

"It saddens me that there isn't a school marm around to discipline you. We just have to play the cards we're dealt, though.

"That said I'll even make another offer to go with the first one. If you leave now and never show your ugly face on the north side of the river, I won't come hunting you and your men." When he didn't reply, I turned to his crew.

"Fellas," I said, "I know how it is when you're riding for a brand. Your boss will send you out to get killed in a war that you have no stake in. I can tell you right now that he won't have the money to pay your final wages due. He'll have neither a pot to piss in nor a window to fling it out. You'll have been shot up for no reason, and you won't even get paid for your sacrifice. I want to invite you to all ride out while you can. I won't be repeating this offer. I will give you a few days to get out with a whole skin."

I turned back to the sheriff and shrugged my shoulders in mock despair. "I gave them a chance, Sheriff. I did my best to give these egg sucking dogs a chance to leave. It's on their head." I turned back to Burly. "You boys are dismissed!"

The sheriff shrugged his shoulders in turn. "Yeah", he said. "Didn't you offer the peace pipe, though?" His sardonic voice seemed the signal for Dobbins and his men to leave, with the enraged Hatch shooting me a look so hot that it was a wonder the table where I had been sitting didn't burst into flames.

Just as Burly reached the door, I called out, "Hey Stud, just a second!" Burly turned back a little apprehensively.

"I just thought that you would like to know that while you were standing here making solemn promises, my men have occupied your headquarters and taken over the herd you are moving across the river!"

Burly's face blanched, and he stood as though petrified.

A muted, but collective gasp went through the room.

"Hey Son, I'm just funning with you," I laughed. I hate to see you leave mad or upset! However, you can go ahead and leave." I laughed loudly as he wheeled and lunged through the door, his crew right behind him. A moment later, I heard their horses thunder off upriver.

I turned to the rest of the men, nearly all of whom were now standing along the bar, talking with each other in an uncertain manner.

"Fellas", I said to the men who were standing along the bar, "My name's Easy Seeker. Please understand I have no intention what-so-ever of crowding any of you off your property. If Dobbins ever threatens any of you, I'll consider it a personal attack on me. I mean what I say about not tolerating him on our side of the river. I also meant what I said about running him out of the country as broke as a cow puncher after a weekend in a whore-house if he carries out his threat to lift a hand against me or anyone else on the north side."

On the way back to my table, I asked Donahue to set 'em up for everyone in the bar.

*

Burly had been completely stunned by Seeker's idea of a practical joke. Who in the hell did he think he was, anyway! At first, he found it hard to contain his fury. After a couple of minutes he decided that he was very content with the way things were going, for there was no way in hell that Seeker could escape his men out on the open range.

A minute later, they arrived back at the herd. He, himself, needed to be back here while the cattle were being worked, for he had some 'strays' that some of his chosen men had stolen from a ranch that headquartered a day's ride to the east. He wanted to make sure that they were re-branded ahead of the other cattle. The cattle his men hadn't stolen had been purchased from another ranch that was situated several miles past the place where the cattle were stolen.

This way, he had a good excuse to have been that far east of his own range, and also for leaving the plain trail of his legally purchased herd. He hid his hate for Seeker from his crew. He didn't want them to know that the man had really gotten to him.

He turned back to where the men were waiting and said to Hatch, "Hatch, I want you to take these men and chase Seeker down. "If you can, bring him to me alive. I want to find out what Seeker is doing in this area. If you can't capture him, kill him and get on back to the herd." He turned his horse away, but then reined back around and asked Hatch, "How many men are you taking with you?"

"Counting me, there are six," came the reply.

"Well," said Burly, "I want you to get six more. Go tell Oklahoma that I said to pick you out six good men to go with you after Seeker. I want you to get the men and be gone in ten minutes."

"Listen, Boss, I know that we six will be more than plenty to kill that four flusher. I don't need any more." Hatch looked at Burly to see if his plea was having any effect. There was no way in hell that Seeker could get away from the six of them. They would run him down and capture him or kill him, just like the boss said.

Dobbins looked at Hatch, inclined to chew his ass out for questioning his orders. However, there was no use embarrassing him in front of the men. "No, Hatch, I want you to get six more men. I haven't seen any signs yet that you and your boys have been close to getting him."

Hatch felt like his ability was being questioned, but he had seen what Burly would do when he got angry. That kind of trouble he sure didn't need. He wheeled his horse and galloped over to where Oklahoma was giving some orders to the men. "Hey, Oklahoma! The boss told me to ask you to pick out six more good men. Don't ask me why. We're just going after that fella Seeker."

"Judging from past performances of every one who has come in contact with him, he must be a real hardcase. I would sure play it cagey if I were you." Oklahoma saw that his words were only incensing Hatch. He shrugged his shoulders and called six of his men over and told them to go with Hatch. Then he turned back to his work with the herd.

Before Hatch and his men rode off, Burly called out to him. "Hatch, I want you to hang back until you're several miles out of town. If I remember right, there's a slope about five or six miles out with no cover for a long way. That would be a good place to take care of Seeker."

"You've got it, Boss! This shouldn't take long." He put his horse into a slow trot and led his bunch toward the Rimrock. He didn't see what the big deal was, but if Burly wanted them to wait, then wait they would. He regulated his speed so they would arrive at Easy's wagon right at the exact same moment they reached the slope. He was elated when they spotted the wagon at the precise moment he had planned.

"Well men," he told them importantly. "There he is. The Boss wants him alive. To get him alive he has to surrender. I don't know how he'll do that unless he waves a white flag. Let's go and get him!" He put his horse into a gallop and the distance between them and the wagon decreased rapidly.

Chapter Six
Leaving Vacaville

A few minutes after the Dobbins bunch had thundered out of town, I said, "Come on kid." We went over to the land office, where I talked with the agent.

He had a map of the region and I showed him the area that I had in mind. He looked at me and said, "I have ridden all over this part of the country and directed a survey crew for the Federal government. I know that there is some pretty good grass in the area you are talking of acquiring, but you have nothing but the Rimrock on your north with some irregular little indentations of the low plains here in the south reaching up into the into the Rimrock. They form some narrow canyons, but nothing large enough to feed a cow. The fertile land that slopes from there down here to the river, is about ten miles across. It has no water at all between the Rimrock and the river. The land is very level and even, with just a very slight slope."

"All of the land that is close enough to the river to water cows is claimed on both sides of the river by Burly Dobbins. There are several small ranchers who have been there since before Dobbins came into the country. Dobbins moved a herd north of the river about a month ago. He is moving another over right now. Just between you and me, I think the little ranchers will be dead or gone before winter. Dobbins is not going to tolerate anyone on the land between the Rimrock and the South Cedar Breaks. That includes the Rogers, and they were the first to bring cattle into the Rimrock."

"That includes every square foot, whether is has water or not. He has visions of owning all of the land, be it usable or not. I would highly recommend that you reconsider taking up land in the area you want. It will buy you nothing but grief."

I contemplated what he had said, and then asked him, "How thorough is your mapping of the little canyons that reach out into the Rimrock?"

"They are very scanty in that area, for they all dead end in a hundred yards or so. Most of the ones that we checked out were only about fifty to one hundred yards in length, and all of them are so narrow that the sunlight never reaches the bottom." He paused for a moment and rubbed his chin. "I have never seen it", he told me, "but an old miner who used to come in for supplies told me that there is a little valley back up along what appears to be an old river bed that comes out of the Rimrock a short distance this side of where the &RR ranch is. The &RR is run by Brad and Earlene Rogers. They have the one known exception to what I have said about there being no valleys of any worth reaching back into the Rimrock. They also have the place that Burly Dobbins has bragged that he will have before this year is out."

"Of whatever length they are, would they be included in the land area I have outlined? I asked. "If you don't mind me saying so, this Burly Dobbins doesn't seem very likeable."

"Yes", he replied, "but they would be of no use to you at all." His voice became soft. "You should be pretty careful in what you say about Dobbins. I might not should be telling you this, but if word ever gets to Dobbins that anyone has spoken of him with anything but respect, Dobbins or one of his hands will make them sorry about it."

"Well," I told him, "I've already told Dobbins that if he comes north of the river, I will kick his ass plumb out of the Rimrock country, with nothing but his long handles. As for those canyons and little valleys, I thought they might at least be good to put a few cows in when the winter blizzards come", I finally said.

"Yeah, they would do that, that is if you had any cattle

to put in them, since there is no water to support them." He shook his head as though I were simple minded when I completed my transaction and left the office.

A few minutes later I stopped by the livery to buy a team of horses and a good wagon. Arnold came over and shook my hand. He looked at me for a moment and remarked, "Some one stopped by half an hour ago and told me some one was over at the bar making friends with Dobbins. Since he also told me that you introduced yourself to Torch, I think you have pretty well proven that you do have a short fuse." He shook his head and slapped my shoulder. "Since you are going to buy a team, I guess you won't need the dun."

"I think I will keep him too. I am going to be building a cabin and doing a few other things and I am going to have to have a team, anyway. I wonder if you will pick me out the team while I go take care of one last chore?" The blacksmith knew that I had accepted him as a true friend or I would never have let him pick the team for me.

"Go ahead," he said. "I'm not busy right now and I'll have the team hitched up and ready to go. You are going to need all the time you can buy. I guarantee you that Burly will try to kill you as soon as you are out of sight of town." He stood for a moment and added, "That is, if he doesn't kill you as you leave town. I'd recommend that you don't believe anything he tells you."

I grinned at him and turned to leave. I was going to walk across to Paddy O'Reilly's to check on my order. Rodney walked along beside me.

"Where are you heading?" he asked.

"I'm heading over to the northwest along the Rimrock. I was hoping you might want to might like to keep me company for a couple or three days."

The kid was sharp and he knew that I was trying to spare him the embarrassment of having to ask me. His face flushed a little, but he said, "Look, Easy. I hate to admit it, but I'm just plain scared of staying in town until the next stage for St. Louis comes in. I know that you are the only one with the nerve to help me." I knew how much courage it took for him to make that admission. The kid had guts.

I assured him that he would be no bother. He told me he had a couple of big trunks that he would like to bring, and I told him I would stop by the hotel and he could load them in the wagon. Since the chore I had told Smith I was going to go do had now been taken care of by the kid dropping by, I turned back to see that the team had already been harnessed and hitched. They were a good, solid and powerful team. I would find out that it was a good thing they were. Rodney went off to take care of the things he had at the hotel and to settle his bill, while I drove the wagon down to the store.

The store was just down the street and I pulled the team up along-side the dock. All I had intended to be carrying was a couple of weeks worth of water and some grub. However, in view of what had happened, I decided to make sure that I had a few surprises in store for the Burly bunch when he came over to carry out his threats. I didn't even *think* the word "if". I knew it would be "when"."

The proprietor already had my order pulled, but I added three twelve gauge double barreled shotguns, half a dozen boxes of double aught shells, a double bitted ax, a pole ax and a hatchet. I added a hammer, a hand saw and a bucksaw, which is a sort of one man crosscut saw, a broad ax for shaping the logs, a post hole digger and a cask of spikes. I thought for a moment and went back into the store and bought an extra barrel and a splitting wedge. If the kid was coming with me, we would need extra water for the extra horses. I was sure that the Rogers would let me refill at their place, but I wanted to have some on hand just in case.

While the proprietor and one of his hands was loading the wagon, he looked at me and said, "I heard what happened down at Donahue's. I can see by your supplies that you intend to at least try to make your statement about staying in the country be a true one." He glanced around and lowered his voice, reaching out his hand to shake. "My name is O'Reilly. There are a lot of people behind you, but few want to go on record as being against Dobbins. Maybe if you live the week out, you'll find out that you have friends." He withdrew his hand. "I wish you the best of luck. I hate to say that you are going to need it." I shrugged my shoulders and clucked the team into motion and pulled up in front of the hotel.

Rodney was standing out front waiting for me. While he and the hotel clerk were loading his gear into the wagon, I got my horse from the hitching rail in front of Donahue's bar. He seemed glad to be able to stretch his legs. He had been hitched there for several hours. I tied him on behind the wagon, along-side my packhorse. I threw the packsaddle into the wagon, along with my supplies. The kid had a nice looking chestnut stabled down at the blacksmith's shop. We stopped by, picked him up and tied him beside my two horses and started out of town.

We stopped in the river and filled the barrels. I had picked up some scrap lumber at the store and put them into the barrels of water to keep them from splashing. Otherwise, we would lose half the water before we got to my canyon.

We rode silently for several miles when the kid looked back. He couldn't stifle a gasp. I looked over and asked him what the problem was. He jerked his thumb back over his shoulder. "That's Hatch coming a couple of miles back. You can see that paint horse from here."

He clambered to the back of the wagon and opened one of his trunks and removed a field glass. "Yes, that's him alright and they're coming fast. What are we going to do now?"

That was a good question, and I hoped that I had a good answer. I told the kid, "Hand me my Winchester from my saddle boot there!"

He jumped to comply and told me, "I have a fine hunting rifle and I know how to use it." I looked over and saw him pulling a truly fine rifle out of the trunk. Another, different but equally fine, was cushioned in soft velvet right next to where he had picked up the first rifle. They were both big bore and equipped with telescopic sights.

"Do you have ammunition for both of those?", I asked him.

"A bushel of it," he exaggerated.

I pulled the team up on a slight rise. There was a clear field of fire for a mile. "Lay out the ammunition! Hurry, we haven't much time!" As I spoke, I grabbed the other English hunting rifle and began adjusting the scope. The kid checked his scope and we jumped behind the wagon and used the side boards for rifle rests.

"When they get halfway down that little slope, shoot the horses from under them!," I snapped. "Forget the men for now! You take the ones on the right. I'll take the left, but I want the paint horse for my first shot."

"You've got it", he replied coolly.

The men came over the little rise at a full gallop. When they were half-way down the slope, I told him, "Now!" We pulled the triggers in unison and two of the front horses tumbled to the ground. One of them was the paint. Another horse pitched head over heels when he ran into the threshing horses. We each shot several times and all of the men were out of sight behind the horses. Not a horse was still moving.

"Hey, you're a good shot!" I praised him. Rodney beamed at the compliment.

"You're not so bad yourself," he replied.

"Where did you learn to shoot like that?" I asked him.

"I went through a shooting school, back home in England," he replied. "We were going on a safari in Africa, and Father told me he expected me to be an example to all of them."

"Well, were you?" I asked, grinning.

"Father said I was," he answered proudly.

"Well, if we're going to make believers out of them, we had better get started," I mused. Since you are such a good shot, I am going to have you take some ammunition and ride over about a quarter of a mile to where that stunted bush is growing." I broke off talking to fire at a man who was making a break back up the rise. He fell, but crawled back into the cover of the horses.

The other men had retrieved their rifles from saddle scabbards on the dead horses. Taking care to keep under cover behind the horses, the men whose rifles had been easily retrieved because their horses had fallen with the rifles on the top were firing a few ineffective shots. They all teamed up to roll the dead horses up enough to get the rifles that were under the horses.

They began shooting in earnest, but the outclassed 44-40s were out of range and each shot was a wasted one. The same was not true of the large bore English big game hunting rifles. I didn't want to kill the men, at least not yet. I wanted to give them the chance to leave the Dobbins bunch and hunt work elsewhere. With Rodney shooting down from one angle and me shooting from the wagon, it left the men little space to hide in. We shot the saddles to rags. I hated to make it cost the cowboys so dearly on this first encounter, but they had to know that we could have killed them.

As it began to get dark, we drove the wagon over the rise and out of their sight; then we rode back toward town, taking care to keep out of their sight. We picked a spot on the west side of the trail back to town. The spot was in the obscurity of a slight draw where the men would be exposed as they went over the hill and were outlined against the rising moon. About fifteen minutes later, we saw their dark figures climbing the gentle grade to the top of the hill.

As they became outlined, we began to shoot all around them, near enough to make them drop their saddles and run for the far side of the slope. After shooting a few more rounds into each saddle, I called out, "Boys, you all know that every one of you is alive because we didn't want to kill you. I want you to know that we understand that you felt you had to come. The next time you come over to the north side, you will be killed, right along with that big mouthed, baby assed Hatch that we let live along with the rest of you. He's just dumb enough to die. Don't be the ones that die with him." We circled back to the wagon and continued on toward the place I had purchased along the Rimrock.

*   .

It was near midnight when the night hawk for the Dobbins herd first spotted the group of men straggling into camp. They were limping along in their blistered feet, cursing the boots they wore for riding. They sure weren't made for walking.

Hatch dreaded with all of his heart having to tell Dobbins that he had failed. He had no idea whether that would bring on one of the rages that Dobbins sometimes had when all was not going as he planned. Yet, there was no way around it. He started for the campfire where he knew Burly would be sleeping.

However, Burly had already been awakened and was waiting to hear his report.

"What in the hell happened?" Dobbins' voice grated like stone against stone.

"We were riding down the slope just this side of where we planned on cutting down on Seeker. I have no idea what he had, but it was like a canon. There were two of them and they waited until we were half way down the slope. Then they shot every horse out from under us before we could get back out of range. I think the second man was the kid we were sent to kill while Torch was alive. In a few seconds, every horse was dead or dying. We pulled our Winchesters and tried to shoot back, but we just didn't have the range. Steavers tried to make a run for it on foot and one of them blew his head off. I've never seen such shooting."

"They split up and one of them, I think it was the Englishman, rode over to our left. He could hit anything he aimed at. If we tried to move around our horses, that Seeker fella could hit us. If they'd wanted to kill us, they could have at anytime. They drove the wagon on over the hill and we thought they had left. It was getting to be dark and we started back. Some of the boys were toting their saddles, although they were already shot to pieces. They must have left the wagon over the hill, for when we topped the ridge on the way back, they started laying bullets all around us. We dropped the saddles and dropped down in the grass to try to get away from their shooting. They just finished shooting the saddles to pieces and then disappeared. We waited until it we felt sure they had left. To make a long story short, here we are."

Burly made no response for a few minutes, although he held Hatch to his place with his eyes. He supposed that Hatch was telling the truth, for there were too many men with him to spill the beans on him if he lied. "Alright, Hatch. I see how you couldn't have been prepared for that. Tell your men to get some sleep. I'll let you go back and do the job tomorrow." He turned his back on Hatch and went back to his own blankets.

The next morning when the cook called them to breakfast, he let everyone finish eating before calling Hatch aside. "Listen, Hatch. I understand that you can't foresee everything. I'm sending you back to do the job that you've had a chance to finish three different times. If you don't get it done this time, you had best just keep riding, for if I see you again, I'll kill you. I don't really blame you, but I can't have everyone thinking that I am going soft. Do you understand what I am saying?"

"Yes Sir, I sure do, Boss. I will kill him this time for sure. The last thing I will do is let him get the drop on me. I am going to be prepared for anything he can do. His luck can't last forever."

"Well get your men together. There is no hurry. Just remember one thing. You said that his luck can't last forever. I want you to be sure to understand that yours can't last forever either. Make sure you're lucky this time." He stared hard into Hatch's eyes and saw the gunman blanch.

Hatch called his men together and told them to cut out some horses and get ready to ride. He picked his own favorite horse and put his Sunday saddle on it. The other punchers went for their own horses, with saddles taken from the camp wagon. Hatch noticed that three of the men were missing. With the one man killed, one wounded by gunfire and one by a falling horse, his initial crew of twelve men were cut down to six. He remembered telling Burly that he was sure that six would be plenty.

He asked around about the three missing men and found that no one had seen them after the midnight watch went out. He shuddered to have to tell Burly that the rats were abandoning the ship. Burly appeared to accept the losses calmly. The truth was that he had been made aware of the circumstances before Hatch had. He asked Hatch if his crew were ready to go. Then he told him to pick out one more man to take with him. Hatch wisely refrained from objecting to the reinforcement. He mounted up and started for his men, who were grouped over by the remuda. He had no more than started when Dobbins called him back.

Hatch turned and waited to see what Burly wanted. Burly ignored him for a moment and called his segundo over. "Oklahoma, I want you to ride along with Hatch. If you have any input or advice, I want you to make it known to Hatch. Sabe?"

"You bet, Burly," Oklahoma answered.

Hatch was afraid to show his anger at having Burly send Oklahoma along like a nurse maid, but he sure wasn't going to make his feelings known to Burly. However, Burly was quick to read the feelings in his face.

"Hatch," he said. "I have known Oklahoma for years. He is a good man to have siding you. You can never have too many good men in your crew."

Hatch straightened up under that veiled praise and told Oklahoma, "Why don't you ride up here with me?"

*

"Kid, see that slight notch along the Rimrock?" I asked after we had been driving along for a while. "Take the wagon and head straight for it. We don't have to worry about Hatch and his gang just yet. There's no way they'd have time to return after walking back to where Dobbins has his herd. It's hard to see in the moonlight, so keep your eye on it while you're driving. This is no time to get lost.

"My nearest neighbors are friends of mine. I'm going to ride ahead to let them know what's happened. I'd have you come along, but I don't want the wagon tracks to lead straight to their house. I won't be far behind when you get to the Rimrock."

"You're talking of that little notch just to the left of that funny looking irregularity in the rim, right?"

"That's the one. I'll see you shortly," I said as I angled off at a lope.

Half an hour later I pulled up at the front porch. Earlene came to the door. "Oh, hi there, Easy"

"Hi yourself, Earlene. You sure look good tonight. Is Brad here too?"

Earlene must have suspected something important had happened since I had immediately asked for Brad. She spoke loudly to her father, "Dad, would you come here for a minute? Easy just rode up and wants to talk to us."

"What's going on?" Brad asked as he and his daughter joined me on the porch.

I quickly sketched in the happenings of the day. "I want to warn you to be on the lookout for that bunch. They are liable to vent their anger on anyone they find. I have to go meet the wagon over at my valley to make sure they don't catch the kid alone. I didn't want to bring the wagon here and have them following the wagon tracks. I want to keep you out of their way."

"Oh, Easy! What're you gonna do? You can't fight that whole bunch alone!" Earlene exclaimed.

I grinned to relieve her stress. "I've done alright so far."

Brad had been standing thoughtfully on the porch. "Listen, Easy. We are on Burly's list right alongside of you. Bring your wagon on over here where we can all fight together. All of this will really have Dobbins on the war path. He has to save face in front of the town and in front of his men."

"I sure appreciate the offer," I said. "Normally I believe that would be the best thing to do. In this case, however, I have to make sure Burly doesn't save face. If he's ever looked bad before, he'll look even worse by the time I get done with him. I'm not being brash. I'm just stating a fact. Please don't worry about me, but do keep your eyes open for your own protection. I'd advise you to stay close to the house until I report back to you."

Earlene started to say something, but changed her mind. Then after a moment she said, "Be careful, and be sure to let us know the news the second you can. We'll be worried until you let us know you're okay."

Wishing I could stay longer, I said my good-bye and headed for my valley.

I reached my destination a few minutes before Rodney. When he finally pulled up, we entered the opening to the valley and rode to the first bend. Once around, we unhitched the team and allowed each horse to drink. When they had had their fill, Rodney picketed them in the lush green grass while I started a fire, taking care that it could not be seen from the entrance.

I had the kid accompany me to the other side of the canyon, and we spread out blankets behind a nest of rocks. This way we would have a clear field of fire if any intruders should drop by earlier than might be expected. The night was pleasant and we passed it sleeping peacefully.

Morning is slow to arrive in a canyon, so we were up long before the sun shed its rays on our campsite. We could look out the entrance and see the rose and gold sunrise gild the grass.

Using the ax and the bucksaw, we felled a couple of cedar trees that were growing near the old river bed. Then I took the double bitted ax and lopped the branches off while the kid used the pole ax on the other tree. Finally, we sawed each one down to fifteen feet in length.

Eyeballing a spot that lined up between the near side of the bend and the opposite wall of the canyon, I picked two spots. Grinning at Rodney, I said, "Here's where you're gonna get some blisters, unless you have some gloves."

"Oh, I have some gloves alright. I sampled some ranch work to see what it was like while I was looking around for a place where Dad might want to invest. I couldn't look like a cowboy without my gloves," he laughed.

"Then dig a post hole here, about this big," I held my hands apart, "and up to here on the posthole diggers. When you finish with it, make another one right here," I stepped off a distance and marked an X with my boot heel.

"I have some things that I have to do, with fixing a breakfast right up at the top of the list." Rodney grinned and licked his lips when I mentioned breakfast.

I left the kid to his work and went back to the wagon with an armload of small dry branches. A few minutes later, I had a pan of bacon frying and a pot of coffee brewing. I took the bacon out of the pan and fried up some bread, as I didn't have the time for baking. I called out to Rodney and he lost no time in leaving his work and coming for breakfast, grinning and rubbing his belly as he came.

"Listen, kid," I said when breakfast was over, "Grab your favorite rifle and some shells, then come with me and I'll show you where I want you to put them." I waited while he grabbed the same rifle he had used so effectively the day before. We walked to a nest of rocks on the far side of the canyon where there was a niche that could provide cover. "Stand your rifle right here where it's easy to reach. You'll be able to move from the niche to the nest of rocks easily, without exposing yourself.

Go back to your gear and get a canteen full of water and a couple of pieces of fried bread and some bacon and make yourself a couple of sandwiches. Wrap them in something to keep the bugs out and put them here," I said pointing. "If we have trouble, I want us to be as comfortable as possible."

While he complied with my suggestions, I harnessed the team and dragged the cedar posts to where the holes were being dug. I went back to the wagon, hitched up and drove back to the holes and unloaded my sign. Taking my ground tarp, I spread it out behind the sign. I took all three of my shot guns, loaded them and placed them on the tarp. Pulling the edge of the tarp back over the guns to protect them from the dirt and sun, I got back in the wagon and pulled it out of sight behind the bend in the canyon.

By then, Rodney had finished one hole and was starting on the other. He might be the son of a rich English gentleman, I mused, but he sure was a willing worker and a good, solid boy. As I watched him work, I quickly amended that thought to "man".

Chapter Nine
Hatch comes calling

Hatch, along with Oklahoma and half a dozen other men rode along following the tracks of Easy's wagon. They appeared to be heading directly for the shadowed entrance to one of the numerous little cul-de-sacs that roughened what would otherwise be the smooth expanse of the Rimrock. He turned his head toward Oklahoma. "I don't know what Seeker has in mind, but he has made a mistake if he thinks he can hole up in there." He reined his horse to a stop, his men right behind. Pulling out a telescope, he looked at the entrance to the cul-de-sac, collapsed the telescope and put it back into his saddle bag.

"How do you like that? He's working on fencing the cul-de-sac off. I guess the dumb son-of-a-bitch thinks we'll just walk right up in front of him," he said to Oklahoma. He looked at the rest of the men and said, "Roper, you take Sam and Pecos and go west. Make sure you get at least a mile down before you swing over to the Rimrock. Stay in by the bluff as you start back toward the entrance." He nodded his head toward the spot to which he was referring. "When you get to the edge of the opening, wait until Oklahoma and I have ridden straight in. Chances are, he's not gonna start shooting at just the two of us."

He turned his head toward the three remaining hands. "Did you hear what I just told Roper?" he asked. He was looking at a big fellow with a scar on his face.

"We sure did, Hatch, the man replied.

His gaze then included the other two men. "You boys go with Hack. Hack, I expect you to stay close in by the bluff and wait for me and Oklahoma to ride past. Don't ride in until we are talking to Seeker. If he has the guts to come out and talk, let us talk for a couple of minutes and then come riding in behind us. Hack, I want you to wait until you see Roper start in. Take your cue from him." He turned to Roper, "You got that Roper," he asked?

"You bet," answered Roper.

"You got that, Hack?" he asked again, shifting his gaze to the scar faced man?

"Yeah, we've got it," came the retort.

"OK, get going," Hatch said. Stay quiet and don't foul up. We'll teach that son-of-a-bitch a lesson that he'll remember the rest of his life." He barked out a laugh and added, "He'll sure as hell not have to remember it for long!"

Chapter Ten
Return engagement

"Grab a root and growl," I said after Rodney and I had finished tamping down the dirt around the second post. I grabbed one end of the big sign and Rodney grabbed the other. "Let's lean it up against the posts," I instructed.

"I imagine it won't be long before we have company. We'll want to keep our eyes peeled now. There's no telling how they'll come at us."

I picked up the shovel and stuck it in the ground beside the posthole diggers, which were also sticking straight up. I wanted it to be obvious that I had been hard at work.

I unwrapped the shotguns and leaned one against the sign behind the post to the left and the other two about three feet further to the right. I had no sooner finished when Rodney shouted, "Hey Easy, here they come!" His voice, while carrying a tone of excitement, held no fear.

"Okay, Rodney, this is it. Get behind the rocks like we planned," I said as I watched the men approaching who were still a mile away. "If you have to piss, do it now behind the wall where you'll be waiting. You don't want to be making a move they might see. Remember, if you have to shoot, shoot straight and shoot immediately. Don't give the dogs a chance."

"You can depend on me, Easy, I'll do my part." He trotted quickly into position. I grabbed the ax by the blade and began tamping the dirt around the post on the side opposite to where the kid was hidden. I wanted to make sure I didn't block his field of fire.

I watched out of the corner of my eye as the men came closer. When they were about fifty yards away, I suddenly looked up as though I had just seen them. I pitched the ax near the other tools and made a show of hitching up my gun belt. I crossed behind the sign and leaned over one end with my hands resting on top of it.

As the men reined in their horses, I straightened up and walked over to the other end of the sign and leaned against the post with my right shoulder. I let my right arm hang behind the post, the barrel of a shotgun in my grip. "You men are a little late for breakfast," I said.

Hatch grinned. "Well, I reckon that we're in time for lunch then." He was perfectly at ease and looked as though he had the world by the tail with a down hill pull. The man with him remained a little more watchful.

"I imagine we can scrape up a meal. After all, it's getting close to that time." As I uttered those words, the reason for Hatch's confidence became apparent. From either side of the canyon mouth, three men rode up. They stopped just behind Hatch and his comrade. "Who's the friend who first rode in with you?" I asked. "I do believe I've seen him somewhere before."

"If you have, you have been in some tougher company than I would have suspected," Hatch replied. It was evident that he was really enjoying himself. "I didn't expect you to be so neighborly. It seems that the last time we saw each other, you weren't nearly so nice. Why do you reckon that is?"

"I'm trying to remember just when that was," I replied coolly. "Just when did we see each other last?"

"You damn well know when we saw each other last," he said, a chink showing in his armor of projected aplomb. "It was just before Burly made me ride out of town with him. You may not realize it, but he saved your life, at least for awhile."

"Hmm," I mused. "I think I remember you now. You were the guy who was doing the most growling and the least biting, weren't you?" I rubbed my chin with my left hand and then said, "I don't know why, but I thought that you may have been with another bunch that I saw a little later than that. I sort of thought I saw you, but the way that guy was running, looking for a place to hide, I just could've been mistaken." I guess he was lucky enough to find a dead paint horse to hide behind."

"You son-of-a-bitch, Burly isn't here to save you this time," he nearly shouted.

"We must be talking about two different times, Hatch. Either that or you were just hatched from a cuckoo bird's egg. I was thinking that you were one of a bunch of wanna be toughs that had ganged up on an English kid. It's a pity there hadn't been twice as many of you. Maybe you would've done a little better."

"Well, be that as it may, I'll bet I have enough this time" he grated.

I had been sliding the shotgun up the back of the post, without moving the rest of my body. I straightened up and stepped to the right of the post, my left hand closing on the shotgun with my finger on the trigger. The barrel swung down and they were looking at the double barrels of the shotgun. "So you think there are enough of you, do you? Why don't you show me just what you intend to do, or are you still in the story-telling phase? Remember how I let you leave the last time? I could've killed you all then. I sort of figured that boys will be boys. I thought you might have learned to stay out of mischief, after that. Good boys can grow up to be men."

Hatch's face was a mixture of purple rage and blanched fear, for the shotgun was centered directly on his gut. The man who had led the group that had come in from the left started moving back in the direction from which he had come.

"Hey, you with the stupid face, get back over there with the rest of your bunch!" I snapped. "Move fast or you won't move at all!"

"You sure as hell can't get us all," he said.

Guts flew in all directions, but mostly out the back of his stomach. He never had time to know what had happened. My shotgun was back centered on Hatch's gut. He sure as hell didn't look so cool and confident now!

"I suppose that now you want to tell me that you have guts to spare, do you Hatch?" My grin was aimed at all of them.

Hatch was ready to leave, but he still had plenty of belligerence left. "We'll be back," he choked out.

"Yeah? You sure are a slow learner. You remember what I told you in town? Well, who will be coming in your place? Do you think little boy Burly will send you again?" It was hard for him to bluster with the shotgun looking him square in the belly.

"I know he'll send me." He was squirming with his rage thwarted by his fear of the shotgun.

"There's a problem more serious than what you think Burly Boy will do." I gave him a friendly grin. "Do you have any idea yet as to what that might be?"

Hatch sat there with a stupid look on his face. "I don't get your meaning," he told me.

I turned my gaze three feet to the left where Oklahoma sat his horse. "Oklahoma, from what I've heard of you, you're smart enough to explain it to him. Of course that explanation does little to tell me how you got yourself mixed up with such a fruit cake, but go ahead and tell Hatch what I meant."

"There are some things a man has to learn on his own. It looks like I didn't learn enough of them my own self," Oklahoma replied.

"Well, Hatch, my ferocious little friend, the reason that you just don't get, is because you won't even be leaving, let alone coming back." I gave him a second to realize what I had said and I blew him off his horse.

Nearly before the shot had left the barrel, I had another shotgun in my hands. The rest of the gang didn't even see what had happened before I cut loose with the next barrel and the next, killing two with the second shot. They were fleeing as if the minions of hell were behind them. That wasn't what they were. They were shots from Rodney's big game rifle.

The fastest man made it fifty yards outside the entrance. If he hadn't been in such a hurry, he might have been able to cut around behind the edge of the cliff. Maybe he would've made it another hundred yards. Well, we don't live by mights and maybes.

Rodney came trotting up with the smoke still curling from his big bore rifle. "Darn it," he said. "I wanted to stretch one of them out on the top of that little ridge."

"Well, that's life," I told him. "Sometimes nothing seems to go right."

Chapter Eleven
Taking it to them

"What are we gonna do now?" Rodney's face was pale, now that the excitement was over.

"The first thing we'll do," I explained, "is fix something to eat. Killing can be a hungry business. Then we'll take the team and wagon and our spare horses over to the &RR. I want you to meet our neighbors. There's something we need to do, and we don't have much time if you want to be in on it and still catch the stage to St. Louis."

Deep inside, I wasn't quite as nonchalant about all the unpleasantries that had just taken place as I had appeared to be on the outside. Still, no one could say I didn't give the men fair warning. At my request, Rodney put a meal together while I hitched the team and tied the horses behind the wagon. We didn't have a lot of time, so after a quick meal, we headed west along the Rimrock. Half an hour later, we arrived at the entrance to the &RR. It wasn't long after that when I pulled the wagon up in front of the house.

I stomped across the porch and was surprised when no one was there to answer my knock. Leaving the team tied to the hitching rail, I slung a saddle on my horse. "Saddle up, kid. It shouldn't take but a few minutes to find them. It worries me they strayed so far from the house, though, when they said they'd stay forted up."

I needn't have worried. Even before Rodney and I could mount our horses, Brad and Earlene rode up from the stream.

"Sorry we weren't here to welcome you," Brad said with a warm smile.

We've been so worried about you!" Earlene said.

"I really appreciate that, Earlene," I said, briefly taking her hand and patting it. As you can see, we're okay. I just need to ask a favor. Would it be alright with you if we left the wagon and team here for a couple of days?"

"Of course we wouldn't mind!" Earlene's voice was warm, but brisk. "We *would* like to know what has been going on. You were expecting trouble. I guess that Dobbins' bite wasn't as bad as his bark?"

"Well, it was pretty bad," I answered. He sent some of his bad boys over to kill me. I doubt that he knew Rodney was with me. Please excuse the oversight, but folks, this is Rodney Hampton. Rodney, these fine people are Brad Rogers and his daughter and partner, Earlene."

Rodney hopped out of his saddle to greet both Brad and Earlene with a warm smile and a hand shake. "Pleased to meet you folks," he said, "I've heard a lot of nice things about you."

Brad said, "You still haven't told us what happened."

"The long and the short of it is that Burly sent eight men out after me. They rode up on me while I was standing by a sign we were putting up. Rodney was hidden out over in a nest of rocks" I grinned, because it sounded like the kid had hidden and left me to face the men alone.

"You left Easy alone to face all those men?" Earlene started to say something scathing, but instead said, "One more person would have made no difference anyway. How is it that the two of you're here now?"

I figured I had carried the joke far enough. "Rodney was hidden, but he wasn't hiding from those men. This is how it played out. A fella named Hatch and a gunman named Oklahoma rode straight in to where I was working. We'd figured someone would be coming, and we were prepared for them. As soon as we spotted them, Rodney went to the nest of rocks where he had his big bore rifle hidden.

I ought to tell you that Rodney is no slouch with that big gun. It has a telescopic sight on it and he could probably drive the nails in my sign from here, if it were out in the opening where he could draw a bead on it."

I turned my head toward Rodney. "Excuse me, Rodney. I meant where you could draw a cross-hair on it."

I turned back to the Rogers. "When Hatch and Oklahoma rode in, they didn't expect me to start shooting with just the two of them coming, as I would have done had it been the whole bunch. They rode in and began to talk to me to take my attention. A couple of minutes later, three more men came riding around the edge of the canyon from the left and at the same exact time, three more from the right. They pretty well had me caught out in the open."

Brad was still listening without comment, but Earlene chimed in, "How could you possibly have gotten away?"

For the first time, Rodney had to interrupt. "You should have seen what happened then! I still can't believe it." He stopped, embarrassed that he had interrupted.

I laughed and said, "You go ahead and tell them, Kid. You had a better view than I did. You know the old saying that sometimes you can't see the forest for the trees."

"No, no, you go on. I'm sorry I butted in." His face had reddened.

"Nah, I'm serious. You tell them." I smiled at him to relieve his embarrassment.

Rodney proceeded with the story where I had left off. He gave a pretty good account of what had happened. He even gave a good account of his part in it.

"You mean you the two of you alone killed all eight of those men?" Earlene asked, incredulously.

"Listen, you two! Believe me, I didn't want to have to kill them, but we'd declared war on one another. When Rodney and I killed all of their horses, I yelled to the men that we could've killed them all, and that if they came back, we *would* kill them.

"You remember what I told you that I told Dobbins in front of the sheriff. We both agreed there was to be no holds barred. I told the cowboys that I would give them time to leave without harming them. I also told them that I would kill them all if they stayed.

"I told Burly that if he stayed south of the river, we would have peace. I told him that if he came north of the river and bothered *anyone,* that I would kill them all or run them out of the country. I told Burly that if he attacked me or anyone else on the north side, that he wouldn't have a cent when he left; that he would leave with nothing. The sheriff reluctantly agreed to our pact."

"Believe me, Easy, I wasn't criticizing what you did!" Earlene said. "I'm just so happy they didn't hurt you. Or you," she added, looking at Rodney.

"What're you gonna do now?" Brad asked. "I would think he'd hire every gunfighter in the west and never give up the chase until he gets you once-and-for-all."

I looked Brad square in the eyes. "What I'm gonna do now is what I'd promised I'd do," I said. "I'm gonna go and destroy every thing he has. I'm gonna run him out of the country. He won't have a dime to his name. He won't be able to hire any gunfighters, or pay his hired hands.

"That's why I need you to keep my horses, and to hide my wagon. I'm hoping he'll be so busy on the south side he won't have anyone to spare for the north side. If he comes over to the north side, that cloud of dust you see behind him will be me, chasing him."

Rogers shook his head. "After what you have already done, maybe I shouldn't ask you how one man can make even a start on all you're planning to do. How can you be so sure you can pull this off?"

"There is never anything sure in something like this. The things that make me *feel confident* I can do it are twofold. The first is that Dobbins will have zero idea of what I'm doing until the roof is already falling in on him. The second and most important one is that I'm *not* alone. I have Rodney with me."

I walked over to the wagon and started sorting through our supplies. I loaded a pile of goods into my saddle bags. Rodney saw what I was doing and I nodded, so he joined me and began loading his own saddle bags. Before we finished, I made sure we had two cans of kerosene. We tied one behind Rodney's saddle and one behind mine.

When we'd finished loading our supplies, Rogers climbed into the seat and took the reins.

"Hey, Brad," I called after him, "maybe we should put the dun where we can grab him in a hurry, just in case I need a fresh horse before Rodney and I can catch up with each other again." Brad waved a hand in acknowledgment as he moved the wagon into the barn. He turned the team loose with the other horses in the pasture where they'd blend in and not look so conspicuous, just in case there happened to be a wandering eye.

Just as I had finished strapping the kerosene to the back of my saddle, Earlene walked over and took my hand. "I know you'll accomplish this task, Easy," she said, "if for no other reason than because you said you will. If you say you can or will do something I believe you can or will do it."

I couldn't help noticing how attractive her flushed cheeks made her look just then, and her bright eyes were more than I could stand. She gave me a quick kiss on the lips and turned toward the house. I wanted to rush after her and give her a proper kiss, but I sensed it wasn't the right place or the right time, so I just stood there and watched her go.

Brad had returned from the barn by then. He didn't look too surprised at Earlene's kiss. As Rodney and I prepared to leave the yard, he reached for my hand. "All the best to you, Easy," he said. "Let me know if you need my help." Then he nodded at the kid and followed Earlene into the house.

Chapter Twelve
South side of the river

There were no incidents as we rode across the river and entered Vacaville. The first thing that I wanted to do was to see the sheriff and bring him up to date on everything that had transpired. We pulled up in front of his office and hitched the horses.

At first Rodney was reluctant to enter with me. I said, "Come on, Kid. The sheriff may want to hear your side of the story." I cuffed my hat back and entered the office. I was amused to see that Rodney did the same as I had. When I hitched up my gun belt, he mirrored that gesture too.

The sheriff was at his desk going through a pile of posters. "Hi, Sheriff," I said. "How's the peace keeping business?"

"Oh, it has been a little on the slow side. I take it that everything has been peaceful for you?" He put aside his pile of fliers, stood up and shook hands, kicked a chair over toward Rodney and waved his hand at a chair for me.

"Nothing quite as boring as that, Sheriff," I said as I sat down and dropped my hat to the floor. "At least our bully boy Burly let us get several miles out of town before he jumped us. After their long walk back to camp, I imagine the men he sent after us wished he hadn't waited so long."

The Sheriff pulled out the makings and spun up a cigarette. "You want to tell me about it? I can see you didn't get killed or shot up."

"No, we came out of it pretty good", I said. The sheriff offered me his tobacco and papers. I waved them away. "Nah, Sheriff. I never picked up the habit."

"You did say *we* didn't you? Who else was with you?" The sheriff was listening intently.

"The same kid old Torch was making it hot for the other day. The same kid who is sitting here by me. You don't want to get the wrong idea about Rodney, here." I grinned at Rodney, who was sitting in a chair off to the side. "You remember him from the saloon. If I hadn't interfered and killed old Torch, he might have killed the whole bunch himself. He can carry his part of the load.

"Anyway, to get back to that little episode you were asking about, Hatch and about ten or twelve of the X-Pand-D boys caught up with us about an hour before sunset. We were out north of here about six or eight miles. The kid spotted them when they were a couple of miles behind us. We pulled the wagon up on a little rise that gave us a clear field of fire. It turns out that Rodney had a couple of big bore hunting rifles in one of his trunks. They both had telescopic sights."

I stopped for a jiffy to shift positions. The chair wasn't the most comfortable I had ever sat in. "We looked through a telescope the kid has and made sure that the paint horse we saw had Hatch riding it. It did. We allowed them to get half way down the slope. I told Rodney to take the right side and I would take the left side and to start killing their horses, except that I would shoot the paint horse, no matter which side it was on.

"The kid can shoot like a professional. He said he went to a shooting school before they went on a safari. Danged if I'm not digressing from my story.

"Anyway, to cut down on the story a mite, we killed every horse and set them afoot. I hated to shoot the horses, but I thought there might be some cowboys who let themselves be forced into something they really didn't want. I wanted them to have a chance to think over what they were getting into and leave before it was too late.

"When we'd made sure every horse was dead, Rodney and I split up. He went a quarter of a mile to the west and we really made it hot for them. Those English rifles sure have the range and the kick to them." I paused in my story to wipe my face off with my neckerchief.

"It was getting dark by then, so I called Rodney back and we drove the team over the rise so it would look like we were leaving. We both rode around them on the west side as they began walking back toward where Dobbins is moving that herd. We got half a mile ahead of them without being seen in the dark. I had Rodney stop and I went on a couple of hundred yards. The moon was coming up and as they topped the rise, they were outlined as plain as day."

"When I started shooting, the kid did too. I had given orders to not shoot the men, but to make them drop the saddles and scatter out. Then we shot their saddles the rest of the way to pieces. I shouted to the men that we could've easily killed them all. I told them that if they came back, I would kill them all, and that there wouldn't be another warning.

After that, Rodney and I went back to the wagon. I've no idea how long they hunkered down before they started their walk on back to the X-Pan-D. I'll bet there were several of them that decided they wouldn't help the X-Pan-D eX-Pan-D anymore. Anyway, I figured that we'd given them a fair warning. I hate to waste a man when he's not aware of what he's getting into."

"Cripes!" the sheriff exclaimed. "So that's why it's been so quiet around here!"

"Well, Sheriff, to be honest, I'm not so sure you can call it all that quiet. That was just the start of the story."

The sheriff shook his head. "Let's have the rest of it then. I figured that Dobbins' ego wouldn't let that go by. I imagine they were a lot more careful the next time."

"Well, yes and no. Dobbins didn't come along that next time either. He sent that fella Hatch again, who was sided by a tough looking yahoo named Oklahoma"

The sheriff cut in, "I have paper on Oklahoma right here in this pile of posters". He slapped his hand down on them. It sounded like a muffled shot.

"That doesn't surprise me," I continued. "Anyhow, Hatch seemed to be in charge, but Oklahoma sure didn't look like he was an underling.

"The kid and I were putting up a sign when the two of them rode straight up toward the canyon mouth. Rodney spotted them and we put a little plan into effect. I guess that with the two men riding in alone, they figured we wouldn't start shooting, since they'd appear as though they were coming in peace.

"Our plan had Rodney hiding in a nest of rocks on the far side of the canyon mouth with his favorite big bore rifle. I was standing by the side of the left hand gate post. Rodney was only forty or fifty yards away." I stopped for a moment to re-create the episode.

"The sign is a big one, about four feet high and maybe ten feet long. Arnold, the blacksmith made it for me. We had it leaning up against the two posts we'd set for the sign, when the two men, Hatch and Oklahoma, rode in with their hands on their saddle horns.

"What I didn't know became apparent a couple of minutes later. Oklahoma kept his hands in sight, as did Hatch, who acted like the cat that swallowed the canary. I saw why a minute later, for three more men came riding around the far canyon wall. Simultaneously, three more rode around from the near side. Old Hatch had the makings of a real general. Now that was the thing that I hadn't known."

"The first thing that they hadn't known was that Rodney was hidden in the rocks with his big bore rifle. The second thing they hadn't known was that I had three double barreled twelve gauge shotguns, all loaded up with double aught buckshot leaning up against the back of the sign with the barrel of one of them right where my right hand would naturally fall if I put it down. It happened that I was standing with my right shoulder against the big gate post. My right arm was out of sight to them, their vision blocked by the gate post. The sign played a big part too.

"Hatch started bragging that Dobbins wasn't there to save me, this time. He was grinning like a wolf over a crippled lamb. While he was making big talk, the leader of the three men who had come in from the near canyon wall started moving over to the left to flank me.

"By that time, under cover of the post, I had eased my right hand down and had the shotgun in my hand. It already had both hammers on full cock. I had eased it up the back of the post. I told the man easing out to my left to get back to the group. He told me there was no way in hell I could get all of them. I sent him to hell to check the accuracy of his statement. I blew his guts all over my grass, but before they had landed, I had stepped over behind the sign and had the shotgun right on Hatch's gut.

"I had told Rodney to make sure that he didn't shoot or disclose his presence in any way as long as I seemed to be in control. Like I said, he's a hell of a lot more man than someone might be led to believe. Anyway, Hatch said that they would be back to kill me later. I asked him who was coming in his place. He said that he was coming in his own place. I told him that he wasn't gonna come back, 'cause he wasn't gonna leave.

"I let him mull that for half a second and blew him out of the saddle. Before the shot got well out of the barrel, I had the second shotgun up and blasted three of the riders out with two shots. The other shotgun was in my hand while the smoke from the earlier shot was still fogging out.

"Rodney shot one man out of the saddle as they tore out of the canyon. My shotgun got the second one just as they cleared the canyon mouth. The other kept heading straight out and was a hundred yards out when Rodney picked him off as clean as plucking a goose. We would have buried them, but we figured it would give the idea that we were too soft."

The sheriff didn't speak for a full minute. "Well, I guess that you can't have people thinking you're soft," he finally said. "After all, when you let them go the first time, that might have given the idea that you're too soft and that led to the second mistake they made." He tried to take a drag on his cigarette, but it had gone out. He threw the butt in an empty five gallon paint bucket that he used for a trash can. "I hope that I'm not being too inquisitive, but what are you gonna do now? Other than bringing me up to date, what are your plans?"

"Sheriff, you remember what it was that I told our bully boy Burly? I don't remember if I said it to you or to the small ranchers that were in the bar the day this all started. I told them, or you, or Burly himself or more than likely all of the above that if he came over to the north side and attacked me or anyone else on the north side that I would run him out of the country as broke as a cowboy after a weekend in a whore-house. He made two attacks on me, and they were both on the north side. Now I'm gonna make good on my promise. I'm gonna run him out of the country or kill him. First, I will make sure that he doesn't have a pot to piss in or a window to throw it out."

"Have you decided how you're gonna do that?" the sheriff inquired.

"Nope, I will just play it by ear. Well, that is not exactly true, but let's just say that you'll know quickly, for I want to get back and see if Earlene Rogers wants to go for a picnic. I don't want to waste my time on Burly Dobbins and his bunch. Anyway, I brought enough food to last us tomorrow and the next day. I figure that should be enough for all but the clean-up." I grinned at the sheriff and got up to leave.

"I guess we will see which way the wind blows pretty soon," the sheriff said.

"That will have a lot to do with the success of my plan," I said cryptically, as I left the office.

I walked into Donahue's Bar. No one else was in the place. Donahue was polishing off some tables. It was easy to see that the floor was freshly swept and the bar shone like a new dollar. Donahue walked back to the bar and smiled at me. "I wasn't sure you would ever make it back," he said, shaking his head in a manner that was nearly wonderment.

"Well," I said, "I did make it back but I can't stay long. I want to ask you a question. If you don't want to get involved in talking with me, forget I asked it."

"What might the question be?" he asked me, idly wiping a bar rag over the spotless wood.

"I was wondering if you know anything about the location and layout of the X-Pan-D." I ordered a beer so it wouldn't appear to anyone who might come wandering in that I had come by just to pass the time in conversation.

"I have a pretty good idea of where the headquarters are located," he answered as he poured the beer into a clean glass, "but I really don't have much idea as to the layout of the corrals, bunk house, barns and other outbuildings," he answered.

"Just where are the headquarters? How does it lie in relation to the South Cedar Breaks?" I paused to give him a chance to answer.

"Wait a minute," he mused. "A cattle buyer came by the other day looking for his place. He had a map of the range. He just wanted me to tell him how to get on the main trail to the headquarters." He rummaged behind the bar for a moment. "Here it is," he said, handing me a crumpled sheet of paper.

I studied the map for a moment, then folded it carefully and put it in my shirt pocket. I took one last swallow of beer before I put the glass down and paid for my drink. "I appreciate it, Donahue," I said, and shook hands with him. Then I went out, mounted and rode back to the blacksmith shop.

When I entered, I found Rodney and Arnold forking hay into some stalls. Arnold climbed down from the loft, stuck his pitch fork into a pile of hay, and walked over to shake my hand.

"Have you ever been out to the headquarters of the X-Pan-D?" I said, by way of starting the conversation.

"I sure have. Several times, actually. Sometimes when he has quite a few new horses he needs shod, he has me come out. Other times he has some equipment he needs repaired. I may not have mentioned it," he said, "but I'm also the nearest thing to a veterinary they have in these parts."

"You wear about as many different hats as anyone I know," I said. "The heart of what I need to know is if you can sketch me out how the headquarters are laid out, and how they shape up with the South Cedar Breaks."

I was in somewhat of a rush so Arnold walked quickly to his office and sat down with a pad and pencil. As he sketched, he gave me a verbal breakdown. "This line represents the river. These marks represent the South Cedar Breaks. The one I'm blocking in now is Promontory Point. It's a sort of mesa with sheer sides. I've heard there's a way up on its south side. The headquarters are located right below it, maybe fifty yards from the foot."

He stopped, pulled out a pocket knife and put a sharper point on the pencil. "As I remember," he continued, "the house is here. The bunkhouse is here and the barn over here. There's a little house located right here that a woman lives in. She's probably some puncher's wife. The corrals are over here and there is a fenced-in pasture over here that usually has half a dozen horses grazing in it."

"What about trees or other cover?" I asked. "Does it look to you like one could pin the men down inside the buildings if one were on top of Promontory Point? Could he do this in relative safety?"

Arnold drew a deep breath. "Yeah, I think it could be done until after dark. Remember, the moon won't light up the ranch yard, once the sun goes down."

"That means that they couldn't get around to the south side to scale the mesa, doesn't it," I asked.

"I would say that would make it more difficult. If they know where the trail up is, they could still pull it off; it would just take a little longer. They wouldn't be able to see which way you went, when you got down."

"I'm sure that you know how important it is that no one know of my questions or anything else that might give an inkling of what I might be contemplating," I reluctantly said, but with a tentative smile.

"You had *better* smile when you ask a question like that, you rascal." Arnold flexed his enormous muscles in a mock show of strength. "You had better believe that your secrets are safe with me."

I slapped his rock-hard shoulder and laughed. "One more thing before I go. What is the safest way to get out of town without being seen?"

"Leave like you're going back to the north side. When you get to the river, ride a couple of miles up river to the west. You'll want to really take care, for Dobbins is still working just a mile up. You can take cover in the trees along the river on the south side.

"When you come to a line of trees along an old dry creek bed, you'll be able to see the wagon road to the headquarters from there, back to your left. When you get to the spot where the roof of the barn first comes into view, circle back further to the west and loop around to the south. You'll come out near the foot of Promontory Point on the west side.

"There's an old game trail there that you can follow around the mesa. Deer and antelope have made a trail that you can get up. If you have a good horse, you can ride up. That would make it a lot easier to get off when the sun goes down."

Arnold handed me the sketch. "All the best to you, Seeker," he said.

"Thank you, Arnold. I'm much obliged." We shook hands; then Rodney and I left.

Chapter Thirteen
The campaign

Rodney and I followed Arnold's instructions. It was the first time that I had been along Wandering River, except to cross into and out of Vacaville. The water was surprisingly clear and had a more rapid flow than I had expected it to have. "Well kid, were you able to keep out of mischief while I was off gallivanting around?" I asked him.

"I tried to, but there were too many dance hall girls hanging off my arms," came the reply. "If I had known there were that many willing girls traipsing around here, I would never have written Dad that I was coming home for a conference."

I laughed and told him, "That is one of the biggest drawbacks to being both a cowboy and gunfighter. It's hard to keep away from the hoards of women who are always hanging around."

He put on a mock look of sadness, and sighed. "How do you live with it?" he asked. Then he added, in false seriousness, "It looks like one of them followed you out to the &RR."

I grinned but held my tongue.

We found the ride along the tree line a pleasant one. As we circled away from the trail, following the twists and turns of the old creek bed, we suddenly began to grow hungry, and we were still a couple miles from our destination. "I guess you can see why we brought along those sandwiches. I know you've heard the old saying that an army travels on its stomach. Since we're a two-man army, we have the prerogative of stopping here in this copse of trees for a moment to enjoy our lunch."

"Now there's an order that I can cheerfully follow, General," he smiled. "My stomach thinks my throat's been cut."

"Then let's disillusion it," I said. "However, let's not get so wrapped up in our little pleasures that we forget to stay alert for trouble." I'd been keeping a close watch as we traveled, never taking my eyes off the path either behind or ahead. I especially watched the range to the west and the trail located about a mile to the east where I had spotted a group of three riders heading toward town. They didn't seem to be in a hurry, yet they were soon fading into the distance.

We had access to plenty of dry wood, so we built a little fire and made some hot coffee to go with our meat and bread. The branches above dispersed what little smoke came from the dry wood.

When we finished, we sat and talked for a while, waiting for dusk to settle in before moving on, knowing it would be a little harder to be seen. When the time was right, we mounted up and headed off to the foot of Promontory Point.

Taking care not to be seen, we crossed the clutter of broken rock and started through the mesquite and cedar trees that grew around the west side of the mesa. In half an hour we found the game trail.

Leaving Rodney and the two horses back in the brush, I scouted out the trail to the top. It appeared to be easy enough to ride the horses up. I was glad of that. One always feels better with a good horse between his legs than he does when he's stranded on foot.

When I returned to Rodney, we set off together. I took the lead on my horse, while he followed ten or twelve feet behind. The trail was fairly narrow, but all in all, it turned out to be easier to navigate than it had looked from below. We were soon on the top and riding across a surprisingly good cover of grass.

When we got near the edge, I dismounted and began leading my horse. Rodney did the same. In another few yards we tied the horses and went on foot to the edge.

We crawled the last few yards and slowly moved forward until we could see the ranch buildings below.

We studied the layout. There were two houses with the smaller of the two situated off to the side and a little behind the bigger one, just as Smith had described. After seeing the layout for myself, I had a better idea how my plans would play out.

"Rodney, what I have in mind is going to take a lot of nerve and skill on your part. Just before it starts getting light I'm going to head to the barn. I'll leave my horse deep in the shadows near the foot of the mesa which should be far enough away to keep any noise his hooves might make on the rocks from giving my position away.

It shouldn't take too long before someone wakes up and finds the barn burning. Once they discover the fire, they'll probably run up and see if they can do something to save the barn. By the time they recover their wits, it'll be light enough for you to start shooting.

"Have your rifle ready with plenty of shells. If there are any horses in the corral, I want you to kill them. It'll be more merciful then letting them burn. Kill every man who tries to leave the house. Remember, the first priority is to make sure that no man gets out of the house. Each time you have a chance, kill the horses.

When you have the men pinned down inside and every horse in the corral is dead, start picking off the horses in the pasture. If even one man gets away, there'll be little chance for me to escape, for there in no telling how close help may be. Let me stress again, if you aren't able to succeed in killing the horses, I have little chance to get away and yours aren't much better.

As soon as you've finished off the last horse, stop shooting. However, anytime that a man gets out into the open, try your best to kill him. We gave them a fair warning.

"Don't shoot unless you have a good target. Hopefully, you'll keep them bottled up until it starts to get dark. If you only shoot when you're sure you can kill a man, they will never know whether you're still here or not. Much of what I plan to be doing depends on you getting this job done. Do you understand what I need?"

Rodney nodded his head. His eyes were bright with excitement and resolve. "Do you mind telling me what you're going to do when you leave the burning barn?"

"What I'm going to try to do is to ride out to the west end of his grass. The hills will be on the south side and the river on the north. The wind blows out of the west at this time of the year. I plan to soak a piece of blanket with kerosene. I'll ignite it and lope along toward the river, pulling the burning torch. When my blanket burns down or disintegrates, I will stop and prepare another torch to drag along.

Even if the Burly bunch is able to get mounted, there will be a solid line of flame between me and them. It will be spreading in length as fast as the horse is loping. I'll make it to the river before they can possibly do anything to stop me. I'll double back on the west side of the fire, so I won't have to worry about the fire burning back toward me. My biggest danger will be men from the herd at the river seeing the fire in time to spot me before I get to the river."

"I'll work back around to about where we are now and we'll decide what to do next. Dobbins will be out of grass and it is too late in the summer for him to be able to depend on new grass. He will be desperate to do something to save his empire. His men are gonna desert him, for the bank isn't gonna finance him with his grass burned and his cattle scattered for a hundred miles to the east. He will be up salt creek without a paddle. If things look right, I will try to burn the rest of his headquarters down tonight or tomorrow."

Rodney shook his head and looked at me. "I'm sure glad we're on the same side," he said.

"When we're fighting ruthless men of their caliber, we have to hit them quickly, and as hard and as savagely as possible before they can even think of hitting us. There are only two of us whereas Burly has a small army. I'm hoping half his army will have deserted by the time the sun sets tomorrow."

"I'll do my part." Rodney said. "I hope you're both careful and lucky when you burn that barn down. I imagine it could be a wasp's nest." Rodney started to say more, but decided not to. He reached over and shook my hand.

"Rodney, picket your horse a little ways back from the edge. You can put your bedroll down here. There're sandwiches for tomorrow, along with plenty of water. I'll leave an extra canteen for your horse. Let him drink half tonight and half tomorrow night. I'd spend the night here with you, but I don't want to be going down the trail in the dark. I'll try to get a little rest when I'm in position. If I happen to be seen before I can burn the barn, my only hope will be you and your rifle."

I grinned and mounted up. After descending the mesa, I rode back to the southwest corner, taking my time. When I arrived, I rode along the west edge until I was able to see the lights of Burly's ranch. I unrolled my soogan in the midst of a thick clump of mesquite trees and grabbed a few hours of sleep. I figured I'd be pretty busy come daybreak.

Chapter Fourteen
The fox is in the hen house

In the darkness that comes just before the dawn, I crept up to the barn. I had constructed three torches and wrapped pieces of an old blanket soaked in kerosene around the end of each one. I opened the door enough to slip inside. It didn't take long to determine there were no horses inside the barn.

I lit one torch and quickly scanned the inside of the huge structure. I was happy to find piles of hay and straw in the empty stalls that lined one wall, for they would make great fuel for the fire. A ladder led up to the loft so I climbed it one-handed while holding the burning torch and the two unlit torches crossed in the other hand.

Using the already burning torch, I lit another and flung it to the center of the loft. The hay burst into flame so fierce that for a moment I was afraid I'd be unable to escape.

Half jumping, half falling, I stumbled down the ladder. I lit the third torch and flung it at the nearest stall. It burst into flame immediately and started rushing down the entire line of stalls. The last torch I threw into the granary. Without taking time to see if it caught, I raced through the barn doors, heading away from the red hot flames.

I walked swiftly toward the little house where Arnold had said a woman lived, taking cover in the mesquites. I paused there to see how long it would take for someone to respond to the fire. A few moments later I heard a shout and then an outburst of shouting, screaming and swearing.

After looking into the fire, it was unlikely that anyone would be able to see into the still darkened shadows from the mesa and the brush. I crouched down and ran to my horse and mounted. Taking care to keep the cabin between me and the fire, I rode carefully to the full cover of the brush and swiftly toward the point where I was expecting to start the prairie fire.

About half a mile later, I stopped and looked back. The huge bonfire was causing eerie shadows to dance on the face of the mesa. The first faint calls of the ranch hands drifted across the distance and their tiny figures moved frantically against the light of the fire.

Dawn swept across the face of the range. I dismounted, poured kerosene on a strip of blanket that I had tied with a piece of old rope, lit it and jumped back onto my horse. Then I started galloping toward the river.

It was soon apparent that I would have to ride more slowly for the dew-wet grass to catch. I pulled my horse down to a trot and began leaving a curtain of flame behind me. It raced toward the east where it would burn out at the East Fork.

My horse jumped a small gully. The fire must have affected his vision, for I felt a rock turn under his left forefoot. He recovered, but I could tell he was favoring the foot with each step.

When the piece of blanket disintegrated, I stopped and repeated my actions. I could hear the boom of Rodney's heavy rifle and I felt a surge of pride in my young friend. Working this way, it took little over an hour to reach the river. I dropped the end of the old rope as I splashed across the river and headed straight for the &RR. I had planned to ride back south behind the fire to check on Rodney. Now, with a lame horse, it was essential that I switch to the dun as soon as possible. I had no time to tarry, for I had to get back to the aid of my young English friend.

I looked back toward the X-Pan-D shortly after crossing the river. The conflagration of the barn was clearly seen, but it was dwarfed by the prairie fire sweeping eastward across the entire front from the river to the South Cedar Breaks. A ragged line of cattle was stampeding ahead of it. The beauty of it was that the livestock would escape danger when they crossed the East Fork.

It was doubtful that the headquarters of the X-Pan-D would be threatened because the ranch yard was pretty well trampled bare by the comings and goings of the livestock and cowboys.

My horse was really favoring his sprained fetlock. I didn't want to ruin him by riding any harder than necessary. I figured that I had until night to get back to Rodney.

A couple of hours after crossing the river, I came into sight of the ranch gate, opening into the &RR canyon mouth and valley. I could see the puzzled looks on the faces of Brad and Earlene when I pulled up in front of the house without Rodney.

"I don't have time to explain," I said tersely as I dismounted. "I have to change my saddle to the dun and get back to where Rodney is holed up. My horse has hurt his left forefoot. If you can take a look at him, I'd sure appreciate it. I would hate to lose that horse.

I glanced at Earlene. "I'm so sorry I have to go, but Rodney's still holed up on the mesa. I have to make sure no harm comes to him. I promise we'll catch up on everything once this whole thing is over."

I had something to say to Brad, but he had already gone off somewhere. Earlene reached out and gave me a hug. "Easy," she said. "Don't worry about a thing here. I understand. Go do what you have to do." She paused and smiled. "Just remember," she said, "when you're done with this thing you have to do, you just turn yourself right back around again and get yourself back here to me before you go out looking for any more trouble, you hear? I'll be waiting for you."

Without a thought, I lowered my lips to hers and gave her a kiss that was backed by all the emotions her warm concern and understanding conjured up inside me. A quick but emotion-filled look was exchanged and I rushed out the front door.

Leave it to Brad to have reacted quickly and practically to the emergency. There he was, coming up from the barn and leading my dun, all saddled and ready to go. "I filled your canteens," he said. We clasped hands silently before I swung aboard the dun and loped out of the yard.

I had changed my mind about riding back behind the fire, because I couldn't afford to be seen by anyone who might still be with Dobbins' herd. They were bound to be swarming around like a hive of bees. There was no way they could have missed seeing all of the smoke from the fire.

I angled off toward the Wandering River at its intersection with the East fork. Then I rode up the East Fork until I came to the South Cedar Breaks, where I turned west. There, riding far enough inside the brushy hills to remain unseen, I rode back to our meeting place on the mesa. There had been no hitches in my plan. Rodney was there waiting. He breathed a sigh of relief when he saw me.

"I was afraid you might have been caught up in the flames", he said. "I had no idea that a prairie fire could be so swift and terrifying. Some of the cowboys tried to run to the mesa to hide in the rocks. I scared them into taking cover in the house or the bunk house, but I know they must have thought they would all die in the fire. The only way they will get out of the ranch and get more horses is for them to walk to town to buy them, but I doubt that there are ten horses for sale in the whole town of Vacaville. I can't help but feel sorry for them," he finished.

"Yeah, I share your feelings, but as the old saying goes, *war is hell.* They didn't show any pity for you the day I first saw you. They weren't playing cowboys and Indians when they came to kill us on the prairie or when they rode in on us at my place.

The men in the saloon would have not only killed you, but they would have beaten and stomped you to death. I have seen such things before. I know how it goes. We warned them. They didn't heed the warning. Come on, let's get a bite to eat and decide what we want to do now."

Chapter Fifteen
A change of plans

While the coffee was heating, I brought Rodney up to date. He couldn't believe how lucky I had been through the whole operation. I couldn't blame him; I could scarcely believe it myself. We continued chatting while we ate a leisurely meal. I had been pondering our next move.

"You know Kid, Burly's bunch is gonna need horses. They would have a long way to walk to get around back of the mesa to the trail head. Coupled with the probability that they will be thinking no one will still be up here on the mesa, it makes me change my plans. Let's spend the night up here. We will sleep where we would be hard to find. I think my horse would wake me up with his snuffling and snorting if someone or something were to come prowling around. I'll have another surprise for them in the morning."

I walked over to a mesquite tree and selected one of the branches. I came back and sat down by the fire and began to slice the little twigs off the branch. Then I peeled it and took a pigging string out of my saddle bag. I had carved a groove around each end of the branch about an inch from the end. I also carved a deep notch on each end. The notches were lined up with each other. The branch had a slight bow in it, and I cut the notches on that same plane.

I made a slip knot in one end of the pigging string. Placing the loop over one end of the stick with the slip knot on the side away from the inside curve of the stick, I brought the pigging string up over the end, pulled it down into the notch and put that end of the stick on a rock.

I pulled the pigging string up to the other end of the stick, placed pressure on the stick and bent it until it had a nice bow in the wood. I measured the string against the stick and tied another slip knot. Again, I bent the bow, pulled the loop tightly into the groove and then bent the bow even further until I could pull the string up over the end and let it slide down into the notch.

It made a pretty credible bow. I placed it in the radiated heat of the fire to harden a little. Next, I started for the mesquite bush to look for some arrow material, but Rodney had anticipated my need and had already gathered eight or ten straight sticks about the right length to be used for arrows.

I cut off enough material from an old pair of leather chaps to fletch the arrows. We split the end of each arrow and placed two pieces of leather in each split. Forming them to make the arrow rotate, we bound the crack shut with pigging string. We dipped the leather in water and placed each arrow near the fire so each strip would harden.

Then we tore pieces off the remaining part of the blanket I had used to fire the pastures. Each piece was of a size to be tied to the front end of the arrow. We intended to soak them with kerosene and use them to set fire to the out buildings and the house. We couldn't imagine they would be able to put out the fire, while we were on the top of Promontory Point with telescopic sights and those high-powered rifles.

I figured that was enough for the night, so we stoked the fire with green wood to keep it burning and grabbed some shut-eye. Tomorrow would be another day.

We woke up early the next morning. I would have liked to have set fire to the buildings early in the morning, so we could make it harder on our opponents. However, there had been a heavy dew and I felt it was best to wait for the roofs to dry a little.

I crawled over to the edge of the mesa and looked down. I was a little appalled at what I saw. The barn was a smoldering area of scattered ashes. As far as I could see, the pastures were nothing but black, scorched earth, with a thin line of smoke here and there, from the roots of some mesquite tree. The ranch was totally devastated. General Sherman would have been proud.

It didn't take long for the roofs to dry, with the breeze blowing in from the west. A fine grit of ashes filled the air. We tied the rags to the ends of the arrows. Soaking one with kerosene and setting it afire, I estimated the angle and let the arrow fly. The arrow struck the side of the house and dropped to the ground. The rag continued to burn. My next shot put an arrow directly in the center of the roof. I could imagine the consternation of the occupants. They probably were wondering what made that thump. They wouldn't have to wonder for long.

Two men made a break for it nearly immediately. I let them get out about a hundred yards from the house and placed a slug out in front of them. They were panicked. They ran a zigzagging pattern, but again I turned them back with shots. They raised their arms imploringly. I cupped my hands around my mouth and yelled, "Corral! Go to the corral." The men went to the corral, fearfully gazing upward.

While I was herding the men back to the corral, Rodney had fired the rest of the outbuildings. The house was blazing so hotly that I knew the other men had to leave it or burn alive. A moment later one man made a break, firing a shot at the rim. Two shots from a Winchester screamed off on the rocks near where I stood. I lay down and peered around a rock. The man who had made the break was headed down the trail, running and zigzagging. I placed a shot so close to him that he threw down his rifle and raised his hands. I waved him back to the corral.

Less than a minute later, a man stuck his head around the front of the house, waving a white flag. "Rodney," I said, "place a slug through a window or two there in the back of the house. Keep them nailed down where they can't shoot. I'm gonna stand up."

Rodney sent a couple or three shots through the windows. I stood up and signaled the man with the white flag to come toward me. He took a few tentative steps and then began fearfully walking forward. I waited until he reached the edge of the cliff.

"What's your name?" I yelled down at him.

"Tom Jenkins," he called back.

"Jenkins, here are my terms," I shouted. "Listen closely, for you won't have another chance. Tell the men to come out of the house with their guns in plain view. Tell them that no one had better come out without a gun and the gun must be in plain sight. They will have to walk over to that clothesline pole. When they get there, tell them to walk, one at a time to the pole on the other end of the clothesline.

"Then have each man pitch his pistol and rifle to the foot of the pole and walk halfway to the corral. Then have him stop and wait until every man has disposed of his guns. If any man tries to run, hide or take a shot up here, he will be killed immediately.

"When you've followed these orders, come back to where you are now, and I will give you further instructions. Get on over and start doing what I told you to do."

Jenkins went back to join the rest of the bunch who were huddled just far enough out from the house to prevent being burned. They'd been easing out from the house, trying unsuccessfully to keep the flames of the house between them and us, so we wouldn't have a clear shot. There was a flurry of conversation among the men when they'd received the orders.

With no warning, one man started running an erratic course toward the mesquite trees and brush. The heavy slug tore his boot heel off and sent him tumbling. He scurried back to the group and no one else made an attempt at escaping.

Before long the unarmed men were finally grouped half way between the clothesline pole and the corral. Jenkins approached the bluff again. He cupped his hands around his mouth and shouted up, "What do you want us to do now?"

"I want all of you to form a line facing toward Vacaville. I'm in no mood to put up with any shenanigans. You saw what happened to the man who tried to escape. A man's head is a lot bigger than his boot heel. You'd all better bear that in mind.

"When the line is formed, I want the first man to step forward toward the bluff five paces and undress. By undress I mean I don't want him to have even a stitch of clothes on, not even his boots. Then I want him to turn slowly around so I can see that he has no weapons of any kind on his body. I'll be watching through my telescopic sights so I can see every freckle. If I have even the least suspicion that he has even so much as a tooth pick, he can kiss his manhood goodbye. When I'm satisfied that he has no weapon, he's to take five paces toward Vacaville, and then go back in line with the other men. When I give a shout, the next man is to do the exact same thing.

"Your clothing will be laid out in a line, so you can put them back on when I give the word. Anyone who fails to comply will be treated in one of two ways, according to my mood. He will either be shot on the spot or will walk to Vacaville without clothes, which means he'll probably die of sunburn. Now get on back and get started."

I didn't catch sight of any rebelliousness or a sullen look from any of the men. Not even Burly and it was easy to spot his big form among the crowd.

It took about twenty minutes for the thirteen men to do as I'd instructed. Then Jenkins once again approached for new orders. I told him to go back and take the first man's clothes.

"Pick them up and shake them vigorously so I can see there's nothing hidden in them. Every pocket is to be emptied so I can put the scope on the contents. Then the man owning those clothes is to take them, dress, and form another line well away from the men who have not yet dressed." I was taking no chances that a weapon could slip through.

When my orders had been carried out, Jenkins again approached. "What now?" he asked.

"Bring the men over here so I can talk to them." I waved him back to the group.

When the men were grouped at the foot of the bluff, I yelled out, "My friend Rodney has a few words to say to you before we decide what to do next. I've recommended he either kills all of you who were hassling him in Donahue's the other day, or shoot you up so bad that you'll never fully recover. It's totally up to him. I turned to the kid. "It's your show now."

Rodney grinned at me and stood up, the heavy rifle hanging from his right hand. "It's easy for me to recognize those of you who are still living. It doesn't seem fair to me that we should have killed everyone but you snakes. Since it was so *easy* to do the job, I think that I'll just let you go, in case we need some sport in the future."

I was watching Burly who was standing well back in the pack. I could guess he was afraid he was gonna be singled out. He was right.

"Burly", I yelled! "Why don't you step forward, so we can have a little chat?"

Burly tried to maintain some bravado, but not very successfully. "What now?" he said.

"What do you think I should do with you? I can't ask you to promise to get out of the Vacaville country, 'cause we all know that you have no honor and would lie like the dog you are. Still, I want you to tell me what you're gonna do now."

Burly looked up at me, "Some..."

I cut him off. "Listen, Dobbins! You're about to say the same thing that Hatch said when I blew his guts out. You had better not repeat his mistake, 'cause I really don't much like you. You don't have Hatch's smiling face and sunny disposition. I might lose my temper with you. I only killed Hatch; I didn't use him for sport." I gave that a moment to sink in.

"You know, on second thought I'm not gonna have a confab with you after all." I rubbed my chin for a moment and then said, "Here is a message to all of you men. Hey Burly, I'm including you in with the men. If I ever see any of you, I will kill you on the spot. If I ever hear anyone say that they saw any of you in this whole state, you can expect me to treat you like you should be treated right now.

Get your asses on the trail back to Vacaville. By the time we get down from here and ride around to the front of this mesa, if any of you are in my sight or ever again come into my line of vision, you'd better give your soul to God, for your ass belongs to me. Get the hell out of here. We're on our way down to kill those of you we can find."

Without hesitation each man turned and set out at a fast walk for Vacaville. "What are we going to do now? The kid asked.

"Well, Rodney, I made a little mistake. I don't want you on the stage with any of that bunch. Unless it's absolutely necessary for you to be on that stage, we'll go back and finish putting up the sign." The kid returned my grin.

"What do you think will happen now?" he queried.

"I can't be sure, but my guess would be that not a man will stay allied with Burly. I do imagine that I haven't seen the last of that individual, though."

"I'll post-pone my trip back to report in to Father. He will sure be surprised to hear about all of my adventures. It beats the safari with excitement to spare!"

I glanced up at the sun. It was not yet noon. So much had taken place in such a short period of time it seemed late enough for suppertime. "Hey Rodney!" I said. "I know you're anxious to leave this little paradise, but I vote for eating our lunch before we go back down to the land of the mortals."

"I was thinking of suggesting the same thing, but I didn't want to appear to be an English tenderfoot," he replied.

We were in good spirits as we grabbed a bite to eat, saddled up and descended from our vantage point. Two hours later we'd crossed the river and were heading toward the &RR.

I didn't want to run back into the Burly bunch until they had a chance to catch today's stage out of town. None of the hands had more than his ass left and no saddle to put *it* in! "Ain't life grand?" I chuckled.

We rode up to the porch of the &RR a couple of hours later. Before we had a chance to dismount, we heard galloping hoof beats from down by the river. My foot had just hit the ground when Earlene flew off her horse and into my arms. A moment later she backed up, her face red. "I was just worried!" she exclaimed, a little embarrassed.

Earlene might have been worried about the way her actions had made her appear, but they sure made my heart swell with emotion. "Well, most of the trouble might be over," I said slowly, wanting so badly to respond to her sudden display of affection. "Then again, it might just be getting started."

Brad's appearance relieved the tension. After shaking the boy's hand, he offered his hand to me, and as I took it, he said. "Earlene mentioned you and Rodney burned out the X-Pan-D. Was it only the big prairie fire you set the other day, or did you burn out his whole place too? I've never seen such a blaze, even looking at it from this far away. The smoke looked as though the world were on fire."

"Well, Brad, you might say we were slightly involved. I set the barn on fire, first, and then while Rodney kept the men pinned down inside the house, I burned their grass off. This morning we went back and burned the rest of the headquarters, disarmed all the men and set them off for Vacaville, riding Shank's mare. We also made it clear to Dobbins that if we see any of them again we'll kill them on the spot. I hope the fact that we let Burly go, instead of killing him, doesn't come back to bite us."

"Why don't we go in for a glass of buttermilk or coffee and you can tell us all about it. There's no need to stand outside in the smoke, if I might make a feeble attempt at humor," said Earlene.

"Are my powers of deduction correct in assuming that your colorful reference to 'Shank's mare' means walking?" Rodney asked. I winked and nodded slightly in reply. Then he addressed Earlene and bowed gallantly. "In answer to your generous offer of coffee or buttermilk, my Lady, I will opt for the buttermilk. I'm tired of Easy's coffee."

"Well Kid, no one hand fed you from a bottle," I laughed. "If you hadn't been such a slacker, we would've finished up the war yesterday. This could be then, with us sitting down in this fine company." I glanced at Earlene as I mentioned the company. She smiled.

Chapter Sixteen
Back home – well, sort of

Time waits for no one; it won't wait for me. I was enjoying the moment just relaxing here with my friends, sipping cool buttermilk and talking. However, I had a lot of work to do, and since talk doesn't make the rooster crow, I pushed back from the table and rose to my feet.

"I apologize for having to leave so soon but my cabin won't build itself," I said. "I'm going to spend some time scouting around my place for a while to see what I have in the way of lumber. I've not had the chance to take a good look at my place and I have a big curiosity about the canyon wall where this valley ends."

"Rodney, we have a couple or three options, as I see it. One is for you to wait a month for things to die down around here before heading back for England, via St. Louis. Another is that you get to Denver and go east from there. There's quite a bit of activity between Denver and St. Louis so it should be easy to catch a stage there.

"Another option is to swing south and catch the stage from Santa Fe to Amarillo that will take you to Fort Worth and then on to Galveston. You can catch a steamboat there on the gulf coast to New Orleans and up the Mississippi to St. Louis. You might even be able to catch a ship from Galveston, either straight back to England or from Galveston to New Orleans and then on to England.

"After considering all the pros and cons, I'd personally recommend catching the last stage named. You'll go through Ft. Worth, but you have good stops from there to Galveston. You'd be less apt to run into trouble going that way."

"Easy," the kid replied, "I know it sounds like I'm running out on you, but I feel that I can't wait the month. Maybe I can find some freighter headed back to San Antonio and travel with it until we cross the stage line. Then I will head on for Galveston to take the fastest way back to England. I have a strong feeling that Father wants to hear from me."

"Don't feel that you're running out on me. You've been a lot of help and a good partner. I have an idea. We can put you on the stage that's headed south after it has already left Vacaville. We will check to see if any of the Burly bunch is on the stage. If not, I think you'll be alright from there through the connections to Galveston.

"Since the stage leaves today, we'll hitch the buggy up now and load your gear. We'll head to the stage road south out of Vacaville. We can catch the southbound stage about ten miles west of Vacaville where it skirts the South Cedar Breaks and turns south."

"That sounds like a winner to me," Rodney said. "There's just one thing I must insist on before I leave. I'd like you to take both my rifles and all my ammunition as a gift for all you've done for me, both in the saloon and afterward." He stood up and made a half bow to Brad. Then he took Earlene's hand, kissed it and turned back to me. "I say, Old Chap, let's get the show on the road."

He exaggerated his normal English accent, with a broad smile that covered us all.

"We'd best hurry," I said. We don't want to have to chase the stage down."

With not much time to spare, we rushed to the barn and got to work. I hitched the team while Brad and Rodney loaded his trunks into the buggy. Earlene brought along a basket of food and a couple of freshly filled canteens. "Easy," she said, "its time I got away for a few hours. How about me riding along to keep you company?"

When I glanced at Brad he just grinned and shrugged his shoulders. "It's okay with me, Earlene, as long as you don't eat my part of the chicken!" I said.

"Oh Easy! Just how much chicken do you think you need?"

"Well, if you eat half as much as Rodney does, and if your chicken is as good as your ham is, you might say I need an awful lot of chicken." I looked at Brad. "Hey, grab your hat and come along with us. We'll have us a picnic along the river while we wait for the stage."

Brad said, "I'm sure tempted, but this will be the first time that I haven't had to be baby sitting Earlene for a long time. I just can't miss this chance to relax without having to tell any bedtime stories or such."

Earlene grabbed the hat off my head and flung it at Brad. When she stood up in an attempt to retrieve it, I had the horses jump forward and she fell backward onto her seat. While she struggled to gain her balance, I jumped from the buggy and took the hat that Brad had picked up and was handing to me, laughing.

When I had climbed back onto my seat, I picked up the reins and then turned to Earlene and gave her a kiss. "I hope you didn't think you could avoid a kiss by coming along," I said. Rodney cleared his throat noisily. Earlene's face brightened and colored. I took up the slack in the reins and clucked to the team. We pulled away and the &RR slowly began to recede into the distance.

As we approached the trail south of Vacaville, Rodney turned to me and we shook hands warmly. "You've heard the story of the bad penny," he said.

"Yeah, I've heard it," I replied, "but England is a long way from here. When you tell your father of your adventures, I imagine he'll have second thoughts about investing out here in the *Wild West!*"

I have to confess that I had become quite fond of Rodney. He had proven to be both brave and resourceful and a great help to me in times of danger.

Suddenly the stage emerged from behind the trees that lined the Wandering River. The driver was cracking his whip and yelling at the team as they approached.

When the stage pulled up, I jumped from the wagon and stuck my head inside. Satisfied that none of the passengers were associated with Dobbins, Rodney and I unloaded his trunks from the buggy. The driver and the shot gun guard lifted them onto the stage.

We waved our final goodbyes as the stage pulled away, crossed the river and rounded a little copse of trees that hid it from view. The sound of the whip cracking and the driver's shouts eventually dimmed and then floated off into oblivion. The only thing left was the dust that swirled up from the wheels and settled on my boots.

Earlene looked up at me and said, "You know, Easy, I sort of hate to see him go. Do you think he will ever return to the Rimrock country?"

"That's a question that will have to be answered by time," I said as I took her hand and we walked back to the buggy. We sat down on the spring seat and I turned the team back along the river to where a nice little grove was situated just off the beaten trail. I wheeled the buggy into a secluded spot in the shade beneath a large tree where it was hidden from view of anyone coming from or going to Vacaville.

I spread a blanket on the soft grass while Earlene got the basket of chicken and fixings, along with a jar of buttermilk. We lay down with her head on my shoulder and talked for a few minutes, growing drowsy in the summer sun. We napped for a little while; then gathered up the blanket and basket, and started back across country to the &RR. I couldn't help marveling at what sweet dessert warm kisses can be.

Chapter Seventeen
A new adventure

Later I stopped by the &RR to drop Earlene off and leave my team and the Rogers' buggy. I was gonna start cutting some poles to fence off the opening to the canyon and thought I might as well get an early start. Earlene wouldn't hear of it. I looked at Brad for help, but he just grinned and told me I would have to shift for myself.

Earlene brushed aside my talk of an early start by reminding me that my cabin was only fifteen or twenty minutes away. When she opened the oven to check on her baking, that clenched the argument then and there. I never could walk away from a peach cobbler, though there were times that I had eaten so much that I nearly had to be carried away.

After the kind of meal that makes a fellow want to curl up and sleep for a week, my thoughts of hitting the sack early were dashed when Earlene invited me to a game of three-handed moon. Table games, such as dominoes, were my weakness. I didn't know how, but this girl sure seemed to know all my Achilles heels. I don't know how one man can have more Achilles heels than he has feet to go with 'em, but I do know one thing for sure; I have 'em.

It'd been a long, long time since I'd had so much fun just sitting around a table playing a game and laughing with a beautiful woman and a congenial companion. Teasing and being teased, joking and frolicking were things I hadn't had much time for in the past. We played one game after another until the minutes turned into hours and the moon was shining in the western windows.

Of course there was no way I was gonna ride home in the dark. Why there are coyotes and, uh things that would go bump in the night if there were something for them to bump against. You must understand that was the reason it was so easy for Earlene to talk me into spending the night.

The next morning I got up bright and early but it was no earlier than the Rogers did. Come to think of it, it wasn't any earlier than any of the three of us ever got up. Breakfast was soon on the table and before I could say a word about heading out to my valley, I found myself the willing victim of a trap.

Earlene handed me the hot biscuits and the jar of butter and said, "Easy, I have been trying to get some things done for the longest time. What would be the chance of you riding out my side of the valley while Dad is checking out his side?" That request was served up with a smile that made the butter melt and drip off of my biscuit right onto my plate of eggs.

Of course I told her no! Well, that's not exactly true. What I really told her was, "There is absolutely no way on earth I would ever let such a proposition go by, but I'm warning you, it's gonna cost you!"

"And pray, kind sir, just what is it that it will cost me?" Her shining eyes and still tousled hair made it easy for me to tell her.

"Oh, let's see. I think a fair price would be another cup of that coffee," I said as I drained the last drop and set my cup back onto the table.

"Pass your cup over here then, and I'll pay that toll in cash, uh coffee," she said, "and even give you a chit for another cup on another day for interest."

"Well, I know that it'll come as a surprise, but I already have a lot of interest. But then, I know that you won't have the least idea of what I mean."

Brad and I walked out to the barn, chatting of how pretty the weather was, but that the feel of rain was in the air and other earth-shaking developments. We saddled up and headed toward the creek, enjoying our conversation as the sun rose above the east rim of the canyon. Since I was riding out the east side, I told Brad I'd see him later and headed up the valley while he continued to the other side of the stream.

I rode along with the warm sun on my shoulders, feeling like a king. Still, I couldn't shake the gnawing concern about what Dobbins might be doing along about now. I had no doubt that he would be back. I also felt sure that he would have an entirely different approach to things than he had shown so far. He was a person so arrogantly sure that everyone would bow to him that he had trouble believing he would ever run into resistance. However, his innate cunning would have by now convinced him that flexing his muscles and waving a six gun around was not enough to win the pot in this game.

I inspected the cattle as I moved up the valley, keeping a mental tally of them. I also kept a wary eye on my surroundings, both on the valley floor and on the Rimrock. I had no desire for Brad or Earlene to have a reason to come looking for my body. I might not have been old and wise, but neither was I a babe in the woods.

The work was so pleasant that it passed all too soon. It seemed that I had no sooner started than I was done, and once again had returned to the house. I had taken a little longer than Earlene usually took, or else Brad had made a faster round than he usually made, for when I returned to the house, Brad met me in the ranch yard and walked alongside my horse as I rode past the barn and on toward the house. I gave him the tally on the east side cattle and glanced down at him.

He volunteered, "Earlene is fixing up a meal and a basket of food. Since we've finished checking the stock for today, it won't surprise me if she wants to ride along with you."

"If it doesn't leave you short handed, I would sure enjoy the company," I said as I swung down from the saddle.

In the west at that time, good women were hard to find. There had been somewhere in between none and few of them in my life up to now, and a lot closer to none than to few, if the truth be known. Although I found it hard to allow myself to dwell on such things, I had to acknowledge that Earlene meant a lot to me. I fiddled around with my horse's mane while Brad saddled Earlene's mount. We walked silently onto the porch.

Earlene must have been watching from the window, for as we stepped onto the porch, she came out, tied a bag of food to her saddle and mounted her horse. We turned and headed toward my valley. We'd ridden a hundred yards before she spoke.

"It's gonna be a warm day," she said, stroking her horse's mane.

"Yes, it seems so," I said. "It usually is at this time of year, but it won't be for much longer now. I hope I have a chance to get a cabin up before that old north wind pours over the Rimrock and right down my shirt collar."

"Let's hurry, then!" She put her mount into a lope and we laughed as the galloping horses made a breeze on our faces.

It seemed but the blink of an eye before I began to pull up as we neared the opening of the canyon. I got off of my horse, pulled my rifle from its boot and eased my head around the edge of the rocky bluff. I studied the rocks and shadows for several minutes. I turned back toward Earlene. She was studying the far side of the canyon. She had her Winchester held across her chest with both hands. It was obvious that she was ready to shoot.

"Earlene," I said. "I'm gonna check the ground between here and the far side of the canyon for tracks. I wonder if you would keep me covered."

"Of course," she said as she moved over to where I had been standing, behind the protection of the wall. "I have you covered, and yes Easy, I can shoot." She laughed softly.

I patted her shoulder and walked slowly across the mouth of the canyon, watching for the slightest sign of man or beast.

Every few steps, I stopped and scanned the canyon rim, paying close attention to the rocky outcropping, the shadows and the camp we'd used a couple of days earlier. There was nothing out of place, not a cigarette butt, not a single tobacco juice stain or anything else out of the ordinary. My sign still leaned against the post where I had left it.

I turned and walked rapidly back across to where Earlene still stood vigilantly. "Let's go. I think all is well, but we can't forget for one minute that there are people who want to kill me. If they find you here with me, I imagine they'll have other plans for you."

We mounted our horses and rode up the canyon. The air was balmy and the sound of Meadow Larks filled the air. Splashes of various colored flowers gave a pleasant smell to the warm air and touched the green grasses and clovers with the soft hues of the rainbow. Outside the valley on the plains, the only green left on the Gramma grass and Curly Mesquite was near the bottom of the stems. The top of both grasses were a grayish brown there, but here in the valley it was still like spring.

We had passed by several places where the Cedar trees would have provided more logs than ten houses and barns could have possibly required, but we were loath to stop. It is so seldom that all of the things that go to make up a day, come together at the same time in such perfection as to create a day like today.

All too soon, we came to the end of the canyon. It was blocked by the wall that was indelibly stamped in my mind. The jumble of rocks that blocked our way at the northwest end of my valley seemed like a massive obstacle commanded by nature to keep the two valleys apart. I made a vow they would be an obstacle that I would overcome.

A tangle of trees and bushes grew at the end of the canyon. Hidden between them was a tiny glen that should be easily viewed from above, but would be virtually invisible from the canyon floor. We worked our way into the small glade, dismounted and picketed our horses.

"Earlene, let's see if we can find a place to scale this wall. I will take the wall on the left; if you walk along to the right, we'll meet over there by the big, flat rock near the center. Just to be safe, take your rifle with you." I took my Winchester from the saddle boot and turned to see that she had done the same. "See you in a minute, Babearlene, I stammered as I caught myself."

"Okay, Babeasy." She laughed and started for the far wall as I pushed my way though the brush.

The far side of the canyon, only yards away, was relatively clear of brush except for a tree or two that grew tall and straight against the wall. A brushy clump hung to the cliff-side near the top of the trees. I had worked my way to the end and was clambering over the stones toward the center when Earlene called to me, "Easy, come look at this!"

"Just a second," I said. "Let me climb down from here." I jumped down onto a rounded rock and made a leap to the large flat stone I had chosen earlier for our meeting place. I half slid and half climbed down to the damp, sandy earth at the foot of the wall where we had discovered the seep on our first trip to my valley. I walked over to Earlene and asked her, "What have you found?"

She led me past the trees to the brush that grew at the end of the wall and pushed through it, while I followed closely behind. She pointed to what appeared to be a pathway but was actually a ledge that sloped from the outside edge downward toward the cliff, while the path led up the cliff.

When it emerged from the brush, it was above the height of a man's head while he was on horse back. This rendered the path invisible to one looking right at it, for all you could see of the actual path was its outside edge. It formed a natural channel, where any water coming down it would flow next to the cliff. It appeared that some sort of a geological fault made a line up the cliff. When it reached the clump of brush near the top of the tall trees, it made a switchback vee and started back the other way which led to the top of the cliff.

"What do you make of that?" she asked.

"Hmmm," I mused. "Let's see where it goes. I'll go first." I chose to go first because I knew what kind of thoughts I would be having if I followed her up the path. Those tight riding pants she wore looked more than kind of good on her body.

She stood aside while I took the lead. The path, although fairly steep, was easy to climb. Although the path doubled back and continued up to the high ground, screened by the bushes growing behind the tree tops, just beyond where the path switched back, was the mouth of a cave. A closer inspection showed marks left by a pick. It was an old mine.

"Wow!" Earlene's exclamation echoed my own feelings. However, at this time I was far more interested in what lay above and beyond the path than I was in the old mine.

"Let's save the mine for a later time," I said. We turned back from the tunnel and continued on our way up the path. As we climbed, I kept hearing what I thought was the wind in the trees that were now below us. However, the sound increased in volume as we progressed. Suddenly it dawned on me. "That's the sound of the waterfall," I exclaimed, picking up the pace.

"It sure sounds like it might be." Earlene picked up speed to match my own and we soon came out on the top of the Rimrock. Stretching away to the north and the east was the broad expanse of the high ground. Looking toward the northwest, we discovered that the Rimrock made a great curve from the north to the west. I could see the desert from here and in my mind I could picture the way I had come into this country. I looked directly to the west. There was the beginning of my oasis. There was the proof that our suspicions were correct.

The huge land-bound "peninsula" that jutted for miles to the southwest was separated from the line of the Rimrock and it was a mystery to me as to whether it was an enormous mesa that abutted the Rimrock, or if its curious teardrop shape had broken off from the Rimrock and caused the huge cracks that formed the one long valley that actually included both the oasis and my valley, except for the jumbled dam of rocks. Another crack running from that one out to the perimeter of the Rimrock where it bent toward the southwest on the right, and east on the left formed the &RR.

The line of the Rimrock to the west made a nearly perfect alignment with the combined canyons of my oasis and my valley. The north and the east walls of my canyon were a continuation of the Rimrock. The &RR was a huge crack that ran from the line of the

Rimrock even with the east side of the "peninsula" to a point a couple of miles west of the "penisula" where it intercepted the line of the Rimrock and opened into the Meandering River Basis.

One could see the line where the huge aberration of the land based peninsula circled back until it lined up with the Rimrock and then swung westward. It was that huge projection that I had circled around days ago to get from my oasis to the valley that contained the &RR.

Earlene and I walked to the edge of the jumbled rock. The cooling mist off the huge waterfall caressed our faces. "There goes the river that once flowed through my valley," I said and squeezed Earlene's hand.

We stood in silence as we took in the valleys below. It was easy to imagine the way it had been when the two valleys were one. The &RR came very close to breaking into the line of the other two valleys. It looked like some force had fractured the high ground at this point and three cracks radiated out from here.

I could imagine the river flowing through my valley and watering the cows that would graze the thick, dense grasses like those that composed the &RR.

I looked at the ridge that hid my valley from the pathway Earlene and I had used when walking from the &RR to my oasis. It appeared that a section of the earth had suddenly tilted up from the southeast side and left a smooth, steep incline. I knew what I would see from there. I knew that I would be able to view the steep ridge that we'd seen when we were walking back and forth between the two valleys.

We must have stood there for fifteen minutes, taking in the wonderful view. We were silent, but that silence held a special communion that caused my heart to swell. I knew from that moment on that I would never let this girl be anything but a part of my life and that I would never let her go.

Earlene's voice was husky as she said, "What do you say we go down and have lunch now?" I wondered if the huskiness of her voice was a reflection of her memories as she thought about that day when we stood so close together in the willows we saw below, nude and near one another, yet nothing more than strangers who had met by chance and been surprised by circumstance.

I reached for her hand and held her back as we approached the rim. I looked carefully down at the horses. They were grazing peacefully in the little glade below us. I inspected the canyon from end to end, especially in the vicinity near our horses and our hidden pathway, but there was nothing to set off an alarm in my mind.

We passed the old mine shaft without comment. When we arrived at the glade, Earlene retrieved our lunch from her saddle bags. We sat down on the flat rock where we'd initially planned to meet and began our meal.

During our conversation, we discussed the old mine. We thought it would be fun to do some exploring, so when we'd finished our meal, I picked up a stick that was lying nearby. I tied a scrap of the old blanket to one end and soaked it with the kerosene I still had strapped to my saddle. "Now let's go have a look in that old mine," I said.

"I thought you'd never ask!" Earlene exclaimed, delighted.

We walked excitedly up the path and paused when we came to the mouth of the mine. The floor of the mine sloped slightly uphill as it disappeared into the darkness. I lit the torch and we entered.

"We'll have to be quick. This torch won't burn for long." We could hear the faint sound of the waterfall as we walked along in the dank air. There was something bothering me that I couldn't put my finger on. Suddenly it dawned on me! The sound of the waterfall was not growing dimmer! It was growing louder!

The sound seemed to be coming through the earth, rather than through the air. A shaft forked to the west from the main shaft which appeared to be running north.　We followed the left fork which was the direction from which the roaring hiss was coming. The shaft went along for a short distance before it abruptly ended.　The ground seemed to tremble beneath the force of the waterfall.

"It's sort of frightening, isn't it?" Earlene hesitated a moment and added, "At the same time it's exciting. Have you ever had the feeling that something was going to play a huge role in your life? That's how I feel about the sound of the waterfall; as though it's about to engulf us and carry us into a new world."

"That's exactly what I was about to say," I said in surprise. "In many ways, this waterfall has already had a distinct role in my life. After all, it *was* at the waterfall where I had caught my first glimpse of a certain water nymph. It may have been only a brief glimpse and I may have thought it was a dream but I'm sure hoping it'll turn out to be just a mere preview of what the actual future will hold for me."

Earlene moved close and rested her head against my breast. I placed my free arm around her and we stood like that for a long while. Finally, we turned and walked down the slight grade to the opening where we stopped to take a good look around before leaving our cover.

After mounting our horses we rode toward a grove of cedar trees that were growing on the northeasterly side of the canyon, just a short distance beyond the point where the canyon widened out into a valley.

I lifted my horse into a slow gallop. "I want to get back to the &RR. I need to bring the team back over here. I'm going to start cutting logs in the cedar grove and dragging them back to the cabin site."

As we rode along the old river bed, we came upon a particularly attractive spot located near the canyon mouth. "That would be a great place for a cabin," Earlene remarked.

The seed of an idea took root in my mind and quickly blossomed into a goal. "Earlene, I think we'd better build our cabin on that higher ground. I stumbled imperceptibly and said, "In fact, I want to build the cabin on that bit of higher ground right over there, because if we build it there where you indicated, I have a feeling we might sometimes have a problem with flooding. By hook or by crook, I'm going to turn the river down this valley where I'm convinced it once flowed.

"Earlene, there are two things that immediately come to mind. The first is to investigate, as well as we can, the course of the river near the waterfall while it is still underground. It wouldn't surprise me if we could put an ear to the ground and get a good inkling of where it's flowing. I want to see if we can determine about where we were standing when we were listening to the waterfall from our old mine.

I'm hoping I can blast a hole through from the mine to the river. Since the shaft runs down hill from its end to the mine's entrance, it's possible that we can divert all or part of the river into the mine shaft and let it flow down on this side of the rock dam at the end of the canyon!"

Failing that, I will try to raise the money to build a flume that runs from high up on the bluff where the water emerges from the cliff-side to a point on this side of the rocky dam and let the water spill down over the boulders and flow into the old river bed. If neither of those is feasible, I will tear the wall down, stone by stone, until the river can flow into this canyon."

I stopped talking to take a deep breath. This was something that *I was going to* do. It was suddenly my mission. It was the mysterious urge that had brought me back to this valley. I was convinced it was my preordained mission in life to bring the river back to my valley. I also believed it was my destiny to rejoin my valley to my oasis. "Earlene, this is my new mission in life!" I exclaimed with conviction. "I will turn this valley into an Eden. You and I will make it bloom like a garden. Look how the land lies between here and the river!"

Suddenly overcome with emotion, I jumped off my horse, grabbed Earlene, pulled her off her mount, and wrapped her tenderly in my arms. I kissed her long and hard, her soft lips answering mine. I pulled away, for I knew that if I didn't I would be unable to control my urges. Earlene studied my face, her eyes so full of expression I could almost hear them consoling and comforting me. I was certain she understood and shared my mixed feelings.

We mounted and galloped nearly all of the way back to the &RR. As we dismounted, Brad came out onto the porch. He saw the excitement in our faces. His eyes searched Earlene's for a moment. He could see our feeling reflected from our eyes. He didn't yet know that those feeling were not the only news we carried.

"Dad, come into the house. We have something to tell you." By the look her father gave her, Earlene was sure he had read the love in our faces. She began to laugh. "No, Dad," she said. "You may be right in your assessment, but you're wrong about our news." She stopped talking for a moment and then directed a question to me. "Easy, do you care if I tell Dad the story?"

"I was hoping you might," I answered. "Please go ahead."

Earlene turned back to her father. With the skill of a born story teller, she relayed the news, detail after detail, holding on to the greatest part for last.

Brad listened with rapt attention. He had been leaning back in his easy chair, but by the time Earlene had finished talking, he was leaning forward and sitting on the edge of his seat.

"We also picked out a spot for a cabin," she said. "We found a grove of cedar trees that we can use to build our home. It will have a view that is reminiscent of our own, in many respects."

"Please forgive me for broaching such a subject, but your words leave me wondering exactly . . ." He never did finish his thought for he suddenly broke off and said, "Forget it. Everything will work itself out." He got to his feet and gave his daughter a big hug. He then took my hand. "Easy, congratulations!"   His lips quivered as he turned quickly away, walked to the kitchen and poured himself a glass of water.

I traded a quick grin with Earlene. Her father came back into the room and asked, "I assume you're going to start on your house immediately?"

I nodded an affirmative and he continued, "Either you can spend the night here and take the wagon back in the morning, or you can take the wagon back now and we will be over in the morning to help you with things as soon as I milk the cow and make my loop around the place." He started for the door and then stopped, one hand on the door knob. "If you or Earlene want to modify those plans, there is no problem. If you should be going back to your place now, we can hitch up while you still have time to get a little work in."

"When I have a hill to climb, I like to get it done. I hate for it to look like the only reason I come over here is show I'm tough enough to drink Earlene's coffee, and sly enough to mooch a good meal, but when we came by that grove of Cedar trees, there hadn't a one of 'em cut itself down."

"In all seriousness, this is the first time I can remember being this eager to do something. Earlene must have been putting peyote in my coffee." I sneaked a look at Earlene and saw her trying to subdue a smile. "I can't wait to get started. Let's get those horses hitched up."

"I figured that was what you would do," said Brad. "That is why I'm standing here with my hand still on the door knob."

Earlene took advantage of the chance to toss in a comment of her own. "I'll have a bite to eat prepared by the time we get hitched." She colored as she realized she had said 'we', instead of 'you'. She colored even more as she realized how it must have sounded when she said, "we get hitched."

The slip of the tongue hadn't gone unnoticed by either Brad or me. Neither of us said a word, but we were both smiling.

Chapter Eighteen
Home springs eternal in the human breast

Opting to leave my pack horse at &RR for now, I tied my horse on behind the wagon. I had a roll of extra bedding in the wagon. I placed it under the spring seat after sliding one of the heavy English rifles into the center. I checked and it slid easily out into my hand. I pulled the team to a stop in front of the porch and tied the off horse's bridle to the tie rail. Both of the Rogers were already sitting at the kitchen table. I quickly washed my hands and joined them.

Rubbing my hands together in anticipation, I accepted a plate with a stack of hot cakes on it. There was a plate of butter and a pitcher of sorghum molasses. I felt like rubbing my hands together again when I saw a glass of cool sweet milk. I knew that I would never be without a milk cow and some chickens, once I got the place built up.

We all fell to and made short work of our plates of flap-jacks. I finished and spoke to my hosts. "I can't tell you how much I thank you for all you have done and are doing for me. I hate to eat and run, but I feel a compulsion to get started."

"Yes, both Earlene and I feel that way about this little spread. We have some high hopes to try some novel things for this part of the country. It would surprise me if some of our plans won't complement yours, and vice versa."

"It would surprise me if that were not true," I agreed as I grabbed my hat and started out the door. I stood there indecisive for a moment, then turned back and gave Earlene a kiss on her lips. It wasn't a long one, but it wasn't all that short, either.

"It wouldn't have been very lady-like if I had had to jerk you off that wagon seat to get my kiss," she said severely.

"That isn't likely to ever be necessary," I replied as I clucked at the team. I pulled back up and added, "I sure advise you both to keep your eyes open for trouble. Don't trust anyone. I don't just mean today, I mean from now on. I've a feeling that this little war between Dobbins and me isn't over. I should have killed him." This last little dialog was aimed at both of them. I had made that obvious by turning my face from one to the other as I was speaking. I shook my reins and the team started off again. If they had known the work I had planned for them, they may not have stepped out so eagerly.

The trip back to my place was a new experience for me. I felt a sort of peace that I had never felt. The sun was warm on my shoulders and the plop of the horse's hooves was tempered by the grass. The trace chains clinked softly and the wagon rattled and squeaked. The wheels crushed the grass with a muted chuffing sound. A meadow lark called out his little melody of two notes repeated twice, followed by his little four or five note warble.

The world was great! A great world didn't make me relax my vigilance by one iota, though.

As I pulled into the canyon, I paused for a moment to look at my sign, still tilted against the posts. The sheriff had come out and picked up the dead we'd left strewing the countryside. I wondered if grass grew any greener when fertilized by blood. I also knew that I had to decide the name of my spread. I needed something to show that I was no longer a rootless drifter, looking for men whom needed killing. I had a new life now. I had my roots. I would let them grow deep.

I clucked the horses back into motion. My goal was the grove of cedar trees. Pulling up near where I planned to begin cutting, the team was soon unhitched and picketed so they could graze. Calliope came next, and with his saddle girth loosened and his bit slipped, he was soon picketed near the other horses, but none of them were near enough to one another to get their ropes entangled.

I had never used a bucksaw. I knew that they were a whole lot faster and more efficient than using an ax to chop the trees down. I also knew that a good sawyer would've used a cross cut saw, but it was an acquired skill that I sure didn't have. Two men usually manned them, but I felt that most of the time I would be alone and I didn't want to squander money on something that would be idle most of the time.

A bucksaw was something that would always be handy for cutting stove wood, fence posts and even for making planks for flooring, and similar things. I took the bucksaw and tried to cut down my first tree. It was a slow go, but it got easier as I went along.

I put the saw back in the wagon and took the double bitted ax. I had used an ax before, but never on the level that I was gonna have to if I wanted to get a cabin built. I chopped into each tree on the side that it appeared it would fall on. This was to keep the saw from being pinched and ruining the set in the saw teeth.

I went ahead and notched a dozen trees while I had the ax out. Then I stuck the ax into an old log and got my saw back out of the wagon. There was something else that had to be acquired when sawing in addition to the skill. One had to get used to bending over and sawing. Talk about something being hard on the back! I would've sawed them off higher, so I wouldn't have to bend so far, but I had an aversion to having the stumps sticking up so high.

I soon found out that there was an art to using the bucksaw too. One had to develop the knack of keeping his pulling and pushing of the saw blade on an even plane with the cut he was making, or the blade would hang and try to kink. With the saw always on the verge of kinking, I slowly, slowly, interminably slowly continued trying to even get the saw to cut a groove deep enough to hold the weight of the saw up, so I could have at least the ghost of a chance of sawing. I finally got a cut started. The side of the tree where I was trying to saw looked like a map of some river, with channels running off at every odd angle. At least it had what would pass for a main channel.

To take a break from that work, which kept me bent over and my muscles aching in places where I didn't even know I had muscles, I took the ax and lopped the limbs off of the few trees I had felled I was glad that I at least had some good gloves. Talk about something being hard on the hands! My gloves would rectify the tendency of my hands to blister. I sure couldn't figure out anything to rectify my aching back.

It was mid-morning when I started cutting the trees. Time seemed to fly until it was time to eat my lunch. My back was soon aching so badly that the afternoon drug as slowly as a balking mule. Eventually, it was too dark to see. I went back into the trees and threw my bed roll out in a smooth place. I felt plenty secure, but that didn't stop me from having my Winchester close at hand. My colt was inside my bedroll with me. I went to bed early because I couldn't see to work. I awoke and got up early, because that was what I was accustomed to doing. As soon as I could see, I started in with the saw again.

I tried a new tack with my sawing. When I first notched the tree on the side where I wanted it to fall, I went to the other side and cut a small notch. I made sure the notch was more or less flat on the bottom. The top was just cut in at the angle the natural swing of the ax made from my shoulder to the cut. This was not the way the lumber jacks did it, but they were experts with the saw and the ax. As for me, it was an enormous help, for it kept the saw from wandering all over the side of the tree before I finally got a groove started that would help support the weight of the saw and also make each saw stroke follow the same path. I'll bet it increased my speed by half again more.

Brad and Earlene must have made an early start on their rounds, for the sun wasn't over two hours high when I saw them ride into the mouth of my canyon. In another half an hour, they had arrived at my work site.

"We came straight to the sound of your ax," Earlene ventured. "It's a good thing you were working or we would have set up camp and eaten our cold fried chicken, potato salad and beans alone, when noon came. I would have sure hated to have to throw out that extra peach cobbler, too!"

"The luck is that I was chopping instead of sawing," I returned. "I spend more time sawing than chopping. Now that I know what I nearly missed, I'll make sure I do my sawing after you leave, so I'll always be chopping about the time you both arrive!"

"This is the first time I've ever been in this valley," Brad threw in. "You sure understated its potential. If you can get that water in that you're talking about, you'll have a place the equal of ours."

"I'm gonna have water in the valley. I may have to build that flume I spoke of, but you can rest assured I *will* have water." My determination was evident in my voice. "Of course, sometimes there is a big difference and a long trail between being determined and turning determination into realization. By the way, I neglected to mention that there is a pool of water at the far end. It seeps out into this side from the other side of the rocks. It has enough water to handle a fourth of my anticipated herd."

"How can I be of the most help?" Brad was pulling his gloves onto his callused hands.

"Let's give it a try with one of us lopping off branches and the other one using this bucksaw," I said. "We can switch off every little while to keep our backs from hurting so much."

Our work went remarkably faster. Every time a tree fell, Brad and I would change jobs. It also is a lot more companionable when working with others, than it is when working by one's self. Whichever one of us was using the ax would cut branches if he finished notching the next tree before the tree being sawed fell.

We continued to apply ourselves to the work. With the two of us alternating on the bucksaw, we were felling at least six trees per hour. We didn't want to use too big of logs because of the trouble it would take to raise the cabin walls and put up the roof. As the day began to wane, Brad told me that he and Earlene needed to get home. The cow had to be milked and the chickens cared for. I told them I would ride back with them as far as the canyon mouth. I wanted to ride in and have a talk with Arnold Smith, the blacksmith.

We left the logging operation and I rode with them, past my sign, and on to the canyon mouth. We said our goodbyes and I headed southeast toward Vacaville while they turned nearly due west along the Rimrock toward the &RR. I kept my horse moving briskly and arrived at the blacksmith shop just as it began to get dark. I was fortunate enough to find Arnold finishing up on a new wheel for a carriage. I told him my problem and he said he thought he had a solution. He asked me to drop back by in a couple of days and he might have something jury-rigged together that would do the job.

I asked him if he had seen any of the X-Pan-D boys in town, with a special interest in Burly Dobbins. He looked at me for a moment and told me, "I hated to ask you what had happened to have every one so up in arms, unless you opened the conversation. The whole crew came in afoot and came into my shop here.

They bought every horse I had in stock. Burly was haranguing them to go with him to do some job. I got the impression that you might be the job he wanted them to go help him with. They all hemmed and hawed around for five minutes when one of them told him, "Burly, there ain't none of us going with you. We've had all of Seeker that we want. You're on your own."

"Burly was some put out, but he was tired, disgusted and on a real low. Besides that, he didn't have a gun." He started to ride off back toward his ranch, but changed his mind. They all rode off to the northeast. I heard someone say something about Denver. All I can tell you is that I doubt any of the crew will be back. As for Burly," he shook his head and started up again. "As for Burly, I just don't know. If I were forced to bet, I would bet you and give odds that he will be back, and that he'll have help with him when he comes. I'll also give odds that you won't see him coming."

I thanked him and told him I'd be back in a couple or three days. I rode back in the dark. When I entered my valley, I kept my eyes open and my ears clean. What Arnold had said about the situation was just about the same as my own idea. I made my camp behind a copse of trees on the darker western side of the valley. There was a little out cropping of rock that would shelter me and my horse from view if the moon came out. I made my normal precautions and got a good night's sleep.

I woke up early the next morning and took a good look around. Then I rode over to the east side of the valley, where the shadows took longer to disappear as the sun broke the horizon out on the flatland. The light penetrated the depths of the canyon on that west wall while I was still in the relative darkness along the wall on the opposite side. I never forgot that if there were some dry-gulcher hiding and looking for a free shot at me, he would probably have the same idea that I had and could be holed up near me.

Light poured over the logging operation as the sun came over the rim of the canyon, a flood of gold against the green of the trees. I took another close look around. Moving quickly across to the other side, I got out of sight behind a pile of rock and inspected the rim on the far side of the canyon through the scope on my rifle. I didn't see anything to arouse my curiosity so once again I picked up the ax and began to lop off the branches of the prior day's fallen timber. I stopped after half an hour and ate a cold biscuit and a slice of beef. I washed it down with water from my canteen.

Chapter Nineteen
The cabin

After my ten minute breakfast, I got busy in earnest, enjoying the play of my muscles as I swung the ax. It felt good to work this way, and that good feeling was spiced by the knowledge that all this effort was for my own cabin, for *our* own cabin. There was an unspoken understanding between us, that is, between Earlene and me. It did bring up another problem, though. I couldn't shake the thought that it would be doing Brad a terrible disservice if I took his daughter away to live with me. That would leave him all alone on the &RR. By the same token, I couldn't abide the thought of not having Earlene with me.

Brad had a fence across his canyon mouth, and it wouldn't be long before I would have one across mine, too. Both our ranches were positioned in such a way that they would benefit by having someone residing in the mouth of the canyon. Over all, it was only desirable for the one of us who had Earlene living with him. It might be best for all concerned if all three of us lived on one ranch together, at least until both our spreads were large enough to require help.

Not forgetting for one minute the danger I was in, I stopped frequently to take a look around, giving special attention to the entrance, for I was anxiously awaiting Earlene and Brad's company. I didn't have to wait long before the two of them could be seen riding across the valley at an easy lope.

After exchanging a quick, but heartfelt greeting, we buckled down to work. I knew better than to tell Earlene to take it easy. She grabbed the ax and started trimming the logs. Although Brad and I were still felling trees, we'd made a change in our method. We used the team to pull a log into such a position that every tree we felled landed across it. This made it easier to saw the logs to length, since the end being cut was held off the ground. This technique kept the blade from pinching as we cut off the excess length.

After working in this way for two more days, we figured we finally had enough logs to raise the cabin walls and serve as rafters for the roof. On the second night we made plans to move the logs to the site the next morning. As Brad and Earlene prepared to leave, they invited me to come along with them; but since I had some plans of my own, I had to turn the offer down. Once they were out of sight, I hitched the team and set out for town. I was hoping Arnold would have the contraption built that I had described to him and ordered the other day.

The contraption was ready and waiting for me when I arrived at Arnold's blacksmith shop, and it took me no time at all to get it back to my spread. The next morning I set it up in a spot where it would be the most convenient. It was ready to use by the time Brad and Earlene arrived.

The contraption was simple enough. It consisted of two heavy wagon wheels, an axle between them long enough to straddle a regular wagon, and two identical "L" shaped frames. The junction of the "L" was attached to the axle of the heavy wagon wheels. The upright arm of the "L" was the longest, and had a place to hitch a team of horses. This gave enough leverage to allow the team to raise the end of several logs at a time, when the logs were chained to the end of the "L". When the team pulled, the "L" pivoted and the logs were lifted.

First we tied the tongue of Brad's wagon to the back axle of my wagon. The two wagons were spotted along-side of the pile of logs we intended to move in that load. The log loader was backed into place so that the ell-shaped extension projected over the wagon tongue between the two wagons. The pile of logs was picked up and the log loader was pulled forward a few feet so that one end of the pile was in my wagon and the other end was on Brad's wagon.

We then hitched the log loader onto the back of Brad's wagon, hitched both teams to my wagon and pulled the entire load to the cabin site.   Picking the most convenient place to unload the logs, we repeated the operation of loading the logs, but in reverse.

Again, we unhitched the team from the log loader, after hitching it to the back of Brad's wagon again.   We hitched them to my wagon in front of the team that was still hitched there, and back we went for another load.

This procedure kept the three of us together.   We carried our rifles with us. We felt that it would be fool-hardy to split our crew up, with the threat of the Burly Bunch hanging over us.

We had to move the logs about three miles. It was a time consuming endeavor, but the work went fast and in three days we had every log moved to the cabin site. We moved our log loader to the cabin site to help get the logs raised into place.

Every morning I utilized my time by notching as many logs as possible and taking the broadaxe to square them up before Brad and Earlene arrived. Later in the day when they left to return home, I continued working until there was no longer any daylight to see by. Between the three of us, it didn't take long before the cabin was finished.

One day Brad and I cut a couple of logs into eighteen inch blocks. That night, after he and Earlene had left, I began splitting the blocks into shakes. Cedar splits easily and the next morning when they arrived, I had enough cedar shakes to shingle the house. With the three of us working, it didn't take long to finish that job, either. It gave me great satisfaction to know that I had security from the weather.

Since the &RR had a lot of work waiting for Brad and Earlene, what with the fall calf crop to look after, as well as the haying to do, the three of us decided it would be best if I continued working on my own. As the old saying goes, I worked from can to can't. In my case, it was from 'can see' to 'can't see'. The fact that I had built a pole fence across the front of my canyon only reminded me that I still had one significant unfinished piece of business to attend to, and that was my sign. I had dragged it from the two gate posts over to where one end was against a gate post and the other end the pole fence. It left room for a wagon to get in and out, but it gave the whole place an unfinished look.

Still, there were other things even more pressing. One morning I drove the wagon into town to pick up some supplies. While I was there, I made it a point to talk to Donahue, the bartender. He mentioned that some men had been in the other day, drinking and playing cards. "I overheard one of them asking the storekeeper if he knew where you lived. He tried to act nonchalant, but I'm sure he had more on his mind than just being sociable. They paid up and left as soon as they got the information."

"Hmm," I said. "How many were there?"

"There were four. They looked like real hard cases."

"Any clue as to what they wanted?" I figured that was a useless question, but I got a surprise.

"Clue enough," Donahue answered. "I heard one of them tell another that Burly would be glad hear that information. That should be about all of the clue you need!"

There it was! It came as no surprise to me. The only thing I hadn't known had been when. Ever since I had burned him out, I had wondered why I hadn't killed him. It had been a very uncharacteristic mistake that was gonna cause a lot of unnecessary trouble.

I drove the wagon up to the store and went inside and gave my list to O'Reilly. "I've been wondering when you would be in," he said. "I have a letter for you." He walked over to the pigeon holes that held the mail that came in on the stages. Sorting through several items, he handed me the letter. It had come from England. I could see him waiting curiously for me to open it. I stuck it in my shirt pocket.

"I'll be back inside of an hour. If you can have the order loaded, I'll be much obliged."

"No problem," he returned.

I walked over to the land office and went inside. The agent looked up and greeted me. "What can I do for you today?" he asked.

"Oh, just curiosity more than anything else. You mentioned that some old miner was telling you about a canyon that widened into a valley. Do you know if he ever found pay dirt?"

"Yeah, as a matter of fact he did. The last time that I remember him coming in, he told me that he was gonna go to Denver and see if he could get a mining engineer to take a look at his mine. He said it would take him a day or two to dig out enough gold to make the trip. I don't believe that I ever saw him again."

I took my leave and walked across to see Arnold. He looked up from his work and said, "I'm glad you stopped by. I've been looking for an excuse to loaf a little."

I laughed and told him, "You can't use me for an excuse for long. I have Paddy O'Reilly loading up a few supplies. Then my own excuse for loafing will be gone, for I will have to go back out to my place and get to work. You remember the old song, "winter's coming on, and cold will be the weather?" Well, I have to get ready for that cold weather."

Arnold rubbed his chin and grinned. "Yeah, but I also remember the next line, "What's the use to live alone when two can live together?" His grin broadened. "Don't tell *me* you don't have your eye on Earlene Rogers."

"Well, as a matter of fact, I do. There is something that gives me a little pause, though. Donahue just informed me that some of Dobbin's men were in the bar inquiring about me. Until things are settled, I will just have to maintain the status quo. When Burly is dead, it will be different. I stupidly let Burly off the hook. I won't have such a lapse in judgment again." I looked at him and said, "Listen, Arnold. If you hear anything at all, even the remotest clue, let me know as fast as you can. I'm not gonna leave this just hanging."

"If I hear anything, I'll drop whatever I'm doing, day or night, and ride out and tell you. I'm ready to side you, anytime you need me."

I had no doubt about his words. He was that kind of a friend.

I walked back to the store and settled up my bill. Minutes later, I was on my way back to the valley. I was keeping my eyes peeled, all of the way.

I suddenly remembered the letter from England. I had no doubt that is was from Rodney. I pulled it from my pocket and read:

Dear Easy,

I have told Father about the circumstances of our meeting. I also have given him my appraisal of the opportunities available. I will be returning to Vacaville within a fortnight. I want to talk to you upon arrival.

Rodney

I thought it would be best if I stopped by the &RR and brought Earlene and Brad up to date with the latest news. Keeping the team in a smart trot, I arrived a couple of hours later. I saw Brad and Earlene working in a flat area down by the stream that cut through their valley. I left the team standing in the yard, grabbed my Winchester and strolled off toward where they were working a team. Surreptitiously I gave the entire area a thorough inspection. There were several groves of trees that would've sheltered a small army, which was enough to keep me on the alert.

The pair kept working until I had reached them. Brad immediately asked me, "What's got you out and about in this neck of the woods? "Has something unusual happened?"

"Isn't it reason enough just to have the feel of the sun on one's shoulders, the scent of freshly turned earth in one's nostrils, and the chance to talk to the prettiest girl in the world?" I grinned and added, "Or at least on the &RR?"

"What kind of left-handed compliment is that?" Earlene was covered with damp earth from her brogans to her knees. Her shirt was wet in a circle down from each armpit and the middle of her back. "You know that any attraction that some idiot might attribute to me only extends to the limits of this plowed field. By the way, ye ain't got nary chaw er 'baccy, hev ye?"

Earlene had never looked more vibrant, more desirable, or more seductive than she did just then. Well, perhaps that didn't count our first encounter at my oasis! The fact that she chose to wear a pair of brogans instead of her riding boots just showed her practicality. I felt a nearly irresistible desire to bury my face in her armpits and inhale so hard that it would suck her entire body inside mine. I walked over and kissed her instead. There was something in her eyes that let me know she both understood and shared my desires.

"Well, I'm an idiot, so I know where-of I speak. When I say the *entire* &RR, I *mean* the entire &RR." I laughed and she laughed with me.

I turned to Brad, "Brad, would you happen to have a plug of Red Mule mountain grown tobacco?"

"Nah, I'm fresh out," he chuckled.

I quit laughing and said, "I do have some news. Donahue told me that some hard-looking men were in his bar and were asking around to see if anyone could tell them where my place is. He also heard them mention Dobbins." I bent over and picked up a clod of the rich soil and crumbled it between my fingers. I raised up my head and looked at each of them in turn. "I'm afraid the vacation is over."

"Well, I've been wondering when it would start," Brad said. "Earlene was saying last night that everything was going too good to be true. She said she could feel some trouble looming over us. I had hoped she was wrong, but I knew she wasn't. I've had the feeling from time to time that we were under observation. I think I'll unhitch the team and we can go up to the house and maybe talk a little strategy." Before he had finished talking, he had already unhooked the trace chains from the single trees of both horses and looped the trace chains over the hames.

Chapter Twenty
War council

We walked silently back up toward the house. Earlene went straight inside as Brad and I continued on to the barn. As we unharnessed the horses, we exchanged meaningless comments about the weather and the approaching winter. We were stalling. We didn't want to talk about the impending problems until we could include Earlene. She had as great a stake in our future as anyone, and her suggestions were just as pertinent.

When we were finished, we clomped across the porch and entered the house. Earlene was waiting for us in the kitchen, so we pulled out some chairs and sat down to a cup of coffee and some sugar cookies.

"Here's the way I see it," I began. "The first thing on my mind is keeping the two of you safe from danger. I'd rest a whole lot easier if you weren't involved. We first need to decide whether we can keep you two out of this. Obviously, I can be more mobile by going it alone."

"No Way!" Earlene exclaimed, "There is absolutely no way we can stay out of it. Need I point out that a lot of folks around here have already discovered where you've taken up land? The land agent, who is more or less the purveyor of news regarding property out here, would have written information regarding who's taken up land and where. It follows that in this nearly empty country, anybody would automatically associate us with you, since there is nobody else living out here but us."

"I have to agree with you," I said. "I would like to keep you out, but wishing doesn't keep the wind from blowing." I looked at Brad. "What do you think?"

"It wouldn't take a genius to see how close we are. Remember I mentioned there have been times when I felt we were being watched? If anyone has seen you and Earlene together, it would be even more than obvious that there is something between you. In my opinion, that makes Earlene the target of anyone who's after you. This means they could target me to get to Earlene. Besides all that, if anyone had been watching from the Rimrock, they would have seen the three of us working together."

"It looks like we're all in agreement. We have to deal with what *is*, not what *isn't*, regardless of any 'if', 'and' or 'maybe', which leads to the second thing on my mind.   Now it's a given the three of us are in partnership, correct?" I paused as they both nodded. "Okay, now stop me if you don't agree, but it would seem to me that since water is available at your house, you have the mouth of your ranch fenced in, and you have corrals, barns and sheds, the best choice would be for the three of us to hole up here together."   I looked from one to the other.   "Any comments?" I asked.

Brad began, "It seems to me that's the only option that makes sense.   We have a lot of work to do here, anyway, not to mention the livestock we have to care for. We wouldn't be able to do that if we holed up at your place. Besides, it would be hard for anyone to bother us as long as you have those rifles Rodney left with you."

"Now that you mention it, I got a letter from Rodney. He's on his way back here. His letter didn't make it clear as to whether his father is accompanying him or not, though. I've a feeling that he's not. He didn't say much to shed light on what he might do here, but I'm led to believe that his father is interested in making an investment in this area."

"I think we'd better go to your place and fetch your horses and whatever supplies you have and bring them over here as soon as possible," Earlene said. From what we know of Burly Dobbins, patience is not one of his virtues. He is gonna strike hard and soon, and in my opinion, it'll be in the next few days."

"One thing is for sure," I said decisively. "We need to consolidate here immediately.   Each day we must presume is the day Burly will attack. I'm certain he will want it to come as a surprise, with the intent to be deadly and without mercy."   I took one last sip of coffee and said, "I'm gonna head for my place now. This may seem like I'm overreacting, but it's my opinion the three of us should ride over together in my wagon. I think we should take your riding horses along too, just in case. You should also bring your rifles. To prevent thievery, I have the rifles Rodney left cached where they are very unlikely to be found."

We quickly left the table. While Earlene put a meal together so we could have lunch on the way, Brad and I headed for the barn so he could turn the work stock out to graze for the night, and I could water my team.

We tied the two riding horses behind the wagon, climbed onto the spring seat and started for the canyon mouth. Brad jumped down and opened the gate and closed it behind us. He clambered back up into the wagon, crowding Earlene just a little closer. I could feel her leg burning an erotic feeling that shot up my leg and deep into my groin.

Instead of turning left to take the little trail that already showed signs of our comings and goings, I drove straight on south for five hundred yards. I saw Earlene open her mouth to say something, but then I thought I saw realization cross her tanned face. I turned the wagon to parallel the cliff.

We were now out of easy rifle range, and could do a much better job of seeing anyone who might approach the edge of the Rimrock. Now that we'd made our decisions, it seemed that it took an interminable time to cover the distance. We actually only took about a half an hour.

Within twenty minutes we had the wagon loaded with the provisions from my cabin. Brad led my stock from the little corral that I had whipped together for a temporary holding pen. To save space in the wagon, I decided to ride my horse. I realized that I would soon have to return Arnold's packsaddle. However, now was not the time, I reasoned, for under the circumstances there was no telling when a pack animal would come in handy. Once again, on the return trip, I swung wide and followed our original tracks back to the &RR.

Once Brad and I had unloaded my supplies from the wagon, I asked Earlene where she wanted me to put them. She showed me a small room that served as a pantry. It had shelves that were stocked with canned goods. The little room ran adjacent to the back porch. The door into the pantry was located in the center space between the kitchen counter and the wall. This made a little alcove to the left and to the right of the door, plus there were shelves straight across from the door.

If one turned to the right and went to the back of the pantry, one would be against the back wall of the house. On the other side of that back wall was the back porch. It one turned to the left and went to the back of the pantry on that side, the kitchen counter, plus some cabinets that were built along the left end of the pantry, but on the kitchen side, took up that space.

There was another surprise. Earlene walked half way back to the right side, bent over, and opened an invisible trap door. It opened into a stairwell. The bottom of the stairwell had another door. It was opened and a large root cellar was exposed. The cellar itself started at the outside wall of the house. It was dug out beneath the porch.

This cellar served multiple purposes. It made a great storage place for food. It was the perfect storm cellar. There were four bunks built along one wall. I didn't ask who the extra bunks were for. I guess that careful people prepare for several eventualities. Despite the interesting things I was seeing, I had something that I needed to tell the Rogers. When we went back up into the kitchen, after carefully shutting the cellar door, we sat down at the table. That is, Earlene and Brad sat down. I put one foot up on my chair and leaned over with my arms folded across my knee.

"Listen," I said. "I need to go back to my spread. There is something bothering me that I need to check out. It shouldn't take me too long, but it is something that I just have to know. I figure the trip to take at least six hours. That will give me two hours for going, two for returning, and two for checking out this thing that's nagging at me.

I don't think anyone will expect me to be leaving tonight. If we have anyone watching us, they will have seen us transporting my stuff over here. They will expect me to stay the night, as per the plans we have. Most likely they wouldn't make a move until they think they know what we're gonna do. Then they'll report back to Dobbins before trying anything. I can guarantee you that Burly is gonna want to be here gloating when they get us. Rather, when they think they're gonna get us," I corrected myself.

Earlene said, "Now listen up! I want both of you to pay strict attention to what I'm gonna say. Based on what you just said, Easy, these men aren't gonna hit us until they have what they think is a good plan. They've lost men, money and face at every turn. They've been made to look like inept fools."

"And the bottom line is what?" Brad was looking at his daughter as he spoke. I knew what was coming.

"The bottom line," Earlene said, "is that I'm going with you, Easy. I don't want to hear any pro or con on the subject. We all know that anyone who might, or might not, for that matter, be watching will be aware that the three of us are here. Since they have been so ineffective in the past, don't you think these men will feel the need for an army? It they had an army with them, we would have seen the signs." She stood up. "Easy, can you think of anything special that we might need?"

I looked at Brad. He looked as helpless as I felt. I looked back at Earlene. "Yeah, there is something special. I want a kerosene lantern. If you have a small maul, that would come in handy too. It would beat my ball peen hammer."

There was no time for idle chit chat or rehashing of things. We needed to get saddled and out of here before the moon rose. Darkness was our ally now.

"There is an extra kerosene lantern in the barn. We'll grab it when we saddle up." She crammed some bread and meat into a sack and picked it up. "Let's hook 'em," she said.

We went out the back door and walked quietly through the darkness to the barn. We saddled up in the dark, and then rode straight into the shadows along the Rimrock and on to the canyon entrance. I decided it would be better to ride out away from the Rimrock, since the moon wouldn't rise before we made it to my place. We put the horses to an easy lope, and made no conversation until we'd turned into my place. Again, we rode near the east wall of the canyon where the shadows were the deepest as the east began to lighten with the coming moon-rise.

When we reached the end of the canyon and arrived at the hidden glade, we left the horses and Earlene took my hand. I squeezed, but then released it and took the maul in one hand and an iron shaft in the other.

Earlene grabbed the unlit lantern and the sack of lunch while I swung a canteen over my shoulder. Without a sound we worked our way to the hidden path that led to higher ground. When we arrived at the old mine entrance, I whispered to Earlene, "Sweetheart, follow me closely. In a little ways, the tunnel will muffle everything so we can talk."

I continued to edge ahead in the darkness until we were deep into the mountain. I lit the lantern and the sudden brightness raised my spirits and fortified me with a stronger sense of courage. Finding one's self surrounded in darkness more intense than the imagination can conjure is disconcerting and not a particularly pleasant feeling.

The lantern swung each time Earlene's arm went back and forth in time with the steps she was taking. With each swing of that lantern, our shadows raced ahead of us on her arm's back swing, and then raced back behind us as her arm swung ahead of us. The grotesque shadows ran along the floor, the walls of the man made cavern, and even over the ceiling, illuminating the moisture that accumulated and occasionally dripped onto the black surface beneath us. As we walked deeper into the bowels of the earth, it was hard to keep the innate superstitions of mankind from our souls.

We turned left into a west-bound tunnel, leaving the main shaft that continued northward and slightly upward. The roar of the falls had been so gradually increasing that it was surprisingly difficult to converse when we reached the tunnel's end. I took the lantern from Earlene's hand and set it in a strategic spot. I leaned the maul and the steel shaft against the rock wall and pulled on my gloves. Earlene stepped closer. I couldn't resist the urge to place my arm around her waist. I brought her to me and pressed her body against my chest and she desperately clung to me as I held her tightly. Slipping my fingers beneath her chin, I raised her lips to mine and we kissed for a long moment. I held her for the space of several heartbeats before I released her.

Then I took the maul, set the end of the shaft against the wall at an upward angle, and began to strike it with short, solid blows. I had no idea how effective the strategy would prove to be. The idea was to loosen the stone dust as I struck a blow, turned the drill slightly, and then strike again.

In a short time, Earlene came forward and gently took the drill from my hand. She placed it into the hole, moved the lantern so that her shadow didn't block the light, and then asked me to start again. Her little gloved hands were as capable holding the drill as they were holding the reins of her horse.

Since I was now able to grasp the maul with both hands, the drilling increased threefold. The solid thunk as the hammer struck the drill, followed by an immediate softer thunk made a weird, but captivating rhythm. The chuffing drill created an echo inside the mine. It was a rather hypnotic sequence, laced together by the rushing roar of the waterfall.

I would estimate that we'd drilled the hole about three feet into the wall and were about to run out of the steel needed to continue when the brownish yellow stone powder suddenly darkened. I dropped the maul and had to begin moving the steel shaft back and forth as it suddenly became nearly wedged in the tight hole. This technique allowed a trickle of thick, pasty water to emerge.

A moment later, the water ran clear and the drill came free. A one inch stream of water squirted out, sweeping all debris from the rocky floor of the mine. We stepped back and watched as a surprisingly strong little stream of water flowed down toward the mine opening. "Let's go," I said. "I've found out what I wanted to know."

We turned and walked swiftly toward the mine entrance. When we came to the place where the tunnel "teed" into the main shaft, Earlene said, "Easy, I've been wondering about this shaft, too. The plan is to redirect the river so it flows through the shaft where we drilled the hole and started this little creek. Now, if you blow away the wall, there'll be no way of ever knowing where this shaft goes. I don't know how you feel about that, but you know the old saying about a woman's curiosity."

"Yeah, I know that old saying. I also know another one about curiosity killing the cat." There was no way of her seeing my grin in the dark, but I could hear her answering chuckle.

To satisfy both of us, I carefully leaned my drill against the wall, placed the maul beside it, and reached for Earlene's hand. Together, we headed up the slight slope. The dank smell became nearly stifling. When we got to the tunnel's end, there was a pile of stony debris where someone had once been digging. It looked like the mine had caved in on one side of the shaft. One could also see the dull gleam of what appeared to be gold. I stopped and picked up a piece of the ore and was examining it when Earlene spoke. "Easy, look here!"

I pitched the piece of ore back onto the pile and turned to see what she had found. She was standing at the wall, pointing at what appeared to be a thick vein of gold. A strategically placed pattern of holes had been drilled to make another blast. I reached out to finger the vein, when Earlene said, "Not that, Easy. Look at this!" I moved closer and noticed, for the first time, the head, shoulder, and arm of a man whose body was covered by the cave-in.

This then, was the body of the old prospector that the land agent had once spoken of to me. Earlene remarked, "I suppose a prospector lives a lonely life, but I can't imagine a more lonely way to die." Her grip on my arm was painfully tight.

I made no answer for a moment. Then I said, "Earlene, with the weight of all that rock on him, he couldn't have lived any longer than whatever air he had left in his lungs. The rock probably squashed the air out of his lungs, and there was no way he would've been able to draw a breath."

Earlene had picked up an old lantern sitting just beyond the cave in. The glass was covered with soot. If the man *had* lived for awhile, I could imagine his feelings as the light of the lantern turned red and smoky as it ran out of kerosene, and the feeling he must have had as the light had first turned feeble from lack of fuel, and then at last flickered out. If he were still living, his last breaths would have been of the poisonous gasses as the flame died, leaving him in perpetual darkness.

We turned to leave, but a thought suddenly struck me. "Earlene, let's estimate the length of this shaft." I will step it off and we'll look at the angle it makes with the cliff-side. I want to know, just out of curiosity, where the end of the shaft is in relation to the spot where we drilled that hole."

"Aren't you gonna start working the mine?" she asked.

"I don't know what I may do some day in the future, Earlene. Right now, I have a far greater interest in making my valley much like the valley of the &RR. I will have every thing I've ever wanted when my place is stocked with cattle and I'm doing the things similar to those that you and your dad have planned."

It may have been the feeling that Earlene and I were isolated from the rest of the world, locked off in a cocoon of darkness and buried together for all time; It may have been that the freedom of the open range was such a contrast to darkness, which loomed beyond the small pool of lantern's light; it may very well have been the sense of being so alone in the open-ended tomb of impending age, that caused me to impulsively say, "My biggest hope is to have you as my wife here on this ranch. I need you so much. The darkness of this mine parallels the darkness that composed my life before I came to the Bend of the Rimrock and found you."

I'm not sure how it came about, but one moment I was just standing there, my lonely life accentuated by the location. Then, suddenly she was wrapped in my arms before I could catch my breath. "I love you, Baby! I think I would just walk off and disappear into the desert if I didn't have you sharing my life," I said. I could feel her breasts heaving as she softly sobbed with emotion.

"Oh my Darling, this is what I've wanted since I saw you lying under the willow tree," she said. "I would never have let you leave this valley. Let me fill your life with light. Let me chase away the darkness." Her lips drew my melancholy mood from my body and made my heart swell. Our bodies were fused into one. The impact that we both must have felt left us panting and starved for air. That is not all we were starved for, but at the last moment, she pulled her face back and said, "Go step off this tunnel and let's get back to the house. I can't stop thinking about what Dobbins may be doing."

Stepping carefully, I measured the tunnel, heel to toe, splashing in a stream of water an inch deep across the width of the tunnel when we came to the side shaft. The current made the water break against the heels of our boots like the prow of a boat as we approached the entrance. Earlene raised the globe and blew the lantern out. We walked toward the slightly lighter black of the opening. The water from the mine flowed down the pathway to the valley floor as we worked our way carefully and quietly down the trail.

I had fears that the water would attract unwanted attention to my mine, but when we reached the bottom of the pathway, it appeared to be seeping from the tangle of plum bushes and the rocks of that jumble of stone that separated my oasis from my valley. It flowed into the little pool that already existed at the canyon's end. I didn't know what would happen when it began to flow into the old river bed, but I doubted that it would ever flow to the canyon's mouth. At least not yet, I thought.

We worked our way back to where the horses were tied. What had seemed to be taking a long time had scarcely allowed the moon to send its beams onto the west canyon wall.

Staying along the shadowy eastern side of the canyon, we rode quietly back to the entrance. Sitting our bit champing horses for a few minutes, we detected nothing to arouse our caution. We rode back out onto the prairie, circled around toward the &RR, and took our gear off the horses at the barn.

When we reached the porch, I seized the moment and pulled Earlene gently to my chest. "I've wanted to do this for the past hour or so," I confessed. We held the embrace for a couple of minutes. Then Earlene rapped on the bedroom window of her father.

A moment later, Brad was opening the back door. "I had a blanket over the window and was reading until you got back home," he said. "It was about some people sharing an adventure. It is a pity things are always so dull around this neck of the woods." He shook his head in simulated despair.

Earlene and I laughed at his little joke as we entered the house. It took a few minutes to bring Brad up-to-date on everything we'd discovered on the little jaunt from which we'd just returned. It was getting too late to talk long though, for were all growing tired and feeling the need for sleep.

When it was time to say goodnight, I started for the back door. "No, Easy, I think it's safer if we all stayed inside tonight," Earlene said.

Secretly pleased, I hurriedly retrieved my bedroll from the back porch and by the time I reentered the house, Earlene had already unrolled a narrow feather bed.

"You may find this a little more comfortable than the wooden floor to spread your bed roll on." As she spoke, I watched her hand disappear as she pressed her palm into the mattress so I could see how thick it was. She straightened from smoothing the bed. "This is what I slept on before we got some beds in from St. Louis."

"Thank you, Earlene; I'm sure I'll sleep well tonight." We whispered our goodnights in an embrace that ended with a satisfying kiss.

As tired as I was, I couldn't fall asleep right away. I just lay there, Earlene's kiss still on my lips, thinking about what she had said. The image of her soft, shapely body lying in this very same mattress that I myself was now lying upon was intoxicating. The sensations this image created stayed with me well into the night. Another thought that I couldn't get rid of was the turns that had been in the main tunnel of the mine. I tried to retrace them in my mind, but found that I was uncertain of the directions of the turns, the order in which the turns went to the left or the right, and the number of steps between each of the turns. I knew in my heart the distance I had stepped off would not be enough to tell us where the gold vein was. However, that was a problem that couldn't be solved by lying awake worrying about it.

Chapter Twenty One
Pinpointing the mine
A surface map

When we were eating breakfast the next morning, I decided to broach that very subject.

"I've been thinking. I might be making a mistake that I could regret someday about the haphazard method that we used to give us a clue as to where we would need to dig to intercept the tunnel of that mine we found. I think that I will run into town and have Arnold fix me up something that will help us be a little more accurate about pinpointing the end of the tunnel.

"I had hoped that Earlene could ride in with me, but in view of the threat hanging over us, I think it's best for the two of you to be able to defend the house and this place, while I go alone. I'll try to get back early, but if Arnold can get to the job today, I may wait until he finishes so I can save a trip back tomorrow to pick it up.

Earlene asked, "Just what are you trying to accomplish, Easy?

"I want something that we can measure the angles a little more accurately than just guessing at it and trying to remember what we guessed. I think we will be able to fix the location within just a very few feet," I replied.

"Let's all keep our eyes open. That snake, Dobbins, isn't going to rattle a warning before he strikes," warned Brad.

I grabbed my hat and headed for the barn, where I saddled up the dun to ride into Vacaville. I figured I would be less conspicuous than if I rode Calliope. Earlene wanted to come with me, but agreed that I was right when I said I thought it would be better if she and Brad both were there to hold down the fort, in case Dobbins happened to show up while I was gone. I remained vigilant, but that didn't keep me from enjoying the ride.

The dun stopped in the river as we waded up into shallow water, and took a drink of water. He started on across without being told and stopped at the livery stable, unbidden. I suppose he remembered when that had been his home.

I swung from the saddle and hung his reins over the corral fence. It was just a few steps to the blacksmith shop. When I stopped by the forge, Arnold told me, "I assume you came here to invite me to a cold beer, and since it's so hot, I think I'll just accept your invitation and we can talk in a little cooler spot, like at one of Donahue's tables." He grinned at his neat way of making me do the buying.

I smiled my acceptance of that little burden and we walked up the street to Donahue's saloon. We climbed the three steps to the porch and pushed through the doors and went straight to the bar and exchanged a few pleasantries with Pat, while he drew three mugs of beer.

"These are on me, fellows. I figure that when you see how good my cold beer is, you'll work a little less and drink a little more. I have to figure out some way to jar you guys loose from some of that money!"

"Thanks, Pat. It's a pity you won't make anything today, 'cause I have to get back out to the spread and don't have time for another one," I explained.

"Danged if you two fellows aren't the hardest to lure into a life of loafing and drinking that I've ever seen," Pat answered back. "I've already nearly gained my goal with Arnold. He's got the loafing part down perfectly, but I'm not very successful with the drinking part. I don't make any money on his loafing, and precious little on his drinking."

I laughed as Arnold made his rejoinder, "You should talk about loafing! Every time I look up from my forge, I see you sitting out on your porch watching me work, and looking for some poor boy to come by so you can talk him into loafing and drinking."

"Well," said Donahue, "It's a self defeating effort. The ones who are working don't have time for drinking, and those that have the time for drinking don't have the price of a beer. That's the reason I'm about to starve out!"

I began laughing and remarked, "Hell, Pat, if there's anything you don't look like you're doing it's starving! Anyway, I have to get Arnold off over here in the corner where none of your bar girls can lure him off before I can lay my problem out in front of him."

I led the way back to a table and Arnold joined me in sitting down and taking a swig of the beer.

"What's on your mind today, Easy?"

"Arnold, I need to fix a contrivance so I can measure an angle. Here's a little drawing that I made to show what I need. It's just to give you an idea of what I expect it to do. You'll probably have a better way to do it, but I need it to be easy to work, even in the dark, and the rods need to be about six feet long so I can eyeball pretty precisely what I have them pointed at. "I need to be able to lock the arms in place securely enough that they can't jiggle loose and the arms need to be of different lengths."

"Well, that looks simple enough to me. When do you need it?" Arnold set down his beer and looked straight at me.

"Darn it all, Arnold, I sure hate to always be rushing you, but we're sort of pressured by the threat of Dobbins taking some sort of action against us, and I really need it as quickly as you can get to it. The job I need to use it on will soon be impossible to do, and I sure would like to get it done while I can," I related.

"In that case, I'll get it done right now. It's going to be easy to fix up, but it won't do to display at the fat cattle show in Ft. Worth," Arnold said. "We'd better stop shooting the breeze and get at." He put down his empty mug and stood up.

I jumped to my feet and followed him out the door. "Arnold, I ..."

"Forget it, Easy! This way you can get right back to the ranch and not leave Brad and Earlene alone any longer than necessary."

Arnold grabbed a handful of iron rods and took them to the forge. He worked with no wasted motions. I worked the bellows while he did a little welding and in less than half an hour he pulled off his apron and submerged the contraption in his horse tank. "It wouldn't do to get that against your horse while it's that hot, he said.

"Talking about your horse, I see you're riding the dun. Is your other horse OK?" Arnold had fished the apparatus out of the tank and was walking with me toward where I had tied the dun.

"Old Calliope is fine," I answered. "I thought I might not be as noticeable riding this horse. I'm trying to keep a low profile until this business is all wound up."

I shook hands with Smith, pulled the dun's reins loose from the corral rail, and mounted up, nodded again to Arnold and headed for Paddy O'Reilly's store. I quickly entered, exchanged hellos with Paddy and grabbed a roll of heavy twine. I turned aside his questions by telling him that I was in a big rush to get back to work.

I had leaned my contraption up against the porch as I dismounted. I mounted and reached over to pick it up, ignoring Paddy's curious looks. Lifting a hand in a gesture of adios, I rode north toward the Rimrock.

At first I rode straight for my place, at an easy trot, but when I came to the long slope where we had set Hatch's crew afoot, I suddenly changed direction for the &RR at a swift gallop. I was throwing a monkey wrench in the plans of any would be bush-whacker.

A few minutes later, I arrived at the entrance to the ranch. I had been scanning the Rimrock ever since I had changed course, but hadn't seen anything to make me uneasy. I stopped before entering the mouth of the canyon, pulled out my binoculars and inspected the entire vicinity to make sure it was clear. Then I put the horse into a lope and rode past the house and on to the barn, unsaddled and turned the dun into the corral.

Earlene and Brad were standing on the porch as I arrived back at the house.

"Were you able to get what you went for?" Earlene asked.

"Yes, and if Brad has no objections, I'd like for you and me to go put it to use right now."

"I have no objections," Brad remarked, "but I do hope you'll keep on the alert. My feeling that we are being watched is stronger than ever. I know that it'll be next to impossible for you to work in the dark, but it would sure be to our advantage that they think there are three of us here, and even more important, for them to be ignorant of the fact the two of you are over at your place."

"That's a point well taken," I answered. "I think that I know a way to address both points. It will also keep us close to this house, time-wise at least."

"Will you be leaving right now, as you indicated to Earlene a moment ago?" Brad's tone indicated that he hoped we wouldn't.

"Actually, Brad, I wasn't speaking literally. I should have said as quickly as possible. I don't want to leave until it is good and dark." I hesitated a moment and continued, "Do either of you know of a good ruse that we could use to go to the barn and saddle up for Earlene and me, without a watcher knowing that we were doing so?"

"Well, we usually milk and gather eggs about this time of day. It would seem natural for you to accompany the two of us while we do those chores. It would actually seem odd if you didn't," Earlene said.

"I have to agree this that," said Brad. "In fact, they will just think you are passing time with us, when actually you can saddle up both horses before we finish with milking and egg gathering. It only takes a few minutes to do both those things and Earlene and I always walk back together."

"It sure works for me," I said. I left my hat on the peg, for the evening breeze always felt so good to a bare head. The three of us left the house together, Brad carrying the milk pail and Earlene the egg basket. Under the circumstances, it didn't seem curious for me to carry my Winchester.

I saddled up the horses and finished a little ahead of either of the other two. This gave me a chance to give a couple of ears of corn to each of the work team and the dun, since he had made a nice little trip today.

I also had a chance to stand in the shadows back inside the barn where I would be unseen as I gave the vicinity a good scanning with my binoculars.

When we arrived back at the house, we washed up for supper in the normal way, and ate a bite. I picked up a deck of cards as the light began to fall and walked out onto the porch briefly, while shuffling the deck. Then I returned and pulled down the blinds as we lit the lamps and appeared to settle down for a game of cards.

"Brad, this is what I am planning on doing. As soon as the darkness is complete, Earlene and I will slip down to the barn. Just before we do, we will step out onto the back porch with a light, for just a moment, to make it look like we are going about normal chores here.

"A few minutes later, we will slip out and go to the barn. However, instead of going to my place, we will go to the end of this ranch and ride up a path to the top. We can tie our horses in the shadows and go by foot over to my place. It will have us afoot, but we will always be within fifty yards of our horses.

"That will save us several miles of riding, counting both going and returning and will cut down on the time we will be away. I think that we can make some pretty accurate measurements in the dark with the contraption that Arnold just whipped up for me. Earlene is more familiar with this place, in the dark, than I am with my place. That can be an advantage."

"That's making the best of a bad situation," Brad mused. "How are you going to mark your pointers? You can scarcely use an X in the dirt," he chuckled.

"I have some cedar stakes I am going to use. I wanted to use some iron stakes, but I'm afraid of the noise it will make driving them in. I have your maul and an old tow sack that you once had corn in. I will put a wad of tow sack on the wooden stake and although it will still make a sound, it will be dull, muffled and hard to hear.

"In the event that I decide not to place visible markers, I have an idea that might be safer than using stakes, anyway. You know someone would become awfully curious if they were to stumble upon the stakes."

While Brad and I were talking, Earlene was both listening and fixing us a lunch. I asked Earlene to get a tablet and pencil before we left the house.

Outside, the darkness was profound. You could hear the crickets chirping and the sound of bull frogs could be faintly heard, wafted by the breeze from down at the stream. The air was full of fire flies; the bull-bats were swooping with their throaty calls heralding their presence.

The call of coyotes from up on the Rimrock made it seem as though there were no human being within a hundred miles. Yet, that silence hid the human wolves that stalked the three of us. There was not the faintest doubt that they were there. Like the four legged wolves, they had learned that it didn't pay to approach us openly.

It was up to us to teach them that it was even more dangerous to approach us in the dark. There would be no quarter given by us again. There would never have been any quarter given by them.

Brad had walked over and peeked out the window. "It looks like it's time for you to go." Brad put his hand on my shoulder. "Easy, don't let anything happen to my daughter! I know that you will be cautious, but I can't help telling you to be careful. Earlene, you watch Easy's back! I wish I could go, but we can't take the chance on leaving the house empty and giving them the chance to hole up here."

"Brad, you can be assured that I won't be fool-hardy. The daughter you referenced is also my own special treasure. I will take the safest way out of each thing that might arise. This will take us awhile, so don't take on any extra worry if we are gone several hours.

I plan to be back before dawn. We won't put speed ahead of caution though." I didn't know what else to add, so I clasped his hand and then stood aside while Earlene kissed him bye, and we slipped out the door.

Sometimes our horses would be so close together that our legs would brush. She would sometimes place one hand on my arm, but since I was carrying the heavy iron rod instrument with me in one hand, I had to keep the other arm free. Each step it was possible that we would encounter those who hoped to become our killers.

"Earlene, would you ride on the other side of me for awhile?" I requested. "I want to change hands with this load, but I don't want it to increase the distance between us."

Her horse immediately dropped back and came up on the other side. It would have been so nice if we could have talked and shared this adventure aloud, but it was more than possible that the man who had lurked in the darkness of my canyon before, would still be staked out, awaiting his opportunity to shoot me from the brush.

Each time our legs would brush, it would heighten my desire. This was not the time that I would be able to tell her this. Now was not the time that I could speak of love or passion; Neither was it the time that I could lay her down in the grass nor cover her face with kisses. More than anything else, this was not the time to relax our vigilance.

Earlene crowded me over a little and then we made a turn and our horses began the ascent out of the valley. It was impossible to make out the shape of Earlene's horse, against the darkness of the sheer cliff that we were riding up. A moment later, we reached level ground and Earlene dismounted. The darkness was not as intense as it had been, and in the east I could see the sky lightening as the moon marked the place where it would soon rise.

We tied our horse near the trail down into our oasis to try to mute the sound of their snorting from anyone in the canyon we had just vacated. I put down the load that I had been carrying, one-handed, for the past hour and stretched my aching arms.

Here was a place where the utmost caution had to be exercised. The contraption was not all that heavy, but it was going to be hard to keep from clanking it against the rocks as we scaled the steep ridge that separated the &RR from my valley. It was also going to be hard for me to properly control the load, while trying to climb one handed. Earlene helped immensely by going ahead of me, having me hand the end of the load up to her so she could hold it away from the rocks while I climbed up beside her.

A moment later, we were ready to climb down the other side. The light of the rising moon began to light our way. It was a double edged sword, for although it made it easier to proceed, it also made us more visible.

It was highly unlikely that we would be seen before we got to the edge of my valley, but that was an unknown in this deadly game of chance.

I silently put down my load and we lay down, side by side, inspecting the area below. I saw nothing, but that was little comfort, for the last time I had only seen the arc of a lit cigarette as it was flipped away. This time, I saw no evil, heard no evil and smelled no evil.

I picked up the load and started to descend, but put out one hand to stop Earlene. She followed me as I took a few steps back and put down my load again. I took her hand and we began to follow the east wall of the canyon, carefully peering over every few steps until we could see the tops of the trees below that marked where the trail doubled back by the mine's entrance.

We were able to pinpoint the mine's opening by the bushes that clung to the cliff at the mine opening. By peering across the canyon, I could see a hole of about one foot diameter in the stone wall of the canyon. It was directly in line with the mine opening. I backed straight away from the canyon edge, so that the mine opening was straight in line with that hole.

Then I had Earlene stand up near the canyon edge. Using her as a sighting post, I turned around and walked twenty five yards away from the canyon. I turned toward Earlene, realigned myself with Earlene and the small hole in the far canyon wall and called quietly for Earlene to join me.

When she was by my side, I had her stand exactly in my steps while I walked back to the canyon edge. Earlene lined me up precisely with the hole and I turned and looked for something to use as a marker. I soon saw a stunted mesquite bush that was alone and in the line we were projecting from the mine mouth and the irregularity in the far canyon wall.

I cut a piece of the twine I had purchased and placed it in an inconspicuous place on the bush. If we had any doubt as to whether we were using the right bush, we could inspect it for the twine.

The two of us returned to where we had left the contraption that Arnold had fabricated, took it and slowly descended the hidden path. When we got to the mine, we entered and walked carefully through the darkness until we knew the lantern Earlene carried could not be seen when lighted.

Setting the burning lantern in the middle of the tunnel, we returned to the mouth of the mine. We spotted the irregularity in the far canyon wall and checked to see how the mine entrance lined up with that irregularity. Since there was a deviation in the alignment, I unfolded the rods that Arnold had prepared. We took one of the six foot arms and aimed it from the center of the mine's mouth at the spot on the far canyon wall. We aimed the other end at the burning lantern, far inside the mine.

I then took my roll of twine and cut a piece exactly the length of the space between the two ends of rods, forming a triangle. I then tied a loose single knot in the piece of twine and told Earlene, "Baby, this single knot is for piece angle number one. She carefully noted this on the paper pad.

We then walked to the lantern and continued to a place where the tunnel veered to the left. We left the contrivance there and went on down the tunnel, carrying the lantern. We came to another fairly sharp turn and set the lantern down and returned to where we had left the rods.

We aimed one of the rods directly back toward the mine's entrance and the other toward the lantern, and repeated the actions we had taken before. When I cut the piece of twine, I tied two loose knots in the string to signify turn number two. I placed it in an envelope, along with the first piece of twine, and drew a line on the back of the envelope, marking the mine mouth with a straight line for an interval and then a bend in the line to represent the second turn, and its direction. Earlene made her own notes in the pad. We repeated our actions for every curve and bend. On the curves, we would measure from the center of the tunnel to the center of the tunnel as far ahead as we could go without the taut twine touching the edge of the tunnel due to the curve.

Each curve and bend was carefully marked with knots and the type of knot was changed with one type knot used for left turns and another type for right turns. Although there were not many turns in the comparatively short tunnel, I wanted to be as precise as possible.

Each angle could be reconstructed by placing the appropriate piece of twine between the ends, while having the one leg of the rods pointed accurately toward the stake that we could drive at the distance where we started the new measurement. There was a corresponding length of twine telling us where the next angular measurement was taken.

The angular measurements would only work if someone had an instrument with the exact same length of each rod. It would be necessary to have the exact distance measurement that was represented by each individual length of the distance twines. On top of that, there was the matter of left turns and right turns.

Even if someone had the twines, they would be useless without the contraption. If someone had both, they would still have to know the code telling which twine went where, and which direction each angular measurement went.

We would have to hide the angle measuring rods so we couldn't be seen carrying them. The place of hiding them would be another part of the puzzle to finding the mine, if we didn't use the mine ourselves, but wanted to give that option to our descendents.

What we had when we finished was the rod contraption, several pieces of twine, identified by knots, and one longer piece of twine with a loop tied at each point where a measurement was taken.

We now had all of our notes written on the envelope and also on the pad of paper. The envelope also contained all of the strings that denoted the angles.

"Sweetheart, it is important that we place this contrivance where only we know the significance. The strings can show the proper angle only for this exact ratio of rod lengths.

"There may come a time when it is imperative that we have more money. Even without that necessity, we will someday want to develop the mine. It would be a shame to let what may be substantial wealth just lay unused, with all of the poverty that exists in the world.

We still have to measure the other tunnel. We can now calculate the exact place where the water will enter the branch tunnel. It is a piece of information that might be valuable to have someday.

We shared a feeling of accomplishment as we walked back to the mine entrance, after Earlene had extinguished the light.

I want us to hide these rods, at least temporarily, before we ride back. There is no use in carrying them back right now. I want them hidden on one of our places, however. We need to hurry, for Brad will be worrying all the time we are gone.

We started up the path, but I had another thought and we turned back and worked our way silently through the bushes to the wall of the canyon, right below the hole we had used for a marker. The cliff-side was too steep to scale, but the hole was close enough to the top that I thought I could reach it with a lariat from the top.

We climbed the path, me carrying the rods and Earlene the lantern. When we had finally worked our way around to a spot right above the hole, I put on my leather gloves and tied the lariat to the trunk of a small mesquite tree, just above ground level. I tied enough loops in the rope to serve as steps in decending and helping when I started my climb back up the rope.

I tied the rods to the end of the rope and lowered it over the edge. Then I lowered myself, hand over hand until my face was right in front of the hole. Luckily, it was deep enough to hide the rods so that they could not be seen.

Standing with my foot in a loop, I pulled the rods up and slid one end into the hole far enough to hold the weight while I took the loop of rope off of them. I then pushed them into the hole to where they were nearly a full arm's length into the hole. I stood for a minute in the loop of rope, resting before starting back up.

I was sure glad that I had put the loops in the rope to provide a resting place, for the small diameter of the rope would have made it very difficult to scale the wall. I was a much easier job with the loops for steps.

After I had caught my breath, Earlene and I walked around to the ridge and scaled it and climbed down the other side. We were now standing in the place where Earlene had dried her nude body, after swimming in our hidden valley.

I said, "Earlene, before I forget it, the first chance we get we must write down the order of the strings, as denoted my the knots. We then need to change the number of the knots, so that the number one knot doesn't correlate to the number one angle. We will keep the code that matching the real number of the piece to the code number.

"I would also like to save the lantern forever, as a memento of the time my life changed from darkness to a new life, full of light and happiness."

We both sat down on the grass, and then found ourselves laying together, fully clothed, but with the heat of our bodies transferred through our clothing, and the hardness of my body trapped between us. Our kisses were like warm honey and we couldn't pull one another close enough.

However, again we had to restrain ourselves. We led our horses down the incline, watching our surrounding with all of our senses honed to their finest. We also were aware of the reactions of our horses, for they might be the first to know of any strange presence. I suppose all of our adversaries thought we were in the house, for apparently no one was stationed in the canyon.

The shadows were deep along the east wall of the valley where the moon light couldn't reach. Soon we were gently rapping on the window of Brad's room, and he opened the door for us. We were surprised to see that it was not even midnight.

Chapter Twenty Two
Rimrock Land and Cattle Company

For the next couple of days, Brad, Earlene, and I spent hours cutting cedar trees for a pole fence we were building near the creek that flowed through the middle of the &RR valley. The plan was to fence off more of the rich bottom land for corn.

There was nice grove of cedar trees growing on the east side of the valley. It was within easy sight of the valley opening. The open pastures left us with a clear field of fire that would make it nearly impossible for any invader to get from the front gate to the house.

It was slow going since we had to work and at the same time, keep an eye out for trouble. We kept our rifles within easy reach. They were a reminder of danger we could not afford to ignore.

We sawed cedar saplings of four to five inches in diameter for line posts and six to seven inches for corner posts. We began fencing off the land that had been picked out for this particular enterprise.

Our supply of posts ran short. Since we had plenty already cut at the grove, Brad decided to go get a load while Earlene and I continued working on the fence. It was just after he left that I spoke, "You know, Earlene, I've been thinking a lot about Brad being alone when we're married. What do you think about the three of us living together?"

"It's a funny thing, Easy, but I've been reluctant to talk to you about it for fear you'd think I didn't want us to have a home of our own."

"Baby, the way I see it, the three of us are family. I don't visualize me going out to look after the cattle while you stay at home looking after the house. I think things are ideal like they are, with the three of us working together. When I say that it is ideal like it is, I don't mean that you and I. . ."

Earlene interrupted by saying, "Easy I know what you're trying to say. Of course we want to be together as a married couple, but we can do that and still be a family. It would be so much easier for the three of us to pitch in as a team to do the things that take more than one person to do.   I'm so happy that you mentioned this."

"I would prefer that you to mention it to Brad while the two of you are alone. That way, he won't feel like he is being coerced into something that he may not feel comfortable with. After all, we would be only fifteen minutes away." I thought highly of Brad and he had been a big help to me. He had made me part of the family, and I had shared their happiness and companionship. I'd felt very much at home as we'd played three handed Moon the other day.

Earlene's face was radiant. "I don't think it would be necessary for me to talk to him alone first, but I see where you're coming from.   I'll take the first opportunity that comes along. That removes the one shadow that was dogging me. Well, the one shadow that doesn't concern Dobbins."

"Okay, Earlene, when Brad gets back, I'm gonna tell him that I'm tired of him getting the easy work and leaving me to dig. Then I'll go get a load of posts. I hope you can discuss our talk with him while I'm gone."   Earlene smiled her agreement and we went back to work.

Half an hour later, Brad returned with the load of posts. "Hmm," he said, do you two always slack off working when I'm out of sight?"

"Slack off? If we're the slackers, how come you get the easy jobs like hauling posts? I'll just string this load of posts and go get another one while you dig holes and work with that sharp-tongued Earlene."

Without a glance at them, I led the team to the fence line and walked alongside the wagon. After a 'whoa' or two, a 'gee' here and a 'haw" there, the team saw what was expected and I had only to jerk the posts off and throw them into place at the proper intervals.

I emptied the wagon, drove to the grove for another load and returned to where Earlene and Brad were working. When Brad dropped the diggers and walked over and put his hand on my shoulder while he shook my hand, I knew that Earlene had told him our plan. It was obvious, at least to me, that he was caught up by emotion. I clapped my hand on his shoulder, picked up the diggers, and went to work.

First, we dug several pairs of holes ten feet apart along a straight line, and then set a pair of posts, two at the start of the fence line, and two at the other end.

Next, I cut a thin ten foot pole about the diameter of a fishing pole and marked it at the ten foot length. I stuck the posthole digger into the ground, while Brad sighted from the first pair of posts to the last set of posts, until he was satisfied our measurements were perfect. We used my diggers and Brad's to make the job go faster.

When we were finished, we would have a fence that was four rails high.

On the fourth day of our work, Brad spotted a single figure riding toward us from the south, and called out to the other two of us. I waited until he was about a mile away, then picked up my English rifle and looked through the scope. I was pleased to see it was Rodney. He rode up and dismounted with a big smile on his face.

We shook hands all around. When it was my turn, I gripped the kid's hand in a warm welcome and told him how good it was to see him again. He looked great and I couldn't wait to hear what news he had for us.

"Let's go up to the house," Brad said. "We can have a bite and catch each other up on everything that's been going on since we last talked."

When we arrived at the barn, Earlene and I unhitched the team while Brad and Rodney went straight to the house.

When we entered the barn, the scent of oats, hay, and seasoned wood met us as we stepped inside. I took a moment to inhale deeply. "I love the smell of a barn," I explained as Earlene stopped and watched me.

We gave each of the horses a few ears of corn. "I never get tired of the smell, myself," Earlene said.

We held hands as we walked back to the house. When we entered, Brad had four whiskey glasses placed on the table. "Rodney says he has some information that calls for a drink. The rascal refused to tell me anything until the two of you were here with us."

"Well, you just hang on a minute while I put some coffee on," said Earlene. "Knowing you men, you'd sit here drinking 'Old John Barley Corn' all day, but the fact of the matter is we have work to do tomorrow. Somebody has to keep you focused in the right direction."

We all laughed and waited until she had the coffee started. Then Brad filled our glasses and the three of us looked expectantly at Rodney.

"First off," Rodney began, "my father wants to thank you, Easy, for saving my life that day Burly sicced his attack dogs on me."

"He also asked me to thank you, Brad and Earlene, for your help as well."

"Now here's the big news. Father's decided he wants to invest in some land and he'd like you, Easy, to be my adviser in the constructing and running of a large ranch." He waited for us to digest that statement, and then he continued.

"He said he would like nothing more than to have all three of you for neighbors. He thinks there could be some mutual exchange of services that could be extremely beneficial to all of us."

"He expressed a desire to combine his finances with your experience. He was very interested in your plans to start a breeding ranch and sell corn-fed beef to the townsmen. He said he doesn't see why we wouldn't be able to form a partnership. While you continue to work your ranches, you would also enjoy a partnership in a larger operation; a cooperative venture that's based on shares rather than an employer-employee relationship. He asked me to stress that if we form this partnership, although the shares might not be equal, the say-so on what we do would be equal, and that each of us, as individuals, would be treated as equals."

"If you agree, he will have legal papers drawn up to that effect. He said that he trusts my judgment that you're as trustworthy as I believe you are. He has great faith that with the support of his funds, and your fortitude and hard work, we can build an enterprise that is not only beneficial to all of us, but that is beneficial to anyone who resides here. It was important to him that I stress how crucial it is that you realize how much respect he has for you."

Rodney raised his glass in the air. "Here's to all of us," he said. "To us and to whatever the future holds."

"To us," we repeated. My eyes met Earlene's as we toasted. I had never felt as close to a group of people as I did just then.

"Easy," she asked, "why don't you and Dad bring Rodney up to date on what has happened since he left?"

"Brad, would you mind starting the story? I've been mulling some things over in my mind, and I need a little time to think. I know that this seems awfully rude, but I need to be alone for a few minutes and try to get some things sorted out. Would you please be so kind as to excuse me for awhile?"

I received some rather curious glances but when they assured me they understood, I rose to my feet, walked out the back door and sat down on the edge of the porch.

In my mind I surveyed the countryside, searching my brain for available land that I thought could be turned into good family farms and ranches.

A thought crossed my mind and began to grow. Just then I heard the door open behind me. Earlene walked over and sat down beside me, her shoulder brushing lightly against mine. "Easy, am I intruding?" She asked sincerely.

"No, Earlene. You're not intruding. To the contrary, actually, I'm glad you're here. I've some things on my mind that I would love to discuss with you. In the past, I've never known a single soul with whom I could share my dreams, plans, or longings. I've always wanted that."

"Do you really believe I'm that person? I so much hope that I am!"

I turned and pulled her tenderly into my arms. My heart ached with emotions that I never knew I had. "There is something special about you, Earlene. You have certain qualities that I admire, that I can't get enough of."

We kissed, softly, longingly. "Earlene," I said, "I know without a doubt that you're the one with whom I want to spend the rest of my life."

We sat on the porch with our arms around each other for the longest time, watching the drifting clouds, listening to the chirping birds, and chatting about our future. Eventually we realized it was time to go back inside.

"It's nearly dinnertime and I have nothing prepared!" Earlene said. "We'd better go inside before we all starve to death."

Chapter Twenty Three
A quandary

Earlene had outdone herself with the evening meal she placed before us. No food had ever tasted better.

As we enjoyed our dinner, passing the gravy across the table, and buttering a slice of homemade bread, I noticed a sense of anticipation in the room as if everyone was expecting me to say something. It was true; I did have something to say. There was plenty that I wanted to say, actually things that I needed to say. However, it required so much presumption on my part that I didn't know how to say it. I had no idea as to whether it was something that would be accepted or not.

I had never had any trouble saying what I wanted to say before, because always before it didn't really matter much to me how it turned out. Don't get me wrong. I've always wanted to live. That is a true statement, but it's hard to resolve the apparent contradiction when I say, I wanted to live, but didn't really care whether I did or not. Now, here I sat, speaking my own secret thoughts to my own secret self. It had always been as though I were starting a race that I wanted to win, but realized it was no big deal if I didn't.

Somehow, since I had befriended Rodney and had become so deeply involved with the Rogers, things had changed dramatically. I not only wanted to live, but I wanted desperately to live. I had to sample the sweetness of Earlene's lips over and over again for the rest of my life. I wanted to sit on a porch, a porch like hers, and look out across something that I had built. Even more important, I wanted 'us' to sit together and look out across what 'we' had built together. I wanted to absorb Earlene into my very being. I wanted to raise a family and have our children live to see what their parents had built.

There was something that I had to do in a way that didn't violate the code of my life. I had assured the small ranchers that I would never crowd them off their property. That assurance also implied that I would never abet the idea of anyone else crowding them, either.

All but two or three of the small ranchers were on the south side of the river, and I had promised my protection only to those on the north side of the river.

Finally, I couldn't hold off any longer. "My friends," I started, "and I include all of you when I say, my loved ones, I have what may be a dilemma. I recognize the fact that Rodney's father is expressing a desire to build a large enterprise here. The only land that could fill the requirements Rodney's father expects lies on the south side of the river. That is the only area that is well watered by the springs that flow out of the South Cedar Breaks.

"The small ranchers on the south of the river are hemmed in by the breaks, which is a starvation position. The only way the land on the south side will ever become available is if and when Burly Dobbins is dead. Now, we all know he has made it inevitable that either he or I will soon die. Since I'm gonna kill him, this is what I propose.

"I want to set up a meeting with the small ranchers from both sides of the river. There are only about twenty or twenty-five of them. My plan is to offer them a proposal they won't want to refuse.

"Before I make the proposal, I have to know what the three of you think. Rodney, you'll be the most affected by what I'm gonna say. Brad, you, Earlene, and I already have most of the land we want here on the north side. Also, we control the water on our side of the river, except for that which flows through the land along the Wandering River.

"My suggestion is to take a block of land that extends from three miles west of the creek that flows from the &RR, to three miles east of the river that will flow from my place.   That block of land will extend to the Wandering River. It will be approximately eight miles wide plus the ten miles to the river, or, in other words, it'll be around eighty square miles, or close to 51,200 acres.

"Now, the X-Pan-D has around ninety-six thousand acres, or 150 square miles. The two tracts together are about 230 square miles, or 147,200 acres.   Rodney, you and your father, and Brad, Earlene, and I would become equal partners in that land, and it would become the nucleus of what might be called the Rimrock Land and Cattle Company. We would have to negotiate a value for those holdings that will be a fair proportion of the cost of the cattle used to stock the RL&CC."

"Shares would be issued to pay for that. Rodney's dad will buy those shares at the actual cost of the investment or the negotiated value I mentioned about the land bearing a fair value in relation to the price of the cattle required to stock the land.   The higher of those two estimates will prevail."

"The Rimrock Land and Cattle Company would also form a bank, most probably the Rimrock Bank and Trust.   Again, stock would be issued, with Rodney's dad buying that stock. The amount of stock each of us would own in the RL&CC would be determined by our original stock as a percentage of the total amount of stock issued. In most cases, if additional capital were needed, it could be in the form of a loan from Rodney's dad to the RL&CC."

"The five of us would have equal voting rights, without regard to the share in the enterprise they hold. Rodney's father has already made that clear."

"We would add to the &RR and what I'm presently calling "My Valley," a one half mile strip that extends from three miles west of the &RR to twenty four miles east of my valley. The title for the &RR would include the strip that runs from halfway between these two locations to the west. I would hold the title to the strip that runs from that half way point on east to the end of the strip."

"This would allow the &RR and my valley access to each other, plus it would allow me to control, not only the main diversion channel that would send water to the small ranches that we are creating, but also the channels that run off of it to provide water to the small ranches we will be creating. That number will depend upon how many of the south side ranchers go for the plan I intend to propose to them. That plan will explain my comment about the water channels."

"It is my intention to activate the old river that used to flow through my canyon. I believe the water can be diverted into a man-made channel that parallels the Rimrock. This would allow for a stream to flow from the main channel to the river on three mile intervals. It would start three miles east of my place and extend about twenty-one miles eastward. Every three miles a channel could be cut, as straight as the terrain will permit, down to the river.

"If it can be done, I would be able to control every side channel that takes water from my valley stream. You realize these are merely preliminary plans. I'm sure there will be a lot of details that will come up for discussion once the papers are drawn."

"There's one other thing I want to mention. The Rimrock Land and Cattle Company should acquire a title to all the land, and then sell it on good terms to the ranchers, to be financed by the Rimrock Bank and Trust."

"Rodney, your father may not wish to build a bank. However, the beauty of it is, he would already have a built-in clientele from the ranchers who would be making reasonable payments to the bank. With the fencing, the work provided by the post cutting, and also the work involved in creating the canals which would run through every spread, the ranchers would make some pocket money. Their efforts would increase the value of their collateral. I might also mention that the merchants, too, would support us, once they witness the small ranchers coming in with cash to spend on their families. They would also benefit from a larger and better school system. The bank would have a strong position in making sure that the ranchers had sufficient livestock and used sound business practices as a term of obtaining that financing."

"Since the ranchers would have a clear view across the plains, it would be much harder for cattle rustlers to go unnoticed. Also, since they would have the ability to band together to defend against both thieves and land hogs, they would feel safer and provide a more secure environment for their families. In addition to all of that, each of the ranches would have access to a road that would run along one side and one end of them. The roads may be planned to run along all four sides. That would make it a lot simpler for the ranchers to move cattle. It would also make it easier for the ranchers to visit one another. This would promote a community spirit."

"I've failed to mention that each rancher's tract of land would be fenced with barb wire. That will make it much easier for each rancher to care for his stock with few problems. All in all, the Rimrock Bank and Trust will have a lot of financing to do, and each of the bank's clients will have solid operations.

The fencing will furnish work for the ranchers, and there is another really big plus. The posts for hundreds of miles of fencing will come from the South

Cedar Breaks. This means the South Cedar Breaks will be getting cleared. We will reseed it with a good grass and it will be added to the RL&CC. Although the RL&CC will own the RB&T, it will be run as a separate enterprise."

I want to emphasize that each part of this enterprise will feed upon the other. It will be a case of the whole being greater than the sum of the parts."

I suddenly stopped. I had allowed my enthusiasm to carry me away. "That is what was running through my head all this time. Now I need to know how you feel. Then we need to start preparing for a showdown with Dobbins and the Burly Bunch." I grinned as I said this, but inside I was feeling anything but cheerful.

Although it was necessary, I was not looking forward to the confrontation. I planned to adhere to my normal approach to such things, however, which is to hit hard and to hit fast and avoid arguing about it. It was with that thought in my mind that I began laying my plans.

"That pretty well sums up what I visualize for the Bend of the Rimrock area. I know this gives everyone a lot to chew on. I'm gonna take a ride to the end of the valley to give you a chance to think about what I just said. I need to do some more thinking of my own, anyway."

I picked up my Winchester and opened the door. In the blink of an eye I was out on the dark porch, closing the door behind me.

Earlene, Brad and Rodney sat silently for a moment after the door softly closed behind Easy.

"I dare say that is as comprehensive a plan as I've ever heard," said Rodney. "I don't see how it could fail, unless Dobbins is able to put a fly in the ointment."

Brad shook his head slowly. "There is an awful lot involved in the plan, but I don't see how the small ranchers can turn it down. Just one of the ranches will be the equal of every ranch in the South Cedar Breaks combined. It's gonna make this into a prosperous section of the country the minute the plan is announced."

Earlene had been sitting quietly, waiting for each of the others to have their say. "I don't know what either of you are gonna decide, but my mind is made up. I don't have to decide, I'm 100% behind his plan. I know there are a lot of things to think about, but the thinking should be about how to proceed, not whether we should proceed.

"I was never any prouder of anyone than I am of Easy. Right now, I'm gonna go catch up with him. He shouldn't be alone after he has laid out such a dream. The bad thing about it, and the one that frightens me so, is that Dobbins is lurking in the background, determined to kill Easy, at what-ever cost."

She got up, picked up her Winchester from behind the stove and reached for the doorknob. "I'm too excited to talk about it tonight," she flung back over her shoulder.

"Earlene, please be careful!" Brad's concern was apparent in his face, but he knew there was no way to stop her.

He looked over at Rodney and said, "Rodney, I don't see how a proposition like that can be turned down. The Rimrock Land and Cattle Company will be a winner while it is still in the womb."

"You won't get an argument from me," Rodney replied.

Chapter Twenty Four
Moving shadow

I kept to the deep shadows cast by the east wall of the canyon as I drifted, silent and hopefully unseen, toward the barn. My senses were honed to their finest point. I stepped softly, pausing now and then to listen. When I arrived at the barn, I pressed an ear against the door. I could hear the horses snuffling and stamping. When I was satisfied all was well, I opened the door enough to squeeze through, and slipped inside.

I saddled my horse in the dark, taking pains to smooth the saddle blanket for folds or irregularities that could cause the horse discomfort.

For the sake of caution, once the horse was saddled, I led him in a meandering path toward one corner of the barn, then back toward the tack room and, finally, I took an erratic path toward the door. Feeling a little foolish, I took the animal outside and shut the barn door behind me.

Leading the horse into the darker shadows, I mounted and rode northward up the valley. The plush grass muffled our footsteps. I could just make out a faint outline of the canyon walls by starlight alone, until the moon rose over the eastern rim of the canyon and the entire valley was bathed in a pale, beautifully transparent silver.

When I had passed this way in the darkness of the night a few days earlier, my love had been riding by my side. That thought seemed to accent my loneliness as I made the ride on this momentous night. The calls of the night birds seemed to have a more plaintive note. The far off call of a wolf seemed a cry from another world.

Before long, I reached the valley's end. I dismounted and slipped the bit from my horse's mouth, and placed him on a short picket.

As I started toward the canyon path that led to the high ground, I remembered the rocky slope I had to navigate, so I turned back to my saddle and slipped a pair of moccasins out of my saddle bags. There was no need to take a chance of turning an ankle in my boots, I reasoned, especially since I had my moccasins handy. When I was ready, I started along the tree line and entered the little forest that grew near the canyon wall.

I climbed the path and each step brought me closer to my oasis. I couldn't stop thinking about the day Earlene had walked this route with me, heading for the cool waters where we'd caught our first fleeting glimpse of each other. When I arrived, I looked down upon the silvered scene and stood, deep in reverie.

Eventually, I turned to leave, and as I did, I had a sudden impulse to scale the ridge to the end of my canyon. Once there, I peered into the darkness where the moonlight couldn't reach, and mused on the future. It was, I thought, as hard to pierce as the deep well of darkness before me.

I was about to turn away when the red glow of a cigarette caught my attention. As I watched, it was flicked into the darkness. Someone was hiding in the little glade where Earlene and I had left our horses the last time we'd been there together.

I considered slipping down and killing the interloper, but decided not to. I had no real knowledge of how many others might be with the man. I also knew that it would take a lot of luck to spot his hiding place in the dark, approach over the debris from the rocky walls without alerting him, and kill him before he could kill me.

I slowly crossed back over the ridge and went down the path, as silently as a mountain lion. I went to my horse, put his bit back into his mouth, coiled the picket rope and heard a voice so low as to nearly be a whisper say, "Don't shoot me, Easy. I came down to ride back with you. I hope that I'm not intruding into your private thoughts."

I brought her to me and clasped her against my thumping heart. "Sweet Baby," I whispered. "You'll never be an intrusion in my life. I was just over looking down into my canyon. Someone is lurking near the glade where we leave our horses. I saw his cigarette. There may be others with him. We can't afford to hang around."

We hurried quietly down the canyon about a hundred yards to where she had left her horse. As she mounted, I let my hand trail slowly down her back until her Levi's brushed my palm when she swung her leg over the saddle. I kissed the burning palm of my hand before mounting.

As we put a little distance between us and the convergence of the three valleys, I did some speculating. "If he were in my canyon," I said, "he could easily get into this one. However, there's a good chance he's not aware of the way these canyons join." I could sense her concern, but like the trooper she was, she showed no fear. She reached through the darkness and felt for my hand. When she found it, she gave it a little squeeze.

It was late by the time we arrived back at the &RR. Earlene and I were both exhausted, so we said a brief goodnight and called it a day. I watched as she walked to her room and closed the door. As I had the night before, my mind danced with fantasies about a girl who lay sleeping, just half a dozen short steps away.

Earlene, Brad, and Rodney had given me the okay to follow through on my proposition, so the next morning, I arose early to ride into Vacaville to arrange a meeting with the north and south side ranchers.

I asked Rodney to ride along so he could get a look at the South Cedar Breaks. I took a moment to write a note which I left on the kitchen table for Earlene and Brad so they'd know where Rodney and I had gone. A few minutes later we were saddled up and heading out to Vacaville.

When we rode into town, a light was burning in the sheriff's office. We pulled up in front of the door and tied our horses to the hitch rail. When I rapped on the door, the sheriff gruffly shouted for us to come in.

"Hi Sheriff!" I pitched my hat into a chair and walked over and shook his hand.

"Hello yourself." He stood up and stepped to the side so he could get a better view of Rodney. "I never thought I'd see you again," he said.

"Well, the bad penny and all that rot, doncha know?" Rodney asked in an exaggerated British accent. "What's the purpose of having friends if you can't see them every once in awhile?"

"I need to fill you in on a couple of things, sheriff", I said. "Do you have a moment?"

The sheriff nodded and took a seat, so I proceeded to fill him in on all of the things that had transpired up to and including my sighting of the man with the cigarette. I omitted the fact that I had been on the canyon rim when I saw him. I felt that would be encroaching on something very private between Earlene and me.

"Well," he said, as I finished, "I'm still holding you and Burly to the contract we made between us. I've no doubt you'll stand by what you promised," he told me. "However, I don't trust Burly as far as I could throw that big hellion." The sheriff stood up and walked over to the window to raise the blind. "Now," he asked, "is there something else you have on your minds?"

"Sheriff, how would I go about getting the word out that I'm holding a meeting for all the small ranchers on both sides of the river?"

"If you have plenty of time, you could leave word with Donahue, Smith, and the land agent. Donahue would let you post a notice in his saloon. It wouldn't take long for the word to get around."

He toed his chair out from behind his desk and sat down. "Take a load off, Fellas." As we took a seat, he pulled a hand-drawn map and a large, blank sheet of paper from out of his desk drawer. "This is a map of the land and these symbols represent the ranches located in the area," he ventured. "The most effective way to get the word around, after all, is to go and tell the men yourself. Copy this map between these boundaries."

The sheriff drew a line on the map around the perimeter of land that represented both sides of the river and took in the South Cedar Breaks. "You can be pretty sure of catching most of the ranchers in or near their houses." Rodney took a pencil off the desk and the sheet of paper the sheriff handed him and began drawing a copy of the map.

"Everyone has been pretty edgy since they heard you burned Dobbins out and told him to get out of the country. They're more than a little worried about what either of you is gonna do now."

"Well, Sheriff, I promised those men that I wouldn't crowd them. I also assured them that I would take personally whatever Dobbins does on the north side."

"Maybe your meeting will give them a little more confidence, at least if it's a fair deal, given in a fair way. Do you feel like cluing me in on this?"

"Please don't take this the wrong way, but to be honest, Sheriff, I'd rather you wait along with everybody else. It's a complicated proposition that I have to offer and I don't think I could tell it twice." I grinned to soften the blow.

"No offense taken," the sheriff assured me. He leaned back in his chair and clasped his hands behind his head. "As I mentioned, if I were looking to have such a meeting, I would first talk to Donahue. He's friendly and fair to everyone and everyone seems to like him. It's true, he, along with every other businessman in town, had to accommodate Dobbins if they wanted to stay in business, but even so, Donahue has his own code that he wouldn't break for anyone, not even Dobbins.

I've also heard him say some complimentary things about you and the way you handled the X-Pan-D boys when they were on the verge of killing that English boy." He paused for a minute, glanced over at Rodney and said, "I meant no offense by calling you "that English boy."

"No offense taken, Sheriff," Rodney smiled affably.

"Although O'Reilly seems to be understanding of the small rancher's plight, I'm not sure if he would go out on a limb to oppose Dobbins," the sheriff continued. His store has had to depend a lot on the X-Pan-D for both hardware and grocery sales. "You realize he expects, as well as everyone else around here, that Dobbins will be back."

He stopped to think for a moment, and then continued, "Come to think of it, I'd ask Arnold Smith, down at the blacksmith shop, if he would donate his big barn for a meeting place. In fact, I believe I would try him ahead of Donahue. Donahue won't take any guff from anyone, including me, and I *am* a duly elected public official, but that Arnold is in a class by himself." He grinned as he placed his emphasis on the word, 'am'.

I reached across the desk and the sheriff and I shook hands. "Sheriff, I assume that I can count on you and your deputies to keep the peace around here before the meeting takes place. I wouldn't be surprised if Dobbins shows up with a display of force at the meeting. I expect to have it at one o'clock on Thursday. I'd hate to have the ranchers intimidated in any way."

"That you can," Easy. "That you can," he said before adding, "Several of the south-side boys were in the saloon when you had your little, ah, should we say altercation with Torch. The authority you exhibited, not to mention courage, duly impressed them. I don't think they'd let anyone intimidate them too much, especially if you have any kind of plan to protect them."

"I do have such a plan, Sheriff. It's all part of my proposal. They'll have to hear what I have to say first, though, before they consider accepting my protection. Then we might just call another meeting and include the whole town, including the public officials. That even includes you, Sheriff," I grinned. "I promise you, you'll be invited in both your public and private persona."

I rose from my chair. "Well, I guess it's off to talk to Arnold then. If he agrees to contribute his barn for the meeting place, which we're hoping to hold on this coming Thursday at one o'clock, we can assure the ranchers we have a date and a location." Rodney took his cue from me and together we said our farewells to the sheriff and headed up the street to the blacksmith shop.

Arnold had just finished working on a horse when we walked in. He straightened up and greeted us with a question. "What brings the cream of the Rimrock into town at this time of day when every decent person is working?"

"We just stopped by to see if you were still sober," I replied. "I see that we're a little late for that, though," I chuckled. "However, there is something I have on my mind I would like to discuss with you."

"Well, imagine that!" Arnold grinned back. He pulled off his leather apron and waved us toward a small pile of sacked oats. "Find yourselves a seat in the drawing room, or should we move to the office?" he joked. Then he turned serious. "I know you boys didn't come in to palaver and enjoy my wit. What can I do for you?"

I gave a sketchy rendition of our plan in as few words as possible, and asked if we could hold the meeting in his barn. He informed us that some of Dobbins' men had been asking around for me, so I told him about the glowing cigarette I saw in the little glade behind my valley. He said he was not surprised to hear we'd been under surveillance.

After I explained the situation, Arnold said tersely, "Of course! You've got it! You have my permission to use my barn any time you want!"

"Thank you," I said, "I'm much obliged. We'll start the meeting at one o'clock in the afternoon of Thursday of this week."

I turned towards the door, "Well," I said, "it's time to get to work. We need to inform as many ranchers as we can about our personal invitation. In the meantime, if anyone drops in, Arnold, we would appreciate it if you would spread the word. It doesn't matter who you invite, not even Burly Dobbins and his bunch. In fact, I hope they do show up. I think it might give the ranchers some courage if I have the chance to talk to Burly in front of them."

We said our so-longs and headed out to spread the word.

We planned on riding down river to the east fork and heading south along that stream. Several of the ranchers were along that river, well back in the South Cedar Breaks. Most of the rest were on the creeks that flowed east into East Fork. Dobbins had been running stock along the creeks that flowed north down toward the Wandering River, into the land between the South Cedar Breaks and the river on both sides of Vacaville.

Chapter Twenty Five
Spreading the gospel

Rodney and I put our horses into a ground-covering trot and headed down river. We carried our rifles in our saddle boots. As had been my habit since Rodney had given me the two English rifles, for quick retrieval, I carried my Winchester with the stock forward on the right side of my horse, and an English rifle to the left with the stock to the rear.

I had been pleased to see that Rodney had brought another of the fine rifles back from England with him. I had the impression that the price of one of those rifles would cost more than a puncher made in a year. I also had the impression that would be pocket change to Rodney's family.

When we reached the East Fork, we were able to see the wagon road which ran alongside the river, just outside the berry thickets and huge trees that grew along the banks. We took a break at the clear-flowing water so our horses could drink. Then we headed up-stream.

Immediately we detected smoke curling up from a house on the far side of the river. I was surprised to find a ranch on that side, for I hadn't seen it when I had ridden up when circling back to Promontory Point on the day we'd burned Dobbins out.

Judging from the headquarters, it was a huge spread, so I couldn't figure out why neither the sheriff nor Smith had mentioned it to me. The building did look new, but it was surprisingly well build and had a solid, permanent look about it.

The only thing I could think of that made any sense at all was perhaps it was located in another county. In any event, something made me decide to by-pass it. I asked Rodney if he'd help me remember to mention the spread to the other ranchers who might be able to shed some light on the mystery.

It was easy to find one's self absorbed in the beauty of the vast reaches of grassland which stretched on both sides of the East Fork where the Wandering River was already lost to sight. The South Cedar Breaks seemed to play out on the east side of the East Fork. I imagined that if one were to turn back and cross the Wandering River and ride on to the Rimrock, the fabled grasslands of the high ground would stretch out of sight to the east, north and westward as far as the line of the mountains permitted.

It wasn't long before we reached the first on our list of small ranches. It lifted out of the grass where a good-sized stream flowed into the East Fork. A man was standing on the porch when we rode up. I recognized his face. He had been in the saloon on the day I had killed Torch.

We exchanged greetings and then I explained about the one o'clock meeting I was holding on the coming Thursday at Arnold's livery barn. I stressed the importance of the meeting and told him to spread the word in case we missed anyone.

When I mentioned the large spread on the far side of the East Fork, he replied, "Ain't none of us made friends with that bunch. They ain't no way friendly. They trade at a good-sized town called Post that is right up on top of the Rimrock. They don't seem to want no friends on this side of the fork."

I filed that piece of information away for future reference.

We continued riding on from ranch to ranch for a good portion of the day. Eventually, we started growing weary, so we counted ourselves lucky when a rancher promised to pass the invitation on to the last three further south. He was on his way to see Heinzer, anyway, and didn't mind making the stops along the way. As it turned out, Heinzer's ranch was the last one on our list who lived on the streams that emptied into the East Fork.

We'd ridden through a lot of land where the grass was choked out by scrub cedar trees, just the right size for fence posts. All of the ranchers that we'd seen were barely subsisting. It seemed to me that my proposal was gonna be seen as an opportunity too good to pass up.

On the backside of Promontory Point, we came to the last ranch on the south side. It was crowded with a brambly mixture of cedar trees, plum thickets, and thorn bushes. We found the proprietor along a scarcely flowing creek. He was a dispirited looking man who was trying to dig out a hole big enough for his small herd to water in. Each time he took out a shovel full of mud, half a shovel full oozed back in. He looked fearful as we rode up. "What do you want? I ain't been nowhere near your cows," he quavered.

"I don't know who you think we are, but we're not here to accuse you of anything. We are inviting you to a one o'clock meeting at Arnold Smith's Livery on Thursday. This fella is Rodney Hampton. You might say that we're partners. My name is Seeker. You can call me Easy."

"I'm Henry Didrikson, Mr. Seeker. Ain't you the guy that killed that X-Pan-D gunman and burned Burly Dobbins out? This here is my ranch. What do you want with me?"

"You'll find out at the one o'clock meeting, Didrikson. All that I'll tell you now is that you'll be very happy you came. We expect you to be there. All the rest of the South Cedar Break ranchers will be there. It's important that each and every one of you have a say in what we're planning."

Didrikson's face still showed apprehension, but he straightened his shoulders a little when I mentioned his importance to the meeting.

"I'll be there, Mr. Seeker. You can count on me."

We waved a hand at him and headed for the west side of Promontory Point. Did we receive a surprise when we came into sight of the old X-Pan-D headquarters! New buildings were going up, and you could see sentries posted in a semi-circle from the bluff on the far side of the headquarters, around the front and back to the bluff on the near side. I turned my gaze upward to the top of the point. My fears were justified. Smoke was curling up from a campfire. Guards were posted on the high ground. We wouldn't surprise them again.

Keeping to the brush, we rode on to the old draw that paralleled the ranch road and returned to the Wandering River. We forded the river and headed straight for the &RR.

Rodney broke the silence. "Looks like Dobbins is back and is loaded for bear."

"That is exactly how it looks," I answered, "and I'm glad to see it."

"Why so, if I might be so bold as to inquire?" said Rodney.

"'Cause now we know where he is and won't have to go hunt him," I answered. We rode in silence for a couple of minutes. "Rodney, I think it is about time for you to start hiring a crew for your spread across the river. We will wait until he builds you a headquarters. Then we will kill him and run his crew all the way to California. This is just what we wanted. I can't believe he is making it so easy."

"I'm glad you feel that way, Easy," Rodney answered quietly. "I hope you'll forgive me if I sound a little dubious."

"Rodney, Rodney, Rodney! What did I do to make you lose the faith? Is it that we had such a hard time running him out the first time?" I asked, grinning.

Rodney grinned back, in the growing darkness. "It's just that you're so timid when things get rough," he replied.

We rode through the pleasant darkness back to the &RR. Unsaddling and putting up our tack, we walked back to the house. Brad and Earlene had been preparing to eat when they heard us ride in. Earlene had set the coffee pot back on the stove to keep the coffee warm, and had two more plates set at the table. We came in and washed up and sat down at the table.

"I presume that you had a fruitful and uneventful trip. It looks like you both still have your scalps," joked Brad.

"Well, being half right is better than being dead wrong," I answered.

"Which half is right?" asked Earlene. She sat motionless, waiting to hear the answer.

"The half about it being fruitful. You couldn't have missed any further if you had had a week to prepare for the uneventful part." I picked up a hot biscuit and began buttering it.

"Let me make a guess," Brad broke back in. "Hmm, you got some information about our mysterious night-time watcher over in your valley. Right?"

"I suppose you could say that you're right, since I didn't stipulate that it had to be direct information. However, I will give you a clue by telling you that it more or less dwarfs the information that your guess encompasses." I turned my head toward Rodney. "Rodney, do you think I'm exaggerating the importance of the information we found out?"

"Not by one whit," answered the kid. "I would say that if anything, you're playing it down."

"Now you have really got us to thinking." Brad looked over at his daughter. "Earlene, what can you think of that is so all-fired important? I feel about stymied, myself."

Earlene sat up straighter and said, "You saw Dobbins?"

I shook my head in bafflement. "How in the world did you guess that?"

"Elementary, my dear Watson."

"What in the world is that supposed to mean?" I asked.

Rodney began laughing. Don'cha keep up with current events, Old Chap? Watson is the assistant of the hottest detective living, albeit in fiction.

When the laughter died off, I decided to get down to brass tacks. "The news that we're trying to tell you is that Burly Dobbins is rebuilding his headquarters," I said. "He has an army on guard, and even old Rodney is afraid we're facing our Waterloo."

I looked over at Rodney and told him, "See, two can play the name dropping game. I didn't have to use a make believe character, or at least event, either!"

"You got me there," said Rodney.

Brad had been sitting and listening to our non-sense. "Tell me about the Burly Bunch," he said.

"Rodney, give Brad a run-down on the whole trip. I have to be thinking about a couple of things, with eating being at the top of the list."

Earlene rolled her eyes and said, "Yes, Rodney. Do tell us of the dangers that are fixing to assail us while Easy beats us to the biscuits."

Without missing a bite, Rodney gave Brad and Earlene a full account of our day's journey. He even mentioned the campfire we saw on the top of Promontory Point.

As for me, I was trying to visualize what might be happening out at the X-Pan-D. What I thought was a likely scenario crystallized in my mind. The more I examined it, the more probable I decided it was. Pushing back from the table, I told Earlene, "I sure hope the word about your good cooking doesn't spread around the country. I'd like to keep that as my own little secret. I don't want every puncher in the short-grass country eating us out of house and home."

"Don't worry, Easy," Earlene said as she cleared the table. "If those cow punchers come around mooching food, they'll have to go hungry. They'd never even find as much as a crumb after you've been at the table."

"What do you say that we all turn in?" I asked. "I have a plan that is gonna keep us working tomorrow. That is, if Rodney isn't off somewhere in the corner reading about Sherlock Holmes. Now if he reads about Napoleon, he might at least bend his mind around a good plan to keep Burly bouncing back every time he tries to breach our bulwarks."

"One, two, three, clap, clap, clap!" said Earlene, clapping in unison with her clap words. Best be bouncing into bed, the bunch of us," She shot back.

We all got up and prepared to hit the sack.

Chapter Twenty Six
The meeting

The meeting was set for one o'clock in the afternoon. Most of the men pulled up in front of the livery stable and entered the big barn as though they wanted to make sure they wouldn't be seen. Every small rancher was accounted for by one o'clock. The sheriff chose a seat on an old one horse shay in a corner at the front of the barn. His three deputies were seated in the remaining three corners.

Rodney sat behind an old roll top desk that was set at an angle that allowed him to see the audience. He was prepared to take notes.

Earlene made herself comfortable on a sack of corn, next to her father who lounged against the wall. The blacksmith remained in the tack room doorway.

The small ranchers were seated in groups on a medley of everything from old cane bottomed chairs, to boxes, stools, and old farm equipment.

There was a murmur when I walked in, then silence as I took my place in front of my audience. "Men, I appreciate you coming here today. I don't want to waste your time, or mine, so I'm gonna get right down to business.

"You know your ranches have been nonproductive for several years. Some of you have felt threatened by large land holders. Well, I believe we've found a way to change all that; a way that will benefit everyone involved. Here is what we propose."

As though entering on cue, Burly Dobbins suddenly appeared, flanked by four hard bitten gunmen. He grinned and said, "Don't let me interrupt the proceedings."

"Don't worry, we won't!" I said, and looked him square in the eye. "We would have invited you, but the rumor was going around you had left town."

"Not now and not ever." Dobbins' voice carried a little sarcasm.

"Alright, folks," I said loudly. "Let's get back to business." As I glanced across the sea of faces before me, I wondered if any of these men were regretting their decision to attend the meeting. "What I have to say is of more interest to you permanent residents of this area than it is to transients."

"I'm sure as hell not a transient!" Burly's voice was hot with rage.

"Oh, I'm sorry, Dobbins, but you don't have to worry. I'll be clearing up any misunderstandings about who's a transient and who's not very soon."

Once again, I shifted my attention to the crowd. "As I was saying, here is what we propose to do. In case any of you are uninformed, when I say "we", I'm talking about Brad Rogers, his daughter, Earlene Rogers, and last but not least by any means, Mr. Rodney Hampton.

"First of all, I'm gonna start off by painting a broad picture of the plans we've devised to make work more productive, and, therefore, life in general, a whole lot better for all of you who reside in the South Cedar Breaks area. I will fill in the details later."

"Now, before we go any further, let me introduce myself. Although most of you may not know me by name, Easy Seeker, I do believe I've met most of you before, and perhaps many of you have heard about my history with this land and some of its more notorious residents. I hope the reputation I've already earned is enough to gain your trust in what I'm about to propose to you today.

"I've drawn up a map that represents the land located on the north side of the river. Mr. O'Reilly, the proprietor of Paddy O'Reilly's General Store, was good enough to run some copies on his mimeograph machine. Miss Rogers, would you mind doing us the honor of passing them out, please.

"Miss Rogers," I repeated to Earlene, "please be sure not to skip over Dobbins and his hired help. Mister Smith and Mister Donahue, please make sure you get a copy, too."

As Earlene made her rounds, I stepped into the crowd, shaking hands, greeting each man by name, and addressing each by 'mister'.

"Dobbins, did you get a copy?" I asked. I had purposely dropped the 'mister' before addressing him. Apparently the fact didn't escape the man, for when Earlene approached him, he rudely snatched his copy from her hand.

When I returned to the front of the group, I said, "Now if you take a look at the map, you'll notice where I've divided the land into several tracts. Each tract represents enough acreage to make a feasible economic unit. How can this be, I'm sure you must be asking yourselves. The answer is simple. For starters, each one will have a stream of good, clean water flowing through its center. Each property will be fenced off with a barbed wire fence, and each will be accessible by road."

"Now, before I continue along these lines, let me address some of the concerns you may have. The first one is monetary. You may be wondering how you're gonna obtain financing to handle such a viable economic unit. The answer is through Rimrock Bank and Trust, whose primary concern will be to service the welfare of this area.

"You may also be wondering how every property could possibly have a stream running through it. Believe me, I understand your concern, and I realize how mysterious this is gonna sound when I tell you that you're just gonna have to wait and trust me on this.

"Very soon you'll have to make a decision as to whether or not you want to be a part of this plan. When that time comes, I want you to say to yourself, *What if he's right? What if there were a stream of water flowing through my property? What if it were surrounded by barbed wire fencing? What if there were a school for my children? What if I were under the protection, not only of our good sheriff, but of the laws that are supposed to protect every honest man in his pursuit of happiness?* These statements will also be backed by the Rimrock Land and Cattle Company, hence forth to be known as the RL&CC."

By now the barn was buzzing with conversation. Suddenly Burly's voice boomed across the room as he held up his map. "What in the hell is this crap?" he shouted, pointing to a spot on the south side of the river. "Where's the X-Pan-D?"

"That *was* the X-Pan-D, Dobbins," I said. "That was before you decided to try to take over the north side. That was before you and all of your hands vacated the X-Pan-D and surrendered it, as open land. That was before you became a transient. That was also before you decided to commit suicide and still be in the Rimrock country when the sun comes up on Monday morning. That was before you got the cock-eyed notion that you were King Dobbins instead of the Donkey King."

I knew Dobbins had no intentions of leaving the country. I also knew the deadline that I had set for Monday morning would enrage him. My intention was to fuel that rage, hoping it would nudge him into immediate action. That had to be his downfall.

The barn suddenly exploded into conversation. I tried to regain order. "Men!" I shouted. "Please, everybody, listen up!" The buzz finally subsided and before long I had everyone's full attention once again.

"Two weeks from now, on a Monday morning, the Rimrock Land and Cattle Company will open an office adjacent to the grocery store in the same location where the cobbler used to have his shop. One thing I still need to mention is the procedure that will be used for selecting each portion of land that will fall under ownership of each rancher who wisely decides to trade his old way of life in for a new start in the chance of a lifetime.

"Every rancher who signs up will have his name entered in a ledger. Each line on the ledger will be numbered. Mind you, this process will make things as fair as we can make them.

"If a dozen people have signed up by the date we establish, we will place a dozen slips of paper in a hat. Each slip of paper will have a number from one to twelve. Each person will draw a number. The person who signed up first will make the first draw. However, when each person has drawn a number, that number will go towards a second drawing. That second drawing will have twelve slips of paper, and each slip will have the name of a participant written on it. The person who previously drew number one will make the first draw. The person whose name that person draws will then choose the property of his choice. The person who previously drew number two will make the second draw. The person whose name he draws gets second choice over the remaining properties, and so on.

"Now, if only five people sign up, only five numbers will be drawn, etc.

"There's one other important note that needs to be addressed. When the drawing is completed, if any person wants to trade his pick for another person's land, and that man is willing to make the trade, they may make the trade within two weeks of the drawing.

"An example of why two people may wish to swap land might be that one person is raising a family and needs to be in close proximity to the school. If both parties are willing, the trade may be made.

"There will be some restrictions on land ownership. No one person may own more than one tract of land within the listed tracts. None of the tracts may be owned by a company. In other words, the land will always be under the private ownership of an individual.

"No part of the stream may be used for irrigation unless a water district is formed and a fair and just amount is allotted to each person. As of this time, it is unknown as to whether or not sufficient water will be available for that purpose.

"Now, keep in mind, this is merely a rough summation of our proposal. If needed, as time goes on, changes will be made accordingly. One thing, however, that you can rest assured of, every decision made will be executed with your needs in mind, as fairly as possible."

I paused for a moment to see if there would be any repercussions. When none came, I went on, "I would like to take this time to invite you to another meeting on Monday two weeks from now. By then we will have some preliminary by-laws drawn up and ready for your inspection. I wish the best of luck to all of you. That meeting will be held at one PM, and as I am repeating, on the second Monday from today, in this same spot which has been made available through the courtesy of our neighbor and the proprietor of the Livery and Blacksmith Shop, Mr. Arnold Smith.

"Before you go, please remember this one thing. If you accept this proposition, you'll be under the protection of the Rimrock Land and Cattle Company, or the

RL&CC. This establishment will not only provide you with all the help you may need in the marketing and purchasing department, but it will also be the place where you can turn for any help in any other department that can be best accomplished through a united effort.

"Before I dismiss you, I want to encourage you to accept this proposition. I hope you can already see the benefits that will be readily available to you and your families.

"Thank you all for coming today and I hope to see each and every one of you at the next meeting."

"Hold it!" The voice boomed out through the bedlam of animated conversation. I turned and saw Burly and his four men, hands on gun butts, standing in the crowd of men. Burly and two of his men faced the front. Two of the other men faced the outside corners of the room, quartering away from Burly's back. "This has gone far enough! It's gonna end right here and now!"

"Burly, Burly, Burly!" I chided. "Don't you remember our contract with the sheriff?"

"Piss on the contract with the sheriff!"

I smiled at him. "Burly, before you let your alligator mouth overload your jay-bird ass, I advise you to look around."

Burly must have thought he was too seasoned to fall for what he imagined was a trick. While he had been talking, the sheriff and his boys had moved in. One of Burly's men took a quick glance around.

"Hey Boss!" His voice was low, but urgent. "We better cool it. Look around you. We wouldn't have a chance!"

Burly took a tentative look around. The crowd had moved against the walls, and four double barreled shotguns were pointed straight at him and his men. He knew that if he made one false move, he and his men would be blown to kingdom come.

He let his hands drop loosely and tried to smile himself. "You guys have a nice day" He jerked his head at his men and they left the room.

Brad, Earlene, and the kid rushed to my side. "OK, we have to hurry," I said to them. "I'm sure they'll be riding hell for leather to beat us back to the &RR. If they start heading off towards the X-Pan-D with the intention of doubling-back once they're out of sight, it will be the only head start we'll have."

Chapter Twenty Seven
A trap is baited with a trap

Arnold had been standing outside the barn, watching the Burly Bunch ride out.

"Did they take the bait?" I asked him.

"It appears so, hook, line and sinker." Arnold said. Then he added, "I sure hope you know what you're doing, Easy."

"I hope so too, Arnold. I'm hoping Burly will be infuriated enough to do something foolish. If he does, we'll probably drop him at the gate outside the &RR, but if he plans to play it smart, we'll get him at that nameless spread of mine. We have to hurry, though."

I reined my horse around. "Let's go!" I shouted to my three companions as we lit off at a gallop for the &RR.

We soon arrived at the gate to the ranch. As we entered, I saw the pile of wood that I had asked Brad and Earlene to gather, while we'd been spreading the word among the South Cedar Breaks ranchers about the meeting.

"Okay," I said. "Rodney, you have had archery classes. I want you to be over at the west wall behind that nest of boulders." I turned to Brad. "You get over here on the east bend. Rodney, start a small fire back in that crevasse where it can't be seen. Have your bow ready. They will be banking on beating us back here. You'll hear them any second. When they start into the canyon mouth, give them time to get halfway between the pile of wood and the east bend where Brad will be hidden. Fire your fire arrow into that pile of kerosene soaked wood. You'll have them outlined against the fire behind them."

"Brad, you can fire the first shot. Make sure it is early enough to keep them from rushing you."

"Rodney, the second Brad fires, you fire too. Pour it onto them and the one's you don't kill will run back to entrance."

"They will know that we are all inside this valley. It may take a few minutes, but Burly will leave a man or two to hold us pinned down here. He will head for my canyon to burn me out."

"Earlene and I will go to the back of this canyon, go up on the Rimrock, cross over to my canyon and go down. I have two horses picketed there and we will try to get to my place ahead of Burly. If he doesn't think of burning me out very quickly, we will get there in time to end this. If he thinks of burning me out right away, he will beat me to my place and we will have to play it by ear and react as best we can to the circumstances."

Just as soon as Brad and Rodney reached their positions, we could hear the unmistakable sound of approaching hoof beats. Immediately, Earlene and I mounted and started up canyon at a brisk walk.

We were no more than a quarter of a mile away when the pile of logs and sticks burst into flames. We heard the crack of rifles for a minute or so and then a sporadic shot or two. Using the noise for cover, we instantly put our horses into a lope.

Half an hour later, we swung down from our horses and stripped them of their saddles and bridles. We hid the saddles behind a big rock shielded by some thorny berry vines and quickly climbed to the high ground. We scaled the ridge separating the heads of the two canyons and quickly trotted down the hidden path.

Our approach startled the two horses I had previously picketed at the bottom of the canyon. Speaking quietly, we gave each a pat to reassure them, bridled and led them to where I had hidden two saddles. Saddling up, we mounted and nudged them back down the canyon at a short lope.

When we neared the house, we began walking the horses and soon got off and led them to just outside the yard. I pulled a shotgun from its boot and held Earlene's reins while she fumbled around for something inside her saddle bag. I had been pondering this situation, and had a plan, but was not sure that it would work.

I saw Burly and two of his men ransacking the house by the light of a lantern. One man came out of the back room where I could plainly hear Burly's voice, "We're not gonna find anything worth stealing, so grab the kerosene lantern and oil down the floor. We'll burn that bastard out, just like he did me."

While the men were speaking, Earlene and I had quietly dismounted and tossed our reins over the saddle horns. As the last word was spoken, I whipped the horses with the end of my lariat. They burst from the yard in a thunder of hoof beats.

"What in the hell is that?" I heard a man yell.

"Get out in the yard and kill the bastards." I recognized Burly's voice.

Burly and his two gun hawks came carefully but rapidly out into the front yard. They were peering through the darkness after the vanishing hoof beats. The man with the lantern had set it down on the porch. The three men were standing like figures in a painting, frozen into stillness by their efforts to hear any movement.

"It's sort of a bad way to get caught, don't you think, Burly Boy?" I said. My voice held them petrified.

"You can't get us all," one man replied.

I let my voice seep into Burly's realization, like molasses into one of Earlene's biscuits. "Burly Boy, you remember how pissed off you were when you found out that Oklahoma and Hatch were dead? What happened was one of your men said those self-same words to me that your gunny just said."

Dobbins had recovered his wits. "Which one of my men, and what words are you talking about?" Dobbins' voice had regained some of its steel.

"Hey you, there closest to the door! What was it you just said? I'm not sure I remember exactly what it was. Would you repeat it?"

The gunman had his lips pulled back against his teeth like a woman's skirt against her legs in a high wind. His hand was on his gun butt. "What I said was, and you can listen carefully, for I won't say it again, you can't get us all."

My shotgun splattered his guts all over my new porch, when the left hammer dropped. The man flanking Burly on the other side had his gun coming up as the right hammer dropped and left his shirt and pants an instantaneous sodden mass of bloody cotton cloth, with some of it peeking from the recesses of his bowels.

"See," I said to Burly, "that is exactly what happened to Hatch and Oklahoma." Burly was looking at the twisted figures. While he was looking, I was reloading. He turned back toward me, "You wouldn't shoot a man when he didn't have a gun in his hand, would you Seeker?" He drew and I let him have both barrels in the bread basket. "No, Burly, I surely wouldn't. I wonder if that's any comfort to you."

If it were, Burly Boy didn't tell me. Burly Boy had bought his last ticket on the black train to hell. My shotgun had punched it for him.

Earlene came out of the darkness and rushed into my arms. We embraced while our shadows made grotesque forms that melted into the black night.

"Sweetheart," I said, "under other circumstances we could both slip into the house and get some sleep. However, your dad needs to know that you're safe. I'm gonna walk back to let him know that you're resting here at my place. It's probable that he and Rodney are still pinned down inside the valley and could use some help."

"That is a great plan, especially the first part where we both could rest together. However, given what just took place here, I wouldn't want to stick around. All this blood and everything would give me the creeps, and I don't feel like cleaning the mess up at the moment. Instead, I'm gonna walk back with you. Then my dad can see for himself that I'm okay.

"If you noticed, I got something out of my saddle bag before you so rudely ran our horses off." She laughed and said, "I'm gonna let you get by with it this time, but don't be making it a habit."

"I promise not to let it be a daily occurrence, but you never did say what you got out of the saddle bags."

"Why I thought you knew me well enough to know without me having to tell you," she smiled.

"Let me guess then," I said.   "Buttermilk and sandwiches."

"Darn it! You're gonna be a hard one to keep a secret from," she said.

"Elementary, my dear Watson," I replied.

We walked in darkness to the far side of the canyon, and sat down on one of the big rocks. It was the same place where Rodney had once waited with his rifle for Hatch and his men to turn up.

We chatted while we munched on our sandwiches, taking turns drinking buttermilk out of the jar. When we finished, we tucked the sack and the empty jar far inside the enclave, to be retrieved at a later date.

As we were about to leave, something caught my eye. I roughly shoved Earlene back into the enclave. "Shhh," I said before she could protest, "I saw something or someone moving."

Carefully and as quietly as possible, I took a cautious step forward and looked around. In a moment I could see what had caught my eye. The two horses I had chased off were heading back this way. When they were close enough, I called them over.

The relief we felt at that moment called for another kiss which turned out to be more intoxicating than any kiss we'd ever exchanged before.

We mounted up and set off at a lope. When we were still a mile away from the canyon entrance, we slowed our horses to a walk and, in a futile effort to avoid the moonlight, we held them as close as we could to the Rimrock.

Eventually we found a good spot to pull up and dismount. I made a thorough check of the area around the entrance, while Earlene waited with the horses.

Twenty minutes later I returned.

"There's no sign of the guard," I told Earlene upon my return. "I don't know whether to feel relieved or more worried than before. If Brad and Rodney defeated the guard, they might be on their way to help us."

"On the other hand," Earlene said, "that might have been the last thing they would have done, because they would have had no way of knowing whether Burly had other men waiting somewhere else. In any event, they may be thinking Burly sent someone for more help."

"As badly as I hate to do it," I said, "we're gonna have to enter the canyon without knowing whether Brad and Rodney are in the house or if X-Pan-D men are in there waiting for us. For all we know, they could be in there hoping for a messenger from Dobbins to come back with news that they hold the canyon. This is one time when I don't know whether to be glad the canyon is as black as a pit, or wish that we had a little moonlight, like we do here outside the canyon."

"One thing's for sure," Earlene said. "We better make certain there's no one behind us before we make ourselves known to anyone occupying the house. They wouldn't have tried to burn us out if they had killed Dad and Rodney. They would have just taken our house for a line camp."

"My thoughts exactly," I agreed. "We can't even be sure whether or not one or both are injured and needing our help. We certainly can't wait around for daylight. We're gonna have to get close enough to identify ourselves, and at the same time find a way to protect ourselves if necessary. Earlene, the only way to do it is to do it. I hate for you to come with me, and I hate even more to leave you behind, so let's go."

"I'm glad you came to that conclusion on your own, for this would be a terrible time for me to have to tell you to go jump in the lake, that I was gonna go, no matter what you said."

I didn't answer. I just squeezed her hand, and then reluctantly released it. After all, we couldn't very well creep up on them while holding hands.

As we slowly advanced, one step at a time, I realized this was the most taxing position in which I had ever been. We had no idea who was in the house, friend or foe. They had no such problem.

I hoped against hope no one was inside the mouth of the canyon. We'd taken our time, creeping through the shadows that pooled like soot along the east wall. When we arrived at the canyon where the east wall jogged even further to the east and then back north for another one hundred yards before both sides of the canyon diverged abruptly and the canyon became a valley, we stopped and listened intently. There was no sound, as though the entire scene were only a picture.

Slowly we eased out from behind the cover of the wall. A voice as brittle as a hunting knife being sharpened against a sandstone said, "You're one step from hell if you don't raise your arms straight up above your heads."

Earlene said, "Dad?"

Chapter Twenty Eight
Consolidating

Several weeks later, Brad, Earlene, Rodney and I were relaxing at the kitchen table in the &RR ranch house. We were discussing the scouting trip Rodney and I had made two weeks earlier. We'd ridden up to the X-Pan D ranch and found it as empty as a ghost town. We also checked out Promontory Point, where we discovered the only signs left were already disappearing, as though the part Promontory Point had played in the ousting of the Burly Dobbins era had been a dream.

We talked about our accomplishments since the day that I had first ridden into the Bend of the Rimrock.

Rodney was expecting some visitors. I had given him a letter of introduction to an acquaintance of mine in Fort Worth. I had requested that he try to find Rodney half a dozen good men to become the nucleus of his ranch crew. Their first task would be to complete the corrals and out buildings of the X-Pan-D ranch. Those men were due to arrive by the end of the week.

It had been decided that the new bank building would be erected on a vacant lot near the center of town. Men had been hired and that building was already well underway. It would also house the headquarters of the Rimrock Land and Cattle Company.

We'd been sending mail back and forth to Rodney's father, bringing him up-to-date on all that was happening. He approved of the proposition I had drawn up, as well as the way we'd endorsed it, including the demise of Burly Dobbins.

Our conversation had covered all those points. Now it was up to me to give my report on the most important point of all. Where was the water for the ranches on the South Cedar Breaks, and when would it be available?

"As you know," I began, "everyone is supporting our proposition for the ranches that will be fenced off. Of course the proposition can't be fulfilled until we can get some water running through those ranches."

"The work crew has finished clearing the channel of brush, thickets and other obstructions. The flowing water will finish the job.

"At ten o'clock this morning, we'll set off the blast that'll turn the water loose. I figure that it'll take about an hour for the water to arrive at the spot where the old river bed meets the Wandering River. That time can vary considerably.

"That's the location where Rodney and I have already made the preparations for the ceremony. Tables, chairs and a speaker's platform are set up and enough picnic tables for the celebration. The ceremony will include the final drawing and the assignment of the tract numbers.

"Construction will begin on the actual water distribution channels immediately upon seeing the water flow into the Wandering River.

"Rodney and I have already had a surveyor stake off the tracts of land where the fences will be constructed, as well as the location of the roads.

"The celebration we've planned will be the kick-off that begins this new era of ranching. It may serve as a pattern for other such efforts throughout the west, in addition to what we will be accomplishing here in the Bend of the Rimrock.

I glanced at my watch, and came to my feet. "I see it's time for me to go and set the charges," I said. "Earlene is going with me to light the fuses. The next time you see us, we will hopefully be galloping along in front of a wall of water that will sweep down the channel. We hope!"

"Don't worry about anything, Easy," Brad said. "While you're gone, Rodney and I will supervise the crowds waiting for the celebration."

Earlene and I mounted up and headed for my valley. Three hours later we pulled up at the valley's end, tied our horses at the foot of the hidden path and made our way up the incline to the mouth of the mine.

I had already drilled the holes and placed the dynamite. I had talked with an experienced dynamite man and he had helped me with advice on how and where to place the charges to direct the stone when the explosion occurred. I had initially planned on setting the charges in a manner that blew the stone wall inward into the mine tunnel, by drilling my holes so they sloped inward toward what would be the center of the circle of the segment being removed from the wall.

After talking to the expert, I changed my mind and drilled a circle of holes that were perpendicular to the wall that was being blown. He had assured me that this would fracture the blown out segment in a manner that would be highly unlikely to end up restricting the water flow. If a significant restriction resulted, the water that was able to pass the restriction would prevent us from being able to take corrective action.

By fracturing the segment being blown out into small pieces, the force of the water would soon clear the tunnel of all restrictions to the water flow. Additional charges were set strategically across the face of the section being blown out, so the debris would be nearly as fine as coarse gravel.

Earlene held the lantern so I could set the caps and cut the fuses. "All the fuses need to be the exact same length," I said. "I'm only allowing two minutes for us to ride a hundred yards or so down the canyon. We can watch the spectacle and judge what the water's gonna do from there. If it starts coming hard and fast, we'll high-tail it to the spot where the canyon widens out. In case there's more water than we expect, we can depend on the width of the valley to keep the depth too low to be a hazard."

A couple of minutes later, I had the fuses set and was ready to light them. "Earlene, it is very important that we don't get in such a hurry that we can make a misstep between here and our horses. Two minutes doesn't sound like much time, but I've rehearsed this by walking normally from here to where the horses are tied, getting on my horse and riding at a walk to the spot from which we will be watching, and still having ample time to allow for problems."

Earlene raised the lantern globe and I stuck the eight fuses into the flame. They sparkled into life simultaneously. We turned and walked swiftly to the tunnel opening, hurried down the pathway and mounted our horses. We rode to our point of vantage and turned to watch.

Just as I began to think the fuses had gone out, the blast finally occurred. It made a dull thud where I had expected a huge blast as dust from the tunnel floor, along with some small debris, gusted from the hole. It seemed that was all that had happened.

Just as we glanced at each other in disbelief, water started gushing from the tunnel. It pushed the brush and the top of the trees from its path and splashed to the ground with an incredible burst of power.

The water seemed to surge in all directions at once, but then a wall of water began to rush down the old channel. It seemed to move like a horse running wild, but when we turned and began loping toward the exit from my valley, we were easily staying abreast of it. It was a wall of mud, tearing brambles, small rocks, sticks, tree trunks and unrecognizable debris from the bottom and sides of the channel.

Earlene and I shouted at each other in jubilation. The water was brim full in the old channel. I imagined that the channel would be swept clean down to the bedrock in a day or two.

We kept loping our horses along, and found that we were actually outdistancing the wall of water as it found places to sweep out across the meadows to as quickly return to the channel. It was like a huge serpent, placing its head first this way and then that, as it searched for prey.

Our horses were foaming with sweat by the time we approached the picnic ground where crowds of people were sitting.

Someone shouted when they spotted us and in a moment the crowd was going wild. Men started flinging their hats in the air; some raced their horses around the perimeter, while still others stood on wagon beds to get a better view. Everyone was screaming and shouting until they covered the roar of the water, which followed us a half mile behind.

Earlene spotted Brad and Rodney, seated on a little stage that had been erected. The sheriff and two of his deputies sat on the edge of the stage. I assumed the other one was somewhere around, or else was back in town keeping his eyes on what was going on. It would've been a good time for an outlaw gang to ransack the town, for the town was empty.

The wall of water rushed by the group without even the tip of a hat. It struck the Wandering River and a huge wave washed across the river and reverberated back until the sweep of the river turned the stream of mud down stream.

The water upstream of the junction flowed clean and clear. The water down stream was a muddy accumulation of debris. I allowed half an hour for everyone to marvel at the spectacle before climbing up to the stage.

The crowd quieted immediately and I began to speak. "Folks, you are witnessing an event unlike any other that's been seen before. This water symbolizes an opportunity for achievements that have never been dreamed of, much less realized before. Best of all, this is just the beginning. The hard work starts tomorrow.

"There's something else that may be even more difficult than the hard work of succeeding with the water project that has just now been put into effect. It may require each of us to re-evaluate the way we look at life. I know that many, if not all of you, have had to depend upon your own ingenuity for everything that you have gleaned from life. I hope that together, as a community, we can change that. I hope that in the future we can start thinking a little more of '_Us_' and a little less of '_Me_'."

"Progress is another word nearly synonymous with cooperation. Civilization is another word for social cooperation. Without the social cooperation of all of us, there will be no schools for the children. Without that cooperation, we can't attract good doctors, or maintain our road system. That cooperation is necessary for us to harvest our crops, to brand our cattle, and especially to band together so we are able to sell the fruits of our labor at prices that will allow us to live comfortably from our efforts. That is the end toward which we aim. By we, I'm referring to those of us who are sponsoring a fair shake for the small ranchers, for our business men and women, and for the community as a whole.

"Our project is like the water we just released down this channel. It may start out with some things muddied up, like the water you have just witnessed. However, if you'll look at the water now, you'll see that it's already beginning to flow clear and sweet. It's that clear and sweet water that each of you'll soon be experiencing.

"Let's all work together toward the same end, adopting a like mind of selflessness; a mind that is geared towards giving and not towards taking. Remember, we are the people of this community. It is up to us to make it what it can and should be.

We have an additional benefit that comes to us because of the confidence the Rimrock Bank and Trust has in this community and the people of which it will consist. We have hired a construction superintendent. He will be hiring men to work in crews of house and barn builders, fencing crews and loggers.

The Bank has agreed to finance the houses as part of the package that will include stocking the ranches, fencing them and preparing them for habitation. The building will proceed in the order the ranches were drawn. The superintendent will be hiring, not only carpenters, but post cutters for fencing, fencing crews and loggers.

A school house and a community hall will begin very shortly, and a school master has been hired.

There was much cheering and applauding. I glanced at Earlene who was displaying her beautiful smile. She was applauding the hardest of all.

"Now, ladies and gentlemen," I said when the crowd had finally quieted down. We've come to the point that has held every one in suspense. We will hold the drawing for the plats of land. I'm sure that you have all read and understand how our drawing will be conducted. However, I'm going to mention how the process works, so there will be no misunderstandings.

"Rodney has the sign-up list in the order that each of you signed up for the drawing. We will start the drawing in that same order. I want you to understand that you're not drawing for your turn to choose your new ranch. The name that you draw will be the person whose turn it is to pick his tract of land.

"Each person whose name is drawn will come up to the table where Rodney is seated. There is a map of the plats, with each one numbered. The map is identical to the ones that have been conveniently posted in several places in town.

"When you make your choice, that choice will be recorded by Rodney. It will also be marked on the master map in your presence. At that same time, it will be marked on another copy of the map, with your name written on the map and signed by both you and Rodney. Your plat will be recorded on the list that Rodney is making up as each person draws his land. The line upon which your name and tract number is listed will be signed by you and Rodney. The names will be attested to by two independent witnesses. Those witnesses are long time residents of your community and have no personal stake in the proceedings.

"Arnold Smith and Pat Donahue will be those two witnesses.

"Your duly elected sheriff, Todd Russell, will sign in his official role as the legal authority that is resident of this county.

"Remember, if there is to be any trading of tracts, it must be made within two weeks from today. Any transactions made after that date will have a transaction fee, which will cover the expenses of the title change and recording.

"Because of our desire to have everything settled as quickly as possible, there will be no exceptions to this rule.

"Rodney Hampton, as the business manager of the Rimrock Land and Cattle Company, and president of the bank, will preside over the paperwork entailed in the recording of the transactions.

"Questions that may arise out of general operations may be addressed to me, if they cannot be handled by the construction superintendent and are not business related. I am the operations manager of the RL&CC. If I am unavailable and the problem needs immediate resolution, you may ask Brad Rogers for help in his capacity as a Director of the RL&CC.

"Earlene Rogers will preside over the drawing, as secretary of the RL&CC. In the presence of the witnesses, who have previously attested to the names entered in this drawing, each name will be called and Earlene will allow each person, in turn, to draw one name from the hat. That person will immediately come up to Rodney's desk and pick his tract of land.

"We will start immediately and will try to keep this grand and momentous occasion moving along rapidly.

"We hope to have each participant make an appointment with Rodney to sign your titles, liens and the other necessary papers.

"With no further comment, we will turn the meeting over to Earlene. Earlene, let's get the show on the road!"

The drawing went surprisingly fast and without a hitch. I enjoyed watching the expressions that played across the face of each of the small ranchers, as first they waited in suspense, and then as they were called, when their name was drawn. The poorly dressed women were every bit as thrilled as the men.

A short time later, the drawing was over and again I took my place in front of the group.

"Folks!" I waited a few seconds and again said, "Folks!! Let me have your attention!" The crowd became very attentive and I marveled at the hope in their faces. "Rodney Hampton has a few things to say that will answer many of your questions about the new conveniences that are coming soon to Vacaville and the Bend of the Rimrock. Citizens of the South Cedar Breaks and the Bend of the Rimrock, I now give you Rodney Hampton."

Suddenly a voice from the crowd shouted, "Let's eat first!"

Rodney had already taken his place on stage. "I'm all for that!" He agreed.

They didn't have to hear it twice. The crowd swiftly moved toward the picnic tables.

Chapter Twenty Nine
Full circle

Time sure flies and it's hard sometimes to fathom all that transpires within a short lifetime. Earlene and I had just been married. We'd decided to spend our honeymoon right there on our own property. We were riding back from town, wanting to enjoy the lazy afternoon, but beneath the surface was a sense of urgency, a need for us to be together.

"Easy," Earlene said as we approached our house, "I have a favor to ask of you. I hope you won't think I'm crazy."

"I can't imagine you asking anything that I would ever consider crazy," I replied. "Earlene, let me say one thing before we go another step, whether in distance, time, love or play. Whether it is strange to others, even ourselves, or things beyond the imagination: in every way that it can be phrased, fantasized, dreamed of or read about, and in every way that I can think of to tell you how much it means to me, let's take a vow, here and now, to never, never, to the end of time, have to fear saying how we feel, what we need, what we want to receive or what we want to give. Let's share what we want to know and experience. Let's never hide ourselves from one another. Let's always have confidence, love and understanding between us.

"I want to be the same as your own soul and the innermost recesses of your own mind. That is what I so hope for you to be to me, too.

"That is what I pledge my honor, my life and my future to give to you. That is the one thing that I seek, above all, to receive from you.

"Now please continue with what you were going to say."

"Well, Easy, this is one of the things that your words so well describe. The favor I'm asking you to do is to ride on ahead of me, and let me follow along by myself."

"As for what you just said, I will make the same pledge to you as you just made to me. This will be an apt example of the things you're speaking of."

"My Darling, I'm so glad of what you just said, for I thought that no one else could ever join me in such a pledge. I feel so much better now about what you just asked me," I replied.

"That isn't all," Earlene looked at me earnestly. "That's not the only thing that I'm asking you to do."

"Pray tell me then, Sweet Baby, my darling," I said smiling, trying to lighten the conversation after I had just bared my very soul. "Just tell me what you would like me to do." I couldn't help wondering what she had in mind.

"You remember the day that we first met at the oasis?" she murmured.

"How could I ever possibly forget?" My pulse was racing and I was afraid my horse would hear my heart beating so loudly that he might try to run away.

"I'd like to re-enact that brief interlude. I'd like you to go back and do everything that you did, in the same order as before, starting with taking your nap. The only difference is I want you to pretend that you're still asleep and whatever you do, don't open your eyes or arise from where you're reclined. Will you do that for me?" Her eyes were shining and the color had risen in her cheeks. "I want to find the answer to some questions that I asked myself after we first glimpsed one another."

"You know that I will, Earlene. I've also wanted to relive that moment with all my heart. One could not count all the fantasies that I've had since that moment, or all the different endings that I've dreamed of since then."

"Easy, let's not say another word. Please ride on ahead. Give me a little time to arrive. Go back to the frame of mind that you had then. Try your best to duplicate everything just as you did before, starting with preparing for your nap. Continue to lie there as though sleeping. I would *love it* if you could actually sleep, although I know that would probably be too much to ask. Now go, without even telling me goodbye. Go, without a backward look!"

It took everything I had to ride away from my new bride without a kiss, without a lingering gaze, without even the touch of a hand, but I did as Earlene requested and rode to the end of the valley and picketed my horse in our glade. Then I climbed the trail to the top, walked swiftly to the path that led down to our oasis, and circled the pool of clear water.

As requested, I disrobed and walked across to the same spot where I had been the first time I had met the water nymph of my dreams. I lay down in what was probably the same impression that my body had initially left on the earth the day of my first encounter. I had relived that episode so many times in my fantasies and dreams that I had memorized the position of every willow leaf, every twig and every bough on the tree.

I closed my eyes and prepared to wait. Although the willow leaves caressed my body just as before, I knew that their sensuous touch wouldn't have been necessary for me to relive that afternoon with perfect accuracy. The thoughts that filled my mind were enough to bring me to the same fever of desire that I had had months ago when I had first arisen from that bed of grass to catch the initial fleeting glimpse of my Aphrodite as she climbed from the pool, golden in the glow of the sun on her wet and shining body, flawless in the new garden of Eden, beyond the imagination of any mortal because of her own rich mortality.

This woman was real flesh and bone. She was no painted figure, dainty and fragile. She was strong, beautiful and beautifully suited to the home we were carving out of the oasis that opened into a barren and savage desert only a few miles to the west of where I lay.

I suddenly heard the soft sound of dripping water. Fighting the impulse to open my eyes, I lay quietly, cradled by the caressing arms of the willow leaves. Oh, how could heaven possibly compete with the anticipated moments that lay ahead?

I sensed, more than felt, a change in the rhythm of the leaves. Then, so gently that I was unsure whether it was a leaf that touched me, or if it were something more, I felt it and then suddenly I couldn't feel it anymore, as if it were wanting me to feel it, yet, at the same time, trying to keep me from feeling it.

I was tense with suspense, trying my best to anticipate where I would feel the next touch. Then I could feel hands, softly sliding over my skin. It was as though a blind person were trying to see me by touch, without awakening me as I lay there, pretending to sleep. I felt the touch sliding along both sides of my face, tracing round my ears, and returning to my forehead. Fingers brushed over my eyebrows, thumbs gently caressed the flesh between my eyebrows and my eye sockets.

They outlined the lids of my eyes, moved out and made light circular motions on my temples. The touch broadened into full palms on my cheeks, with thumbs sliding along the sides of my nose. They came together on my upper lips and then, ever so lightly, they moved over my lips several times, met from both sides of my face to the center of my chin then along the bottoms of my jawbones and lightly followed my throat to the indentation where the two sides of the breastbone meet.

Never breaking contact with my skin, the thumbs remained centered at that point, while the fingers came down to each side of my neck, and moved along so that my entire neck, that was not against the cushion of old willow leaves were encased by those wonderful hands.

Such a position must have become uncomfortable, for I felt her body straddle mine, but with her weight supported mostly by her knees as her left hand slid out along my right arm, seized it by the wrist and brought it up across my chest. She then began to squeeze the flesh along my arm from my hand to my shoulder. She would close her hand upon the flesh and then release it and move another couple of inches toward my shoulder.

When she had worked her way to my shoulder, she gently smoothed her hand along that arm before laying it back out to the side, with my palm turned up and my elbow bent to place my hand on the same plane as the top of my head. She then reached to her right and took my left arm and did the same.

When she finished doing it as she had done my right arm, she began to lightly knead the muscles on my chest and abdomen. Then she turned her body with her back to me and moved downward to where she could rub my feet and legs in a manner similar to how she had done my arms.

When she got to my knees, she slid back up my body so that she could finish my legs, in their entirety.

No word had been spoken, and my eyes were still closed. Despite the passion raging through my body, I was succumbing to the light massaging and was lying between wakefulness and sleep when she completed my legs and slid off of my body and made a slight effort to turn me over. I rolled over on my stomach and she began to follow a procedure to cover my arms.

When she had finished with my arms and the back of my neck, she again moved backward to allow her to rub all of the muscles in my back. At times she would trace the outline of my muscle with her fingers, and there were times that she seemed to be writing words on my back. I can't vouch for the accuracy of my interpretation of the words and sentences she wrote, but they placed me in a mood beyond explanation, and still in a trance.

She was sitting with her weight on my butt as she finished her massage as low as she could reach from her sitting position. Then, once again, she reversed her direction and moved down enough to bend each leg up, in turn, and knead the muscles of my calves.

With each movement of her body, I could feel her muscular little butt twisting against my own. She moved up my back enough to get all of my muscles upon which she had been sitting, and once again reversed her position and began at my neck and began to make circling motions around each of my vertebrae, in turn, as though examining each one separately, as she counted them, one by one.

As she got to the last one, she was extremely thorough in her circling. Then she moved further down and began to lightly spank me. The spanks became more and more vigorous and stung quite a lot, but the more they stung, the hotter my flesh felt and the higher my desires rose.

Once again she let me know that she wanted me to roll back over into my initial position, lying on my back.

The sky descended and all sensations blurred into one great, unending spiral of pleasure as she explored every place she had missed on her first pass of my body.

There was never a fantasy that had passed through my fertile imagination that could have touched upon the reality of the first co-mingling of our two beings.

Time had stopped at the moment that I descended into our oasis, and did not begin again until we dressed to leave our refuge from all the loneliness that we had felt in our lives before this moment. That would be three short days later.

We lay unmoving, fearing to change anything that might disturb the perfection of the moment. Suffice it to say that every dream had been realized, every fantasy fulfilled, and every promise we had made one another had been cemented with the glue of an impermeable love and devotion.

At last we lay, tangled in willow leaves as the sun began to lose its battle against the cool of the evening. Too enthralled to even think of separating, she raised her lips from mine and asked softly, "Are you as happy as I am?"

"I honestly feel I've been exhaling all my life, and have only now been able to draw oxygen deeply into my lungs," I answered. "I can't see how there is room in the universe for another feeling equal to what I've just felt and still feel.

"Earlier, as I was lying in anticipation, I wanted so badly for you to hurry a little faster. Is it fair for me to ask what took you so long to get here?"

"You would never guess in a thousand years," she answered. "so I'm going to stay right here forever and never release you unless you can guess the answer."

I lay quietly for several minutes. "If I guess it right the first time, will you promise that you won't release my body for a while longer, and that you'll never release my heart?"

"Yes," she whispered, "but there is no way you could ever guess what delayed me. Not ever, and for sure not on the first guess."

"My guess is that you were on the Rimrock with your binoculars watching me," I said.

She sprang straight up into a sitting position in one graceful and exceedingly pleasant movement. "How did you ever guess? Were you peeping, after you promised you wouldn't?"

"No, Sweet Baby. I promise that I didn't cheat in any way."

"Then how did you know?" she insisted.

"It was elementary, my dear Watson. I relied upon my fantasies to guide me," I said, drawing her forward into my arms. We stood up to dress, but Earlene had one more question she wanted to answer. She answered it by using me as the tool with which she wrote our initials on the sandy bank of the glorious pool.

*

We sat on our horses in front of our canyon, looking at the large sign that graced the entrance to our ranch. So far, there was only one thing painted on the sign, in bold black letters. There was also an enlarged profile of our brand, burned into the wood of the sign. Arnold had erected it while Earlene and I were spending our first three days of married life at our oasis.

The sign read:

EEZ SEEKER'S VALLEY EEZ

"Oh, I just love it, Easy!" She reached over and took my hand. "It's just perfect!"

"Okay, Miss Brand Reader, how would you read that brand?" I asked.

"Why, I would call it the Easy!"

"And how did you arrive at that?" I smiled.

"Why, I would call it the E's Zee! It could also be called the Easy! E for Easy and E for Earlene!" she smiled back.

"Well, I figured it with the first E for Earlene and the second E for Easy"

"Hahaha, I was sure you would say that," she laughed.

"Oh, and how could you have been so sure?" I inquired.

"Elementary, my dear Watson! Elementary!"